Also by Andersen Prunty

Squirm With Me

Creep House: Horror Stories

Sociopaths In Love

The Warm Glow of Happy Homes

Bury the Children in the Yard: Horror Stories

Satanic Summer

Fill the Grand Canyon and Live Forever

Pray You Die Alone: Horror Stories

Sunruined: Horror Stories

The Driver's Guide to Hitting Pedestrians

Hi I'm a Social Disease: Horror Stories

Fuckness

The Sorrow King

Slag Attack

My Fake War

Morning is Dead

The Beard

Zerostrata

Jack and Mr. Grin

The Overwhelming Urge

THIS TOWN NEEDS A MONSTER

GRINDHOUSE PRESS

For Carrie—

Thanks for the past five years. You're my best friend in the world.

THIS
TOWN
NEEDS
A
MONSTER

BEGINNINGS

Where am I?

I'm in Gethsemane, Ohio. It's the same place I've been for the past forty years. It's where my parents brought me home from the hospital. I didn't think I'd still be here but there's no place I'd rather be.

It's the beginning of a new life but it feels like the end of a journey. A long, circular journey. I always thought I'd have to go far from home to find happiness but, and I know this sounds clichéd, it was practically in my backyard the entire time.

Oh, a backyard. I have one of those now.

Because I have a house for the first time in my life. It's not a huge house but I don't really need a huge house. This is adequate. It's probably more than enough. It's perfect.

I have a partner—a woman—who I know isn't going anywhere. We have similar goals in life and that's what really matters. I don't know if she loves me or not. You can never really know that about a person. I'm not even entirely sure she *is* a person. Besides, love fades. Love dies and goes away. What I need right now is stability. It's what I've always needed but never had. As long as we're both serving our community, both doing our part, then I don't see any catastrophes happening. As long as we never want *more*.

The community is what's important. With the community comes service. The community is responsible for this life. This is the best life for me. And that's perfection.

I used to feel so alone and disenfranchised. I sought answers and, in my own way, I sought happiness. I never found them because I was always putting myself first. The only thing that came from that was starting over, time and time again. Bringing a modicum of happiness to myself while ignoring everyone around me if not making them outright miserable. A new beginning every few years, all of them leaving me feeling broke and broken and hollowed out.

None of them were like this.

This one will be different.

I finally found someone who could give me a voice. Someone who could give all of us a voice. A voice for the voiceless.

It was exactly what I needed.

I'd never really known darkness.

I'd never truly fucked up.

I'd never really done much of anything.

Before coming in contact with the community, those were often the thoughts that swirled in the gray area between consciousness and sleep.

When I thought back on my life, I thought about it in terms of absences, things not done, emptiness. I didn't realize how terrifying this should have been. The most frightening thing about a void is not the emptiness, it's that it's just sitting there, waiting for something to fill it . . .

That's what I have now: a full life.

I'm sure there will be consequences but the rewards will fully outnumber them.

Everything has consequences.

If I ever have any doubt, all I have to do is pull up the video files on my laptop. All I have to do is focus on the Brad Renfield in those videos, the close-ups of my face, the look in my eyes. The only thing I see there is guilt and shame and fear and paranoia and anxiety and longing and lust. A man, more than old enough to know better, doing things simply because he's told to without knowing why. Without knowing the answers.

A man without a life.

A man without knowledge.

A man without a community.

A man without happiness.

I imagine how horrifying it would be to wake up and look at that face in the mirror every morning.

Horror. Yeah, it's all around us.

We can shut our eyes and try to block it out but it's happening anyway. Happening all the time.

This is how I opened my eyes to it.

How I learned to embrace it.

This is how I found happiness.

DAWN SYNDROME

"I need you to meet me in the field."

Travis had woken me up. I never turned the ringer on on my phone and was surprised the vibration had been enough to rouse me. I'd unthinkingly answered it and wished I hadn't.

"Are you there?"

He sounded frantic. He usually didn't get like this unless he'd been drinking.

"It's late, Trav. I have to be at work in a few hours. You do too."

"Fuck that."

I continued pulling cobwebs out of my dusty brain. I'd quit drinking a few months ago and, once the insomnia passed, I began sleeping deeper and dreaming more than I ever had. Sometimes the dreams were so vivid that, upon waking, it was tough to separate them from memories.

"Okay, but I'm not leaving unless you tell me why."

"I'm fucked, man."

At least, it didn't *sound* like he'd been drinking. But this was the sort of thing he came up with when he had been. I'd always thought of myself as a fun, happy drunk. Travis was the opposite. He grew sad and melancholic, became a colossal downer. Quitting drinking gave us one less excuse to hang out together. Probably one of the reasons I'd stopped.

This was the sort of late night attack he'd lobbed at me on My-Face once we'd stopped hanging out every night. Ultimately I'd had to quit that too. It was probably for the best. Social networking did nothing for my anxiety.

"Just take a deep breath and calm down, man."

"I've already done that, Brad."

I couldn't remember the last time he'd said my name aloud. The effect was surprisingly chilling.

"Okay. So you're finished. What does that even mean?"

"Not finished. Fucked. Completely fucked, man. It means I want you to shoot me in the face. Put me out of my fucking misery."

I coughed out a laugh. Maybe he was just putting me on. I realized I was smiling.

"It's not fucking funny!"

The smile dropped away.

I tried not to sound mad. "You can't call someone up in the middle of the night and ask them to shoot you in the face and expect them to take you seriously."

"You know I can't do it myself. It would kill Mom and Dad. It has to look like an accident. I thought you'd want to help. It's going to happen one way or another."

"Just calm down and go to bed. Are you drunk?"

"I'm not fucking drunk or stoned. I'm as sober as I've been in two decades. I have clarity. For the first time in I don't know how long, I'm seeing things clearly. That's how I know I'm fucked. You're fucked too. We're all fucked. I don't expect everyone to have the balls to remove themselves from this . . . this *conspiracy*, but I'm not taking part in it another fucking day."

"I just . . . I can't do anything like that. Maybe you need help. Have you thought about calling someone who can help you?"

"It has to be you. You're the only one who can do it. You're the only one I trust. I don't *think* you're a part of it yet."

"I'm . . . not a part of anything. I don't even know what you're talking about. But I can't do what you're asking me to."

There was a pause. I heard him nervously breathe out before saying, "Then I'm going to share the photos."

He'd thought this through more than I'd given him credit for.

Now it was time for *me* to do some thinking.

It sounded like he was having some kind of psychotic paranoid episode. What the fuck did I know about that shit? I was a landscaper, not a doctor. I wasn't even that great at empathizing. The simple fact that Travis was reaching out to me instead of practically anyone else in the world was incredibly sad. I had tried to distance myself from mental illness as much as possible. It seemed like one of the most truly terrifying things in the world. But, with the threat of sharing the photos, Travis was hellbent on getting me there. I didn't need to ask which photos. I knew. The threat of sharing them even made Travis's reasons for wanting me there irrelevant.

"Fine," I said. "Give me about a half hour."

"See you there."

Then he was gone.

My phone winked out in my palm.

Now I had no choice but to go. There wasn't any way I was going to shoot my best friend in the face, even if he was a terrible friend, probably even a terrible person. He wouldn't do anything until I met him. That would force him to think about it for a few more minutes, at least. I assumed he already had a gun. If he wanted me to shoot him, getting the gun away wouldn't be a problem. Once I had that, I could find out where he had the photos. Probably on his phone, but maybe on his laptop or even printed out. Maybe I could convince him that destroying or deleting them was a good idea. The photos had been a really stupid idea. Sometimes you do things in the heat of the moment without thinking it could possibly lead to death or, at the very least, a horrendous beating. Sometimes you do things you have no recollection of doing and yet it occupies some alley of your brain like a malignant ghost waiting to spring forward during the quietest, most unexpected moments.

I slid on my jeans and t-shirt, thankful it was a warm night in June and not freezing cold. I grabbed my keys and took a deep breath before heading out of the apartment.

I should have felt bad about feeling put out but this thing with Travis had been building for some time. Possibly another reason for giving up drinking, hoping Travis would follow my example. If I wanted to feel really altruistic about it.

We both worked for the same landscaping company—Billups' Interior and Exterior. "Keeping You Green Inside and Out!"

Travis had gotten me the job. Lately he'd been calling off more than he'd been coming in. I went every day because I had to pay rent and bills and buy groceries and gas for my truck. Travis still lived with his parents, was an only child, and his mom did everything shy of wiping his ass for him. We were both forty and I wondered why he didn't have any desire to at least try acting like a grownup. He said it didn't matter. It was just buying into the experiment, the conspiracy. Also, he said people scared him. I tried telling him people had always been kind of terrifying but he swore it had gotten worse the past couple of years. Like society itself was coming to some kind of critical mass. He blamed all kinds of things: corporate America, prescription medication, the internet, social networking, alcohol, marijuana, heroin, narcissism, television and the media in general, the nearby air force base, colleges, the prevalence of the commercial medical industry. He said the only reason we had jobs in landscaping was because people were too incapacitated to do it themselves but still had the need to keep up appearances because Gethsemane was such a staunchly middle class conservative town. Some places we took care of the outdoor landscaping as well as watering and pruning the plants in the house. Travis swore some houses were completely abandoned, that he hadn't seen any signs of life there for years. He also said some of the houses contained dead people, lying in their beds, turned to rust. Others contained hollowed out shells of people, food for whatever his evil of the day was to latch onto and drain of life and soul. All of this, of course, led to him thinking the town was some kind of military installation, ground zero for the Grand Experiment. He was always a little hazy about what all the Grand Experiment entailed.

I couldn't help but think this was all in Travis's head. That, deep down, he *wanted* it to be this way. Gethsemane was not without its quirks. Nearly a decade ago there was a rash of suicides that, for a town of around five thousand people, struck a chord. The suicide virus (what the papers called it) ended with a bizarre storm killing several more people. The townsfolk came to a general consensus it had been a tornado, but it was never verified by the National Weather Service. The people of the town seemed to pull together. Tragedy had a way of doing this. I started seeing flyers for something called The Healing League. Naturally, there were a number of theories surrounding the suicides—a suicide pact, a monster, Satanism, possibly even a very sly murderer or something supernatural—but people seemed to agree it had been largely caused by economic hardship brought on by the market collapse, the closing of the nearby GM plant, and a strain of bad drugs. Never mind that the suicides had been teenagers with little to no connection to any of these things. The solidarity sweeping the town in the light of these events inevitably dissipated and people went back to their old ways. Being a small, conservative Ohio town, this meant people went back to being isolated, hateful, and rude. All of which prompted Travis to say one night around a campfire: "This town needs a monster."

Maybe I should just shoot the miserable fucker in the face.

The field was a vast expanse of grass a few acres behind Travis's childhood home. It couldn't even really be called his childhood home since he was currently living there. Maybe calling it his forever home would have been more accurate. He'd made a couple of attempts to get out—one of those attempts had us renting an apartment together—but he always ended up back there. Gethsemane was about ten miles west of Dayton, about an hour north of Cincinnati and south of Columbus, five hours from Chicago, in the middle of a country that could be traveled coast to coast in less than a week and, still, we had both failed to escape. We'd both turned forty the previous year, so I guess we still had the rest of our lives to get out but it was starting to look a little less likely every year. Eventually, I would just become complacent with it, tell myself it wasn't that bad, and resign to stay there the rest of my life. Maybe I already had. As it was, I had to work so hard just to keep my head above water I couldn't even really think about leaving. My parents had me later in life and had both passed a few years ago, within months of each other. Other than lack of funds to go elsewhere, there really wasn't anything keeping me there. Travis was the only person I even considered a friend and, these days, I spent most of my time trying to avoid him.

The field was accessible by a narrow gravel lane cut through a thick swath of woods. I don't know why the grassy field hadn't been tilled up and used for soybeans or corn like most of the other property but, then again, I didn't really know anything about that kind of stuff. Maybe the ground was no good for it. Maybe it was cursed or something. Maybe one of the previous families who owned the land had been buried there, the grave marker long since disintegrated or stolen.

I pulled into the turnaround and angled the truck toward the field, flipping on the high beams. A low fire burned in the middle of the field but I didn't see any sign of Travis. Maybe he'd calmed down and hadn't bothered coming at all. Maybe he'd gotten tired of waiting and decided to take care of things himself. Either of those scenarios would have pissed me off but at least I wouldn't have to reckon with shooting him in the face.

I pulled the truck forward so the woods shielded it from the road. We didn't have a lot of cops in these parts but, at this hour, they got bored and tended to explore any possible situation that would keep them awake. That is if they weren't already napping in the parking lot of the Snack Barn or on some abandoned country road.

I shut off the truck and scanned the field, all purplish and dewy in the moonlight.

No sign of Travis.

Why had I even bothered coming?

I should have just called 911 and reported a person in distress. I could have done it anonymously and maybe the shame and embarrassment of surrounding Travis's stupidity with some obnoxious fanfare would keep him from being so thoughtless in the future.

Or at least keep him from dragging me into it.

No. That was a terrible thought. I was just tired and cranky and lazy. For me, suicide had never been an option. I felt like life was one long, brutally sick joke and intended to stick around for the punchline, even if there wasn't one. But I could see how the thought of it comforted some people. It was like poor man's insurance. Or insurance for the hopelessly broken.

I opened the creaky door and stepped out of the truck and into the susurrating rhythm of insects, the country version of quiet. I thought about leaving the headlights on but the moon was full and high and the fire provided a focal point so I reached back into the truck and turned them off.

I again scanned the field, giving my eyes time to adjust.

Still no sign of him.

I could have called out for him but I wasn't even the type of person who talked to myself when I was alone so it would have felt really weird surrounded by that insect hum.

I pulled my phone out of my pocket. Eventually technology would render talking, and probably even noise, obsolete, as it silently glided along in some spooky, unseen place of its own. It was the cold distance of space, reaching down to us through a glowing screen. We were all connected to satellites by the devices we carried in our pockets, that much closer to the heavens.

I half expected to find a text from him, something unfelt amidst the rough truck ride, saying "Don't bother" or something to that effect.

I hadn't received anything.

I thought about sending him a text asking where he was before stopping myself. I didn't really *want* him to be here. I decided to send him something asking if he was okay. It was now so easy to edit ourselves it amazed me we weren't all paralyzed with indecision.

Just as my thumb touched the screen I got a text from him.

"Dont wury bout me. Go on home. I dont even hav gun. Theres whisky by the fire."

Travis wasn't great at spelling and probably saw autocorrect as some form of mind control.

I felt immediately angry Travis had wasted my time, relieved only by the fact I didn't have to deal with any of his whiney bullshit. Most of all, I felt stupid for coming, for buying into his bullshit. He got me every time and it was like I never learned. Then I started feeling like a piece of shit. Was I so inaccessible Travis had to stage these antics to get my attention?

I took in a deep breath of the perfumed summer air, looked up at the stars sprinkling the clear sky.

Whiskey by the fire . . . It was like Travis was mocking my attempt at sobriety. I walked over to the fire, through the knee-high grass, and looked down at the bottle of Jack. I picked it up. It was a little less than a quarter full. I uncapped it, held it up to my nose, and took a deep breath of its familiar and comforting scent. It was tempting. It was a gorgeous night. It would be nice to sit down on one of the stumps by the fire and polish off the bottle. There wasn't really much in there. I'd be able to make it home just fine. It had been long enough since I'd had a drink that I doubted it would throw me back into what I'd called Dawn Syndrome.

That was ultimately what stopped me.

I'd always drunk socially. When I did that, I'd go home and go to bed when the bar closed and that was it. Then I stopped going to bars because they got too expensive and started drinking with

Travis. If we were drinking at my place, he'd get to a certain point, the sad point, and just go to sleep on my couch and I'd go to bed. I stopped drinking with him on a nightly basis because he became annoying. I liked being drunk and he ruined it. So I started drinking alone, staying up later and later, eventually not going to bed unless I'd seen the sun come up. It became as much of an addiction as the alcohol itself. I decided going to a bar would help curb this. That was what led to the girl and the photos and we ended up staying up all night and when she left I felt like I'd done a terrible thing, a dangerous thing, and decided to stop.

When Travis got me the job at the landscaping company, I was still staying up all night. Only, instead of going to bed when the sun came up, I went to work. I couldn't go to work hammered so maybe that helped keep me off the booze. I'd come home around five or six in the evening and go to bed, exhausted, not waking up until midnight.

Over the past few weeks I'd managed to work into a slightly more normal schedule.

One sip of the bottle I held in my hand could undo all of that.

I poured it out in the grass and dropped the bottle into the fire.

I felt exhausted.

I had to work tomorrow and all I wanted to do was go home and go to bed.

I went back to the truck, climbed in, and started it up. I backed it up and turned toward the main road.

If I didn't have to work tomorrow, I would have probably hung out by the fire for a little while. It really was a nice night.

I started down the gravel drive, wishing the sounds of the night could penetrate the sound of catastrophic mechanical failure coming from my truck.

Something greenish and illuminated flickered on the left side of the road. I glanced in that direction and didn't see anything. I turned my attention to the road and caught a shadowy shape standing there. My first thought was that this was Travis and this was how he was going to trick me into ending his life. I jerked the wheel to the right but went too far off the road and into some shrubs.

The truck came to a stop.

Fuck.

My heart raced.

I turned back to the drive to see if whatever I'd swerved to avoid was still there.

It wasn't.

My heart continued to hammer.

What had I seen?

It definitely wasn't a deer.

It had looked like a person but not really. More like a shadow.

Christ.

Was I losing it?

If I had seen something, where was it now?

I checked the dirty rearview mirror and saw nothing. I looked out the passenger window and saw nothing but the blackness of the woods.

I took some deep breaths and calmed my racing heart. I was

tired. I had probably just hallucinated something. I'd done that before when driving while tired.

Okay. I was now going to continue on my way home.

I threw the truck into reverse and . . . it didn't budge.

Christ. Fuck this night. Fuck Travis. I was going to passive aggressively cold shoulder him for at least two fucking weeks.

I took another deep breath and stepped out of the truck.

The front tires were at least three inches off the ground. I couldn't see up under the truck very well. I must have run up onto a stump or something.

I reached in and turned the ignition off, moved around to the front of the truck and tried to push. It went nowhere.

Fuck this.

I pulled my phone out, ready to text Travis, and thought better of it.

As much as he deserved to be pulled out of his comfy bed and subjected to possibly backbreaking manual labor, he would be in absolutely no condition to help me. And I didn't think I wanted to deal with him right now.

I could call a tow truck or something but then I'd have to pay for it with money I didn't have.

I popped back into the truck, rolled up the windows, and grabbed my keys.

If I started walking now, I could get to the apartment in an hour or so. I'd send Travis a text telling him he needed to pick me up for work tomorrow. Then, after work, the stupid fucker was going to help unleash my truck from this whoremongering stump.

Seemed like a plan.

I began walking down the narrow gravel lane.

A car's lights illuminated the main road.

I paused, moving off the gravel path and into the murkiness of the woods. I didn't want to be seen and I didn't want to startle anyone.

The car passed very slowly.

And it was a cop car.

Shit.

If a cop noticed me, he was going to ask why I was out here. If I told him about the truck, I felt like he would be insistent about doing something about it, which would end up costing me money.

As the car passed, I had a quick feeling of regret. I should have flagged him down. If he was bored enough and in any kind of physical shape, maybe he would have even offered to help me. Just because I assumed everyone was a lazy asshole didn't mean they actually were. But he'd inevitably ask why I was out here and I'd have to make up something about Travis. It was much easier to hide in the woods, wait for him to pass, and hope I didn't run into him the rest of the way back to town.

The cop car stopped and backed up.

I remained frozen. After seeing so many videos of cops shooting people, I stayed hidden because I thought surprising him in the middle of the night could be potentially lethal.

Suddenly there was a blinding white light coming from the cop car and the sirens emitted a brief *bloop*.

I'd been found.

I tried to think of what I would say to him.

Usually, cops out here were looking for people hunting deer off-season, teenage vandals, or entrepreneurs performing a late night harvest of some illegal crops.

I became immediately nervous. It didn't help that I was still spooked by whatever I'd seen in the middle of the road. I took a deep breath and told myself I hadn't done anything wrong. I hadn't committed any sort of crime. Travis's parents owned this property. Travis had invited me, so it wasn't like I was trespassing. I'd just tell him I was hanging out with Travis and was on my way home. I didn't see any reason to mention the truck. I glanced back toward the truck as covertly as I possibly could which, in the blinding glare of the searchlight, probably wasn't covert at all.

The truck was plainly visible.

Why was my truck off the road?

I swerved to avoid a critter. Lost control. It wasn't a deer but it was pretty fucking big. Nerves. I certainly hadn't hallucinated some kind of apparition.

Why was I hiding in the woods?

Who was hiding? I wasn't hiding. I love cops!

I raised my hands above my head and slowly moved toward the car.

I squinted dramatically so whoever was inside might realize how intense the light was and turn it off. I waited for a voice to come from some kind of loudspeaker. I thought that was usually what happened. My experience with law enforcement was, thankfully, pretty limited.

The light didn't flick off until I was nearly close enough to touch the car.

The passenger window was down and a young pretty girl leaned across the seat.

"Get in, chubby," she said.

In the course of my years on this planet, I've done a few things that go completely against my better judgment just to see what would happen. I often used that as an excuse as to why my station in life had never really improved. Anyway, this was one of those things.

I got in the car.

As soon as I pulled my door shut the girl pulled the car back onto the road and accelerated to a speed I wasn't entirely comfortable with. No introductions. No questions. No inspections.

I glanced over at the girl and, seeing that her eyes were glued to the road, let my glance linger and turn into something more.

Dark hair. Dark eyes. Tan skin. Athletically built. Wearing a Tiffany blue tank top and very short white shorts. Nothing about her really screamed cop. I wasn't great with ages but would have put her somewhere between fourteen and twenty-five. Although she was driving, so she had to be at least sixteen, right?

"So," I said, "my name's Brad."

She glanced over at me, looking somewhat annoyed, almost like she'd already forgotten I was in the car.

"I'm Dawn," she said. "Dawn Bando."

"Are you, um, a cop, Dawn?"

"Fuck no. Do I look like a cop?"

"No."

"My dad is, though. A cop. So I decided to borrow his car."

Fuck. This girl was joyriding around in a cop car. This was probably not at all where I should be right now.

"Tell me about your situation, Brad."

I thought about it for a second.

"I'm not really in a situation."

"I don't believe you."

"I mean, it's not serious."

"Maybe I can help you."

"I don't really see how you can help me." I suddenly felt like we were talking about more than my truck being off the road.

"Well, we won't know until you tell me, will we? Look, my dad's a real cop. He's the sheriff. I'll be able to get you help if you need it. And if you're in trouble for something you've done then don't you think it would be better to tell me first anyway?"

I felt a glimmer of panic. Dawn made it sound like I'd committed a crime. Like I was in some kind of trouble. I thought about the photos I'd taken. I guess if the wrong people—specifically, the wrong guy—found out about those, I could probably be in some form of physical danger. But that wasn't the kind of thing you went to the police about.

"Sometimes it feels good just to talk about things. No one's perfect. I mean, look at me. I spiked my dad's evening beer with Ambien, took three days' worth of Adderall and stole his car so I can find someone old enough to buy me beer. You might ask yourself why I would need to go through all the trouble to buy beer when my dad probably has some in the fridge but that's just the fuck of it. He's a recovering alcoholic and I think he's afraid of spiraling back down so he buys one tall boy can of Miller Lite on his way home from work, drinks it while he watches the evening news, and then goes to bed. He says the beer helps him sleep and is probably ultimately safer and more natural than prescription drugs. But tonight he's sleeping a little harder than usual. He didn't even make it to bed. Just conked out right there in his easy chair.

"By the way, you're the guy."

My brain was not the fastest moving machine and I was still trying to digest everything she'd just said.

"Huh?" I said.

"You're the guy who's going to buy me beer. You look old."

"I'm . . . I don't think anybody sells beer at this hour. And I'm not *that* old. I'm forty." And now I knew she was under twenty-one.

"There's a carryout on Route 4 at the edge of Dayton that does. But they card. I guess they don't want to break too many laws at once. So that's where we're going. Leaves you plenty of time to tell me what's going on."

Dawn seemed like kind of a psycho and I really didn't want to tell her what was going on. What kind of attractive teen girl goes out joyriding to look for a strange older man to buy her beer? Probably the same type of person who abuses Adderall and drugs her father. It was hard for me to have contempt for youth, but I felt like Dawn could get really irritating really quickly. Like, I didn't think she was going to leave me alone until I told her something.

Also, like an old pervert, and despite the fact she was kind of irritating and clearly deranged, I began wondering what the possibility of fucking her was.

"It's no big deal, really," I said. "I was just going to meet a friend and he wasn't there and I, uh, ran my car off the road."

"Why were you going to meet your friend so late? Are you a fag?"

Her use of that word was jarring. I thought the only people who ever used that were old rabid right wing types and jocks.

"No. I'm not gay. I was, uh, going to buy some weed from him." Why did I even say that? Why say I was going to do something illegal when I was there for a completely respectable, possibly even noble, reason? Was I trying to sound cool? Were people in their forties who smoked weed cool or pathetic? I didn't even smoke weed. Whatever. It was a neat and tidy answer and the truth wasn't and it wasn't something I really wanted to talk to a stranger about.

She breathed out a short, sarcastic laugh and said, "Weed's so lame. I can get some for you, if you want."

I hadn't smoked it since high school and didn't have a particular desire to start.

"I think I'm okay."

"Pretty ridiculous that I have to drive all this way for beer when I have access to just about anything, huh?"

"I guess."

"I appreciate you doing this for me. Let me know if there's anything you need."

I glanced over at Dawn, ran my eyes up her fit legs, realized my gaze came to rest on her crotch, and looked away. I wasn't going to mention the myriad ways she could make it up to me. If she offered, I'd take her up on it in a heartbeat. As long as she was legal, I had absolutely no problem with it. But I wasn't going to put it out there. I didn't want her to see me as a sleazy older guy, which I probably was. Younger girls no longer looked at me as a potential hook up. It was a somewhat heartbreaking realization but was probably synonymous with maturity.

"Do you think you'd be able to take me home after this? That's all I really need."

"Sure," she said. "Well, after we get beer I need to pick up a couple of people but, after that, yeah, we'll be headed back to Get so I can drop you off. No problem."

I wasn't sure how I felt about the picking up a couple of other people part. It seemed to complicate things. Plus unfamiliar people made me nervous. I should have just called a tow truck after crashing my truck. Until getting in the car with Dawn, I hadn't really done anything wrong. Now I was probably an accessory to stealing a cop car. Soon I would be guilty of buying alcohol for who knew how many underage people. I tried not to panic too much. If she was a sheriff's daughter, I imagined she had some level of immunity.

"So what's the youngest girl you've ever fucked?" Dawn asked.

I still felt a million miles away and couldn't figure out if her question seemed completely bizarre or just out of place. I had to put things into perspective. She was a teen girl out for a night of summer hijinks. I was in the middle of a situation that had the potential of turning into an existential crisis. Maybe it would just be best to play along until I could get home. Besides, her question made me hard for some reason and whatever endorphins were released by that felt good. I tried to swallow down the probably one-way sexual tension.

"Probably . . . sixteen."

"Really? You don't sound so sure."

I didn't feel the need to go into great detail with this girl. She didn't need my sexual history.

"Yeah. I guess. I hooked up with her at a friend's party at his college. She was at least sixteen. Could have been older. All I know is what my friend told me."

"Is this the same friend you were trying to buy weed from?"

"No."

"How old were you?"

"I think, probably, nineteen."

"Did you fuck her good? Fuck her hard?"

I didn't answer. This felt like too much for my nerves to take. I didn't know why she was talking about this stuff. There was absolutely no way she was interested in fucking me. She was probably mocking me.

"Does it make you uncomfortable to talk about this stuff?"

"Maybe." I thought she would stop but I really didn't want her to.

"Why?"

"I don't know."

"Because I'm a girl?"

"Maybe."

"Because I'm young?"

"Might have something to do with it."

"Teen girls have sex too, you know. I'm just curious." She glanced down at my cock straining against my jeans. "It kind of looks like part of you likes talking about it."

Maybe the best way to get her to stop talking about this was to turn on the creepy old man vibe, the exact thing I was trying to avoid.

"Why are you asking?" I said. "Do you want me to fuck you?"

The ensuing laugh could be gently described as derisive.

"I don't really have much need for men in my life."

She was silent for a minute or so, plucking her phone up from between her bare thighs and checking something. It made me nervous but I figured people in her age group had managed to master this art as well as I used to manage smoking, drinking coffee, and fumbling with the stereo while driving or how people of my father's generation had managed to drive drunk.

"Would you, though?" she asked out of nowhere.

"Would I what?"

"Fuck me."

Back on the sex thing. Jesus. Where was this carryout?

"No." But, of course, I would.

"Why not?"

"Too young."

"Bullshit."

"I'm serious."

"Do you jerk off to porn?"

"Of course."

"And you, what, look for sad old women to jerk off to?"

"No."

"Most of the girls you jerk off to are probably about my age. Maybe even younger."

"That's different."

"How's it different?"

"I don't know. I've gotten older. The younger girls are the crazier they seem."

"Wow. Thanks."

Given the current scenario, how could she possibly be offended by this? She was the embodiment of that statement.

"What you mean," she said, "is that you don't want to be in a relationship with a girl my age. You would totally fuck me if there were no strings attached."

This was completely true but her confidence annoyed me.

"There are always strings attached. That's why I said jerking off to porn is different. That underpaid Serbian actress is probably not going to call me up in the middle of the night and tell me she's going to OD on pills if I don't start paying more attention to her. She's probably not going to size shame me on MyFace."

"That's pretty good. Has someone done that to you?"

"What? OD?"

"No. Size shame you on MyFace."

"Not personally."

"And the other thing?"

"Not personally."

"So all your ideas about crazy young girls seem theoretical. Not experiential."

"Sure. I guess."

"That just makes you sound like a scared little boy."

"Okay."

"Okay?"

"Yeah. Okay. It's just not something I think about a lot. I go to work. I exist. When I get horny I jerk off to porn. It's simple. Maybe I'll want something more someday."

"Sounds boring."

"Some of us are fine with boring."

"Not me."

"Clearly."

"I wasn't trying to make you feel bad with all the porn stuff. It's an interest of mine, that's all."

"Porn?"

"Yeah. Well, what guys jerk off to. Actually, what people watch in general."

"Why?"

"Why not?"

I shrugged.

"I don't want to be *in* porn. I make it. Like directing and filming and shit. All types of content, really."

"That's . . . one career path, I guess."

"So now you're going to be condescending?"

"I'm not being condescending. It just seems like there are probably other things you could do."

"Okay. I might listen to you if you can prove you know what you're talking about. So I'm curious to see where you live. Maybe when I drop you off you can invite me in and show me all of your nice things. Show me everything that being boring gets you."

"All right. You got me. My life is shit. I guess I never had the porn option."

She reached over and slapped her hand down on my thigh.

"Maybe it's not too late."

By the time we reached the carryout I was just happy to get out of the car and take a break from the verbal assault. My erection was nearly painful.

Dawn handed me a fifty and said, "Get a case of whatever. Nothing light. Coors. Bud. Whatever. Maybe Heineken if they've got it. No craft beer."

The carryout was called Gas n Gas. I didn't see any pumps anywhere. The outside lighting was yellow and there were bars on the windows, plastered with ads for the lottery and cigarettes. It seemed to be in the middle of nowhere. Gunshots and sirens provided a distant soundscape.

A painfully skinny girl wearing a red swimsuit top over nonexistent breasts and shorts even shorter than Dawn's stood beside the door, smoking a cigarette. I glanced at her and nodded before opening the door displaying a typed sheet of paper stating customers had to remove their hoods before entering and that ice cream cones were not permitted in the store. I wondered what had happened to make this a problem.

The inside lighting was bright and harsh or maybe it just seemed that way after being on the dark country road. The clerk glanced up at me, probably to confirm I wasn't wearing a hood or enjoying an ice cream cone, before going back to his phone. I went to the coolers in the back, prepared to grab the beer and head back up front.

I paused.

I texted Travis.

"Are you awake?"

The second after sending it, I wondered why I'd bothered. Was I going to tell him about Dawn? Was I afraid something was going to happen to me?

Maybe.

I focused my attention back on the beer cooler. It had been a while since I'd done this and it amazed me how readily the checklist resurfaced. The most beer for the money, the highest alcohol content, the best beer for the weather, the stuff I liked, the stuff I knew I didn't like.

Fuck it, I thought.

I wasn't buying it for myself.

I opened the cooler door and grabbed a case of PBR. It would either be exactly what Dawn wanted or she would ridicule me because of it.

I took the case of beer to the counter. The obese clerk stood up, looked like he might fall down, and lurched toward the old yellowed register.

He jerked his head toward the door and said, "That girl din't ask you for nothin, did she?"

"No." I instantly resented the clerk for trying to drag me into some kind of conflict.

"I gotta do more to keep the trash run off. Too much trash around here. They come around stinkin like dicks and hustlin my customers for drug money."

"I . . . I'm not really from around here."

"You a cop?"

He must have noticed the cop car for the first time. I glanced out and saw Dawn standing next to the car talking to the skinny girl.

"Nah. I'm just out for a ride along."

This situation should have seemed absurd to anyone who hadn't spent his years working third shift at a store on the edge of the most dangerous part of Dayton serving people's legal addictions.

"Yeah," he said. "I guess you guys get to have all the good shiny fun."

After taking a long, leering look at Dawn and the skinny girl, he scanned the beer and gave me the total. I handed him the fifty. He held it up above his head and inspected it closely before marking it with a special marker and tucking it in the drawer.

"Um . . . do I have any change?"

"I know what you're up to. No change."

I thought about bringing the cop car into it but this guy's spooky knowledge of the situation told me it probably wouldn't do any good.

I knocked over a rack of ChapStick and grabbed the beer. While I went out to my night of good shiny fun, he'd be battling his girth to pick ChapStick up off a dirty floor.

"We need to go," I said.

"Okay, Barcie's coming with us."

I assumed Barcie was the skinny girl. I took a quick glance at her, just long enough to take notice of a few things. Her thin brown hair was pulled back into a ponytail, but that still didn't hide the bald spots on her head. She had a jagged scar in place of one of her eyebrows, was missing an ear and, when she smiled, I noticed she was also missing a lot of teeth.

"You mind driving?" Dawn asked.

"Um, I'd rather not."

"Maybe it's not really a choice? I mean, like, you can either drive or walk."

I knew where we were. She knew where we were too. The really rational part of me knew that if I were forced to walk home, nothing would happen to me. The reasonably heightened paranoid part of my brain, however, more or less assured me something would happen and whatever it was would be terrible.

"Fine. Let's just get out of here."

I got behind the wheel. Dawn and Barcie got in the back. I pulled out of the parking lot and thought I had yet another, more serious offense to add to my growing list.

Dawn and Barcie sat in the middle of the backseat, Dawn more toward the driver's side.

"Where am I going?" I looked at her in the rearview.

I was hoping this was the person she had intended to pick up and I'd be able to go home. I knew she'd said 'a couple of people' but my brain had gotten overzealous and edited that out.

"Just drive around for a bit."

"Any particular place?"

"Just drive around. We're going to eventually have to go to Kettering, so I guess if you wanted to start off in that direction, that'd be great."

I had absolutely no sense of direction. I knew we were in West Dayton. Kettering was south of Dayton. I started back to Gethsemane, about ten miles west of Dayton. From there I knew how to get to Kettering.

"Hey, um, Barcie?" I said.

"Yeah, man," she said slowly.

"Would you happen to have a cigarette I can bum?"

She handed a cigarette and a lighter up to me with a wildly shaking hand.

"Thanks."

"Yeah, man."

I lit the cigarette, cracked the window, and handed the lighter back to her. It was the first cigarette I'd smoked in months and it was great.

I continued down Route 4, going back the way we'd come. I expected the girls to be chatty but they were mostly silent. I took another deep, satisfying drag from the cigarette and glanced in the rearview mirror.

The girls were kissing, Dawn's hands working between Barcie's legs. Barcie's head was leaned back, her mouth open. Something about the image struck me as slightly grotesque and I had to tell myself exceptionally ugly people were allowed to experience pleasure also. Dawn broke the kiss and I snapped my attention back to the road in front of me.

"It's okay if you want to watch."

I could feel my face flush with embarrassment.

"I, uh, probably need to watch the road."

"Pull over if you want. There're quiet little roads all over the place. You can pull it out, if you want."

By 'it,' I assumed she meant my cock.

"I think I'll just keep driving."

"I changed my mind. I want you to watch. I think you'd be fine watching this on a computer screen. Maybe you need to experience it in real life."

I took another drag off the cheap cigarette. It didn't taste good anymore so I tossed it out the window.

"I think I'm just going to drive myself back to my apartment. I got you the beer. I did what you wanted me to. I don't have to stick around and let you humiliate me."

I glanced back in the mirror. Dawn had her phone in her hand, Barcie smirking next to her.

"*Actually* . . . you kind of do. After all, you're driving around in a stolen cop car. If I were to call 911 and tell them how me and Barcie ended up back here, you'd probably be in a lot of trouble. Just pull off on the next side road."

Why was I even fighting this? An extremely attractive girl was asking me to watch her make out with another girl who looked kind of like a monster. How was this not something I wanted to do?

I made a right on Jefferson Straight Road, drove down it about a mile, and pulled off into the gravel on the shoulder.

Dawn leaned forward between the seats and pulled the keys from the ignition and pressed a button. The spotlight burst into life, shining into the overgrown bushes that crept nearly to the road.

"Makes it look like you're looking for something," Dawn said.

Why was there no separation between the front and back? I'd never been in a cop car but I thought most of them had some sort of mesh to keep the criminal from the cop. Maybe it was retractable or something. Maybe Gethsemane was such a small town they didn't fool with it. Maybe 'sheriff' was more of an administrative position than anything. Maybe Sheriff Bando didn't haul around criminals. I started to wonder if it was a cop car at all, but the shotgun locked between the two front seats and the laptop in front of the dash seemed pretty legit.

"Okay," Dawn said. "Move the mirror around where you can see us. It should make you more comfortable that way. It'll be more like a screen. If I look up, I want to see your eyes, okay? I want to know you're paying attention to us. And like I said, feel free to jerk off if you want."

I didn't say anything. My mouth had gone dry. I wasn't a prude or anything, but I couldn't pull my cock out in front of these two girls. I felt like they would end up ridiculing me if I did.

Dawn leaned over Barcie and began kissing her again.

She broke the kiss and glanced in the rearview. She smirked a little when she met my eyes.

"Hey," she said, "Barcie'll totally suck your dick if you want her to."

I swallowed and my throat made a dry click.

"I, uh, think I'm okay."

"You don't think she's pretty?"

I looked at Barcie in the mirror. She blinked so slowly it looked like she was about to nod off. The eyelid under the scar didn't work as well as the other one and they moved out of sync with one another.

"It's not that. I just don't know her." But that wasn't it at all. It wasn't even that I didn't find Barcie attractive. It was more like I didn't want to feel indebted to either one of them. If Barcie were to give me a blowjob, who knew what they would ask me to do next.

"I want to watch Barcie suck your sad little cock."

My erection had come back in full force and it was going to be hard arguing with her. I knew it would be something I regretted doing. It had been less than an hour and I already regretted getting in the car with Dawn.

"Come on." I tried hard to think of a legitimate excuse.

"*Come on*," she mocked. "That's like the worst argument in the world."

"I'm married," I said. There, that should do it. Marriage didn't carry the weight it once did, but maybe it would work.

"You're lying."

"No I'm not. I've been married for five years."

"Where's the ring?"

"We don't wear any."

"Why not?"

"I don't know. Because we're not sixty. Because we're progressive people who respect each other and don't view marriage as ownership."

"What's her name?"

"Kathleen."

"What does she do?"

"Teacher."

"Where did you meet?"

"Community college."

"Show me a picture."

"I don't have one on me."

"Not even on your phone?"

"I don't take many pictures with it."

"Nice one. Whatever. That makes me want to watch more. Now you'll be cheating on your wife too. Double fun. Wait. Is oral sex even cheating? I think the jury's still out on that. Get back here, hoss."

"Seriously . . . can we just *not* do this? It's been a long night. You wanted me to help you and I did that. I just want to go home. I'm tired. I have to work in the morning."

She leaned over the seat and looked at my distended crotch.

"You're also very hard. It's not like I'm asking you to take it up the ass or something. The scared little boy is still going to end the night safe and snug in his little bed and when you wake up tomorrow, you can get back to your sad little life. But if you tell me no again, then I'm going to take out my phone and press it one time and your life is going to get really *really* complicated and you're probably not going to like any of it."

"You're not even the one doing it!"

"Barcie doesn't mind, do you?"

"Whatever, babe," Barcie said.

"Is that why you're arguing? You want *me* to suck your cock?"

There was absolutely no right answer to this. But, yeah, that was probably the actual reason.

"I don't want *anyone* to suck my cock."

The girls started laughing and when I thought about what I'd just said I realized how ridiculous it sounded. It needed a lot of qualifiers, a lot of clarification. On its own, it had probably never been uttered by anyone who actually had a penis.

"Get back here. Otherwise you'll be the one who ends up sucking cock. Besides, I don't do that, so it's not happening with me."

What was the worst that could happen?

I was pretty good at avoiding things. Once I got away from these girls I could probably stay away.

I got out of the car, opened the back door on the driver's side and got in. I tried my best to will my erection away. Dawn rose up off the seat and pressed her back against the roof. She turned around and kicked the passenger seat as far forward as it would go to give herself more room. Barcie made a slithery movement and was suddenly resting on her elbows, her head above my lap, her fingers working the button and zipper of my jeans. Dawn rested her ass against the back of the passenger seat, reached down, unbuttoned Barcie's shorts and pulled them and her underwear down her thighs. The girl's white ass was so bony I told myself it reminded me of a concentration camp prisoner's and thought that would do wonders for stifling my erection but the girl had tugged my jeans and underwear down far enough for my cock to pop out and I felt the slightly cool air hit it followed by the heat of Barcie's mouth and before I knew it I was hard and no longer looking at Barcie's bony ass but letting my eyes run up Dawn's tanned thighs and resting on the crotch of her shorts before traveling up her stomach and taking in her small firm breasts. She was watching me look at her. I immediately felt shame and embarrassment.

Dawn made a cone of her hand and began pressing it against Barcie's cunt.

Barcie's mouth was doing things to my cock I'd never felt before.

"Feels good, doesn't it?" Dawn said. "You don't have to be afraid to like it. Barcie's never gotten any complaints."

It did feel good. This poor, unfortunate looking girl was giving me head while Dawn did god knew what to her. Why should I act like I wasn't enjoying it?

"Yeah," I said. "It feels really good."

"You gonna come?"

"Yeah. I'm gonna come pretty soon."

I was pretty pent up. It had been a few days since I'd even masturbated. Months since I'd actually touched a real girl.

I watched Dawn's hand continue to press against Barcie. I looked down at Barcie, her head moving up and down, all the cords standing out in her neck. Dawn's fingers began disappearing.

"I'm coming," I said. I wasn't trying to be dramatic or anything. I just thought the girl should be given the choice if she didn't want to drink me.

"Go ahead and come in her mouth. That's what she likes. She'll milk you dry. Unless you want to come on her face."

But my muscles had already constricted. I felt Barcie jerk a little with the initial shot. She did her best to keep going but ultimately pulled her mouth off me to gag while Dawn, now in up to her elbow, began punching her arm in and out of Barcie. Barcie's eyes were closed, drool and come dripping out of her mouth, as she squealed and moaned. Dawn's arm moved faster and faster until Barcie collapsed on the seat in a shivering heap.

The car was filled with a humid, smelly silence as we all sat on the backseat.

I slid my pants back up and fastened them.

Barcie pulled her cigarettes and lighter out of her shorts on the floor, not bothering to put them back on.

Dawn held her fisting arm out in front of her and studied it.

"I like the way it looks as it dries," she said.

"Can I get one of those?" I asked Barcie.

She handed me a cigarette and I lit up.

"How was it, Barse?" Dawn asked.

"Nutritious." Barcie smiled.

Dawn said, "You know all of Gethsemane's cop cars are equipped with cameras inside and out?" She pointed at a red light on the dash. "So, congratulations, Brett, you're officially an accomplice."

"My name's Brad," I said.

Once we were ready to go, Dawn reassumed driving privileges. She told me I had to sit in the back, "like a criminal."

I felt dazed and weird and like anything I said would be something else for Dawn to humiliate me about so I just looked out the window. Dawn's constant banter became a human equivalent of the road's hum, countered only with Barcie's slow, laconic responses. I hoped we'd be going back to Gethsemane after our stop in Kettering. Barcie had asked Dawn if the people we were picking up would be ready and Dawn said they were, she'd just texted them.

I imagined a whole society of young people, never really sleeping, never really eating, sitting around and feasting on anxiety while waiting to be rousted from their permanent semi-stupor by the vibrating of their phones. I think I dozed off for a bit.

The intermittent popping of the beer cans kept waking me up. I didn't know if my half-sleep state was distorting reality or if the girls really managed to pound that many beers before we got to Kettering. Kettering wasn't that far away. They'd pounded like five beers each. I'd come to with the pop of the can and then again a couple of minutes later when they rolled down their windows to throw the cans out. I really wanted one and knew it would help calm my nerves and make the situation a little more tolerable but I stopped myself from asking. It wouldn't end with one and I would ultimately get stupid and lose all initiative. The same as if I'd taken a sip of the whiskey back at Travis's. I tried forcing myself to doze back off but it wasn't working.

Dawn pulled the car into the driveway of a definitively middle class neighborhood, which Kettering seemed to have in abundance. She pulled out her phone and typed something, probably letting whoever know we were here to pick them up.

I remembered my text to Travis and was pretty sure my phone hadn't vibrated with a response. I didn't want to pull it out in front of Dawn, although I wasn't sure why. It wasn't like she was going to beat me up and take it from me. At least, I didn't think she would. I made a note to check it the first chance I got.

A heavily muscled young guy and a small young woman emerged from the house.

Dawn and Barcie got out of the car. Barcie didn't stand so well. Dawn seemed unaffected.

"You're gonna have to drive," Dawn told the massive guy. "We're too wasted." She didn't slur or sound the slightest bit drunk and I wondered if she was just concerned about being over the legal limit. But who pulled over a cop car? Maybe she was just too lazy to drive anymore.

"That's cool," he said. "You want to just do it here?"

"Nah. I've got someplace better."

"Right on."

While everyone seemed distracted, I quickly slid my phone out of my pocket and clicked the button to turn the screen on.

No text from Travis.

Dawn said to the girl, "Nice to see you again."

The girl didn't say anything. She just blinked and smiled.

The girl was really pretty but in a completely different way than Dawn. There was something about Dawn that seemed slightly exotic and, maybe, a little tomboyish. This girl seemed preppy and clean, like she'd just wandered out of a sorority. Blond and blue-eyed, her body was lithe and petite.

Everyone got back into the car: the guy behind the steering wheel, the girl in the passenger seat, Barcie to my right and Dawn to my left.

"Oh, guys, this is Brad," Dawn said.

"Hey, man, I'm Klint with a 'K'. This is Taylor Dream. She's gonna be real famous."

"Great." It wasn't the best thing to say but I didn't even really know how to respond to a statement like that. Klint's alpha frat vibe made me immediately uncomfortable and there was something weird about the girl too. Maybe they both just seemed too normal.

"Isn't Taylor pretty?" Dawn asked.

"Yeah," I said.

"Relax, bro," Klint said as he backed the car out. "I'm the only one who fucks her."

"It's okay," Dawn said. "Brad doesn't like to fuck real girls. He likes jerking off more. Would you jerk off to Taylor?"

My face was again hot with embarrassment but I knew she wouldn't let it rest until I said something so I just said, "Sure."

"How would you want to see her get fucked? Rough? Do you want to see her get tied up? Do you want to see her choke on some guy's huge cock? Do you want to watch her get fucked by some gross old fat guy? How about, like, ten gross old fat guys? Oh, I bet you want to see her take it up the ass, don't you?"

I didn't say anything.

"You'll have to excuse Brad. It's probably hard for him to think about sex right now. He's already shot his load into Barcie's mouth."

Klint glanced into the rearview and said, "Yikes."

Something about that rubbed me the wrong way. I cleared my throat and said, "I don't really pay a lot of attention to the guys in the video. I'd like to see her get fucked hard, definitely in the ass. But when the guy finishes I'd like to see her put on a strap on and fuck the guy in the ass."

Dawn smiled. "I like that idea."

"I am not taking it up the ass," Klint said.

"We can talk about it when we get there," Dawn said. "Speaking of which . . ." She pulled out her phone, pulled up a mapping app and placed it on the laptop below the dash.

Then she leaned her head against the window and seemed to doze off. I don't think she actually dozed off. I think she just closed her eyes. The car was silent for the duration of the ride.

I was surprised when the cop car pulled up in front of my apartment nearly a half hour later. My first thought was not that she had brought me home but that she lived in the same building. I quickly dismissed that as absurd. I would know if the sheriff lived in the building. I would've noticed a police car parked in front or a uniformed man exiting or entering the building without removing someone in handcuffs. Besides, my building was not really for professionals or families. It was for poor people and old people. There were only about twelve apartments in the old three-story building and it was only about half full at any given time.

"We're going to need to use your apartment for a couple hours," Dawn said.

What was the point in arguing? At least I was home. She hadn't lied about that.

I led them to the door of my building. Dawn said she and Barcie needed to get some stuff out of the trunk and would be up in a few minutes.

I led Klint and Taylor Dream up to my sad second floor apartment. I had this momentary fear that if I stuck around I was going to be asked to participate and was pretty sure my head was going to explode if I had to be in the same room as Klint for more than five minutes. It was nearly six in the morning. The sun was coming up and the birds were chirping outside.

"Well, folks," I said, "I'm exhausted."

I pulled all the covers and pillows from my bed. Klint had brought the case of beer up with him and I grabbed one of those too. I took everything into the bathroom. I knew if I didn't disappear before Dawn came up she wouldn't let me leave. I didn't lock the door because I figured they would need the bathroom. I threw the covers in the bathtub, pulled the shower curtain, chugged the beer, and drifted off.

When I woke up the first time, the shower curtain had been pulled back and Taylor Dream was on her knees, naked, vomiting into the toilet. Dawn stood in the doorway, filming it. I woke up again to see Klint, naked and staring into the vanity mirror, breathing hard and flexing, blood running down the backs of his legs. I thought he was shaking and looked pale but that could have just been my imagination.

I woke up for the final time sometime that afternoon. I was still in the bathtub but I was soaking wet and imagined everyone pissing on me at some point.

My phone sat on my chest.

There was one text message and three missed calls.

The text was from Dawn Bando.

Nice to see she'd added herself as a contact.

The calls were all from work.

I opened the text.

It was a photo of my text to Travis on Travis's phone.

"Are you awake?"

Did that mean she had Travis's phone?

The text accompanying the picture said: "Remember to ask me about Schrodinger's cat."

HUMILIATION REEL

"We done had three people call in today," Ted Billups said. "It's the busiest time of the year."

"I know. I'm really sorry. I'm going to get the truck towed today. I'll be there tomorrow."

I had called work before even getting out of the bathtub. Now, lying there, I wished I hadn't. I was wet and there was a dank foul smell in the bathroom. I was pretty sure it was coming from me.

"You'd best or I'm gonna have to hire me some new folks. You heard from Travis?"

"No. Why? Did he call in too?"

"Didn't bother callin. I tried textin him but I just keep gettin pitchers of a hairy ladies' parts." It was hard not to laugh hearing Ted Billups say those words. "I don't know if that's his way uh quittin or whut."

"I'll see if I can get hold of him."

"I best not see you boys out runnin around together."

"I wish I had a car to run around in."

"Welp, I better get back to it. Gonna be a long day."

"See you tomorrow. And thanks again."

"Yep."

I clicked off. Today was a pretty good day to miss. Today was Chamon day. Their kids had been home from school on summer break for the past couple of weeks. They had an irritating daughter, about seven, who followed me around the house and asked what I was doing the entire time I was there, despite the brevity of my answers.

"I'm watering plants."

"I'm trimming plants."

"Still watering."

"Still trimming."

Their mom never suggested to her that she might be bothering me. Never offered up any alternatives for her to go and do. It made it even more irritating because the girl was typically staring into the screen of her phone while she accosted me. Creepier than the girl was her older brother who sat in the corner of the living room scratching at various parts of his body. He had bloody patches on his face, hands, and arms. A corona of dead skin surrounded him on the dark wood floor. So somebody else would get to deal with that.

I removed everything from the tub, stripped off my clothes, and took a long, hot shower. After my shower I had to walk through the apartment to get clean clothes. By the time I reached my chest of drawers, I felt like I needed another shower. My first instinct was to just walk away from the apartment. Go to a hotel until I could find another apartment and know I would never see my security deposit again.

Thankfully there were no people in the apartment, but it looked like it had been the site of a weeklong party. There were ashes and cigarette butts everywhere. Beer cans. Dark stains on the floor and bed. I couldn't tell if they were shit or blood or both.

Despite my nausea and sense of sinking dread, I was incredibly hungry. I had food in the kitchen area but couldn't even think about preparing food, let alone eating, in the apartment until it had been cleaned.

I got dressed, grabbed my wallet and phone, and headed to the diner on the corner. I stopped by the bank of mailboxes just inside the main entrance. I threw everything in the trashcan by the door. There was a lost dog flyer taped to the door. It was a different lost dog flyer than the one from a couple days ago.

While eating, I tried to clear my head.

I had successfully pushed the girl from the photos out of my thoughts weeks ago so it had been a while since I'd had to think about anything other than what I was going to eat or read or watch on my laptop. It was easy to get overwhelmed. Now Travis had me thinking about the girl from the photos again. I didn't have any feelings for her so the only thing I really associated her with was panic and fear. And now there was the shit with Travis and that girl from last night, Dawn. That had been insane and she had been on my mind since waking up. And what was the shit about Schrodinger's cat? I knew a little about it but hadn't given it much thought since, well, since I was about Dawn's age.

I tried to push it all away until I powered through my meal.

I knew I'd have to spend a lot of time cleaning the apartment, probably the rest of the day, and would use that time to sort things out. While I didn't love the idea of cleaning up other people's bodily fluids, I had never minded cleaning. I found something very Zen about it. Focusing on one thing and then the next until everything was neat and orderly. Maybe that's why I didn't hate my current job as much as I'd hated many other jobs. Landscaping is essentially being nature's janitor.

Once stuffed on cheap and greasy breakfast food, I headed back to the apartment. I pulled out all of my cleaning products from beneath the sink and set them on the small stove, which was still remarkably clean. I filled the mop bucket with cleaner and water. I would probably need to empty and refill this several more times. I strapped on some rubber gloves and prepared to dig in.

My phone vibrated.

I took the gloves off and pulled my phone out.

It was a text from Dawn.

"Why didn't you answer me?"

I was going to immediately respond with something like, "Dunno. Just woke up," but stopped myself. Why did I have to respond at all? If I were smart, wouldn't I just try to avoid Dawn forever?

I knew I couldn't really do that.

Well, I probably could do it, but knew I wasn't going to.

She might know what happened to Travis.

Not just that. It was everything else. True, if every night were like last night, I'd find it exhausting but . . . But more things had happened last night than I'd witnessed the last five years, easily. While I didn't feel good about everything that had happened, I didn't feel great about going to work every day, either, but still did it.

My phone vibrated again.

Another text from Dawn.

"Come down to the street."

The phone vibrated again before I could even put it back in my pocket.

"I know you're in there."

I didn't kid myself. I knew I was going to go down there, but there was something I wanted to check before I did.

I pulled up the browser on my phone and typed:

"sheriff bando gethsemane"

I half expected it to turn up nothing, but I was taken to the very professional looking website for the Gethsemane Police Department. The image of Sheriff Charles "Chuck" Bando, portly and smiling, but still dead-eyed, stared back at me. Of course it occurred to me this was public knowledge, meaning just because a Sheriff Bando existed didn't necessarily mean the girl I'd met who called herself Dawn Bando was really his daughter. I quickly typed in the name "Dawn Bando." The first link was to her MyFace page, naturally, and below that was a link to the Gethsemane High graduating class of 2017, which meant she'd just graduated this spring.

I tapped on the MyFace link. It was set to private, but her profile pic was visible. She smiled in a way that was soft and inviting, not demented or crazed, and she held a small dog and wore a conservative sundress. It was unmistakably the girl I'd met last night, although this one seemed to have a less malevolent tone.

I put the phone back in my pocket and headed down to the street.

She stood on the sidewalk in front of my truck, wearing a pair of skintight black yoga pants and a tight gray V-neck t-shirt. I didn't know if I should thank her or be immediately suspicious.

"My truck," I said.

"I had it picked up for you."

It didn't look that bad. There were some new dents and scratches on the passenger side but they fit in with all the preexisting dents and scratches. The all-encompassing rust had really been the main focal point since buying it, anyway.

"How did you find it?" I said.

"Thanks, Dawn. I'm really glad you did such a nice thing," she said in a husky, terrible imitation of my voice. But it seemed moderately playful and I liked that.

"Yeah. Thanks. Sorry. So . . . how did you find it?"

"You got my text, right?"

"Yeah. It was confusing."

"Not really. You're just being willfully ignorant."

"What do you mean?"

"I asked you why you were where you were last night and you lied to me."

"Is Travis okay? Did you do something to him?"

"Who's Travis?"

"He's the guy I was going to meet last night. You sent me a picture of his phone."

"Shhh. Want to take a ride?"

The dread came back. I don't know why it hadn't occurred to me earlier. Maybe it was because Dawn had been alone and young and seemed incapable of doing what I now thought maybe she'd done. I tried to put the thought out of my head. It was a dumb idea. Probably an impossible idea. There was no connection between Dawn and Travis, so there was no way Dawn had done anything to him. So why did she have his phone? Maybe she'd gone and dug around in the field today. Maybe that was how she turned up the truck, even though I remember it being plainly visible last night when she had found me, so that didn't really involve deep sleuthing.

"The correct answer is yes."

"Okay." Just seeing her again, being this close to her, seemed to cause whatever was left of the rational part of my brain to leak out. I didn't want to argue with her. I wanted to fuck her. I also had to remind myself she wasn't interested and probably just wanted the attention a pathetic older guy could give her.

I expected her to hop in the passenger seat of the truck but she walked to the car parked in front of it. I hadn't even noticed it. This was the car she'd been driving last night. Looking at it in the bright afternoon sunlight, I could now tell it wasn't a cop car at all. I mean, it looked like it had been a cop car at one time but there were no decals or anything on the doors. No sirens. It was the type of car I typically associated with plainclothes detectives and warrant officers. Maybe it wasn't the same one as last night. If her dad was the sheriff, it was possible he owned a whole fleet of decommissioned cop cars.

We got in and she pulled away from the curb.

"Where are we going?"

"I don't know. Is there anywhere you want to go?"

"Is this all a game to you?"

She made a pouty face. "Why? Are you not having any fun?"

"Do you know what happened to Travis?" I felt like it was safer to ask this now that we were in the car. Now that she couldn't take off and leave me standing on the curb. Now that those large, eerie eyes were fixed on the road and not me.

She shrugged. "All I know is what you told me. You went to buy weed from him and he wasn't there. Where's Travis? I guess that's a mystery."

"What does it have to do with Schrodinger's cat?"

"Are you familiar with that?"

"It's a theory or a thought experiment or something. Something to do with quantum mechanics. Put a cat in a box with something potentially lethal and, before the box is opened, the cat is considered to be both alive *and* dead."

"That's pretty close. See? A mystery."

"So Travis is both alive and dead?"

"That's impossible. He's probably alive *or* dead, but isn't that the same for everybody. We're alive. That's what we should focus on. Besides, do you really think I'd be capable of doing anything to him?"

"How did you end up with his phone?"

"Maybe I found it."

"Did you?"

"Find it? How else would I have it? I guess the real question is where I found it."

"Where did you find it?"

"Why would I tell you the truth if you're not going to tell me the truth?"

"I'm still wondering why I *should* tell you the truth."

"Suit yourself. You know, I couldn't help noticing your number was the last one he called."

"Yeah. Probably."

"Might look bad. I mean, if he's missing. Or dead."

"I hate you." I was half joking.

She laughed. "That's why it's so much fun being around you."

Maybe she was waiting for me to say something else but I couldn't really think of anything to say that wouldn't serve as more fodder for her to manipulate me.

"You know," she said, "you were pretty much the only person besides his mom he ever called or texted."

"Probably. Travis didn't have a lot of friends. *Doesn't* . . . have a lot of friends."

"Is that why you sent him those pictures?"

I put my hand over my forehead and massaged my temples. The pictures. It felt like they were going to haunt me for the rest of my life.

"Let's just say if I ever gave you my pussy and you sent naked pictures of me to your best friend, I wouldn't be too happy." She paused and shrugged again. "Actually, I probably wouldn't give a fuck but I'm not most girls and, wait for it, I'm not married. I mean, you're not married either but . . . I'm pretty sure *she* is."

I wondered how far in she wanted to plunge the knife.

"Why did you tell me you were married?"

"How do you know I'm not?"

"I knew you weren't as soon as you said you were. You seem desperate and sad but in a different way. Like there's no one really looking out for you. Plus I researched you. Found no record of any marriages. Ever. I would have assumed you'd at least have given it a shot by now. You kind of have something about you that screams failure."

"Maybe I never even tried."

"That's what it is. That's even worse."

"Yeah, well . . ."

"Did you know who that was before you fucked her? I'm assuming you did fuck her."

I was going to tell her it was none of her business but then she would just bring up the pictures on Travis's phone again so I just nodded slowly.

"Yes you fucked her or yes you knew who she was?"

"Both." My voice sounded hoarse.

"Stasia Warner," Dawn said. "She's fairly well known in Get. Do you know why she's fairly well known?"

"Afraid so."

"That's right. She's well known because she's married to Larry Warner. Do you know what Larry Warner's nickname is?"

"White Power Larry," I mumbled.

"I'm sorry. I didn't hear you," she said.

"White. Power. Larry," I said more loudly.

"That's right! White Power Larry. Tell me, Brad, do you think White Power Larry's into wife swapping? Actually, it's not even wife swapping since he didn't really get anything in return. So I guess it would be more like wife loaning. Do you think White Power Larry likes loaning out his young, drunk wife to pathetic losers?"

"It was a while ago," I said. "I used to drink quite a bit. I did a lot of things I wouldn't have done otherwise."

"Really? Because she's super hot. I would have fucked her in a heartbeat. Congratulations on nailing that, by the way. I'm not sure if it's worth dying for but . . ."

"I didn't even know I'd sent the photos until the next day. I haven't taken a drink since."

"Until . . ."

"Until last night."

She had a loopy, shit-eating grin plastered across her face.

"Remind me to show you some of the footage if I get the chance."

I felt queasy. The greasy breakfast wasn't sitting so well.

"Will you pull over?"

"Awww," she made that insulting pouty face again. "Is widdle Bwad going to be sick?"

"Please."

"I'm not pulling over so you can vomit like a teenager who can't handle his liquor."

"*Please.*"

"Just vomit out the window."

I rolled down the window. Maybe the breeze would help stave off the nausea. Maybe she would have to stop for something and I could throw myself out of the car.

No.

It was definitely coming up.

"Oh, man," she said. "I gotta get this."

She pulled her phone from between her thighs and tapped it a few times before fixing it on me while continuing to drive.

"Can you not record me?"

"That's perfect. Keep saying shit like that."

"Fuck you."

"*Fuck you,*" she mocked.

I unfastened my seatbelt and leaned my head out the window.

"Try not to get any on the car!" she called.

I retched. At first it was nothing but bile and shame. I retched again and it felt like the entirety of my breakfast came up with one heave.

Dawn laughed. "Oh, man! That was a lot!"

She stopped the car, backed up, and got out to film my puddle of vomit.

I could have run then but the only thing I could think about was how it would look as she filmed a grown man running in terror from a small teen girl.

She got back in the car and said, "Know where you want to go yet?"

"Yeah," I said. "Take me to where you found the truck."

"Why?"

"I need to check on something."

"You know," she said, "I'll admit I'm a little surprised you knew about Schrodinger's cat."

"Why? Because you think I'm an idiot."

"I've seen your apartment. It doesn't exactly seem like you've done well for yourself. Plus I don't really remember seeing a lot of books but I was somewhat preoccupied. I'll have to go back and review the footage. Are you sure you didn't just look it up after I mentioned it?"

For some reason it bothered me when she said she was 'preoccupied.' I wondered if Klint had fucked her. I wondered why I cared. I wondered why the thought of it gave me a slight erection. I wondered how I could think about any of that with the smell of puke still drying on my lips.

"I sold most of my books during the Great Simplification a couple of years ago."

"Let me guess . . . Some kind of break up. Like, of a long term thing." She put on her baby voice again. "Bwad's mad. Bwad's gonna sell all his stuff. Dat'll show her. He doesn't need you. He doesn't need nothin!"

Her smile would have been a beautiful thing if it weren't brought on by derision and self-satisfaction.

"Yeah. Something like that." I wasn't going to go into details with her. "Did you fuck that guy last night?"

"I told you. I don't really like cock. Why? Would you be jealous if I did?"

"No. I was just curious. He seemed like a douche."

"I don't think he'll be around much more. Besides, I thought you were kind of sweet on Barcie."

I didn't want to say anything mean. "Barcie's not really my type."

"Why? Because she's ugly?"

"I just don't think she's really for me."

"It's not very nice to just shoot your load into a girl's mouth if you don't really like her."

"That wasn't really my choice. You know that. Stop trying to make me feel bad about it."

"Fine. I like Barcie, anyway. I think she's unique and tough. And *I* think she's beautiful. Did you see how much I got into her last night? I was in almost up to my elbow!"

"Yeah," I said. "I, um, I was there. I saw it."

"Right. Because your cock was in her mouth while that was happening."

"Are you taking me where I asked you to?"

"No," she said.

"Why not?"

"Because I don't want to."

"That's childish."

"So says widdle Bwad. Maybe because you still haven't told me the truth about why I found you hiding in the bushes on the side of the road."

Since she already knew about the pictures, I didn't really think there was anything to hide.

"Travis seemed self-destructive. He wanted me to shoot him in the face. I told him no. He used the pictures as blackmail. When I got there he was gone. See? Not too exciting."

"I guess I can see why you're worried then. Sounds like maybe he was mixed up in something. There's some pretty dark shit that goes on in this town."

"I guess. I don't know. I hardly leave the apartment."

"Unless it's to fuck the wife of the local hatemonger or shoot your best friend in the face."

We were now in the nature reserve covering much of Gethsemane. Miles of well-maintained roads wound through the slightly hilly deciduous woods, the sunlight strobing through the trees. My stomach had settled somewhat. That was something, at least. I wondered if Dawn would just spend the rest of the afternoon driving around if I didn't give her somewhere else to go. I also wondered if she would find some reason to not take me wherever I asked.

As if reading my mind, she said, "You know, I'm just going to keep driving around until you tell me to go somewhere."

"I've already told you where I wanted you to take me."

"Yeah. I'm still not going there."

"Fine. Let's go to your house."

"Why?"

"I don't know. It's someplace, isn't it? You've seen my apartment, now show me your house."

"It's actually my dad's house."

"Okay. Let's go there."

She glanced at her phone. "Okay. Dad's going to be at work for a couple more hours. I guess we can hang out there for a bit."

It turned out we were only about five minutes away. She lived in a cabin in the woods, one of four or five surrounding a small lake. Describing it as a cabin made it seem too modest. It was actually a massive house that happened to be made out of logs. Two stories with walkout decks on both floors.

She stopped the car in the circular blacktop driveway and we both got out.

"This is really nice," I said.

"I guess."

"Does your mom live here with you?"

"No. She died a few years back. Someone actually accused my dad of killing her but it wasn't taken too seriously."

"Did he?"

"I don't know. I don't think so. I wasn't around much then."

She unlocked the door, punched a code into a security system, and walked into the house. I remembered the dog from the My-Face profile pic and expected to see it running around but I didn't see any sign of it. Maybe it was just a prop. Someone else's dog used to soften her up and make her seem less like a psychopath. Maybe it was one of the ones that had gone missing.

"I'm already bored," she said. "Wanna lick my pussy for a few minutes?"

The request was so out of the blue I didn't know if I'd heard her correctly.

I swallowed roughly and said, "What?"

"You heard me. Want to?"

"Do I have a choice?"

"You always have a choice, but decisions have consequences. Besides, do you really want a choice?"

"Who doesn't want to have the right to say no?"

"A lot of people probably. I mean, think about it, it could seem emasculating if you're doing it and not getting anything in return. But if you don't have a choice then it's just something you have to do. And you do want to. You'd probably do just about anything I asked you to because you think that maybe, one day, you'll finally get to fuck me."

I was already slightly hard just thinking about it. How could I argue with her?

I followed her into the living room. She tossed her phone onto the couch and shucked out of her yoga pants. There was something completely utilitarian and routine in her movement. I would have thought I wanted to watch her remove her pants slowly but there was something arousing about her blasé nonchalance. She sat down on the couch and spread her legs. She picked up her phone, looked into the camera and smiled before training it on me. I got down on my knees between her legs and began kissing her pussy. I licked up and down her labia and reached my hand up to spread her open.

"Just your tongue," she said. "I don't want you to touch me."

I glanced up at her. Her eyes were glued to her phone, which was focused on me. She showed no signs of enjoying it. I pressed my tongue against her clit, closing my lips around it and sucking her into my mouth. Her cunt had an almost acrid chemical tang and I told myself that was probably from all the pills. I was rock hard. I pulled back and looked up at her again. She was still focused on her phone, no sign of pleasure on her face.

"Can I jerk off while I do it?"

"No. I want you to concentrate. You can afterward."

I went back to eating her out. I'd always thought I was okay at this. I'd been in a couple of long-term relationships and saw myself as being properly trained but no matter what I did, I couldn't elicit any pleasurable response whatsoever. I thought about biting her just to see if she felt anything. I just kept going and going. There wasn't really any way to gauge the time and I didn't want to look around for a clock or something because I was afraid that would make me seem disinterested. And I didn't want to stop. I sucked and licked and probed and nibbled for what felt like an hour. It could have been longer. I would have stayed down there as long as she wanted me to. There was something about her juices that had a nearly narcotic effect. I didn't think about anything other than her and her cunt. Physically, I felt nothing but the silky texture of her skin on my tongue. My knees and back should have hurt but it was like I lost all awareness of my body. I couldn't remember the last time I'd felt this focused and clear-headed. My cock was hard and throbbing the entire time. It was like I didn't even need to masturbate or be inside her. Even before stopping, I thought about the next time I'd have the chance to do this.

Finally she said, "Okay, that's good."

I stood up and stretched.

"Did you, um, do anything?" I asked.

"Do anything?"

"Did you come?"

"A little, I guess. I didn't have an orgasm if that's what you meant. No ego boost for widdle Bwad. Sorry."

"I could keep going."

"But that was exactly what I wanted."

"Okay."

I was a little confused. I'd always assumed most people had sex to get off.

"Did you want me to leave my pants off while you jerk off or can I put them back on?"

My erection had wilted the moment I'd pulled away from her and I felt oddly satisfied so I'd kind of forgotten about jerking off.

"I'm okay," I said. There was a part of me that felt like I'd regret that decision later.

"Oh," she said, "you're definitely jerking off. That's not the choice. Your choice is whether or not I have my pants on."

"Can I touch you while I do it?"

"No. Gross."

"Leave them off them. Can I watch you touch yourself?"

"I don't do that."

Dawn was perhaps the first sexually liberated prude I'd ever met. So she would fist another girl, let a practical stranger go down on her, but didn't masturbate?

I unfastened my pants and pulled them down a little. She kept the phone pointed at me the entire time, capturing my gaze trained between her spread legs. I was hoping she'd break down and play with herself but she didn't. Just stared into her phone and jostled her legs back and forth and up and down out of boredom. My eyes feasted on her while I stroked myself faster and faster. Something about her complete disinterest was driving me insane. I thought about burying my head back between her legs. I thought about fucking her. I thought about getting her on her knees and ramming myself into her as deeply as I could, my hands on her hips, yanking her back against me, plunging my thumb into her asshole and pulling her hair so hard she couldn't close her mouth. I wrapped my free hand around the tip of my cock because I'd forgotten to grab a paper towel or anything. I came several hot spurts into my hand.

Dawn stood up and took a couple steps toward me.

"Let's see it," she said.

I held out my hand.

"Now drink it."

"No way."

"So it's good enough for Barcie but not for you? I guess I've got some pictures I need to send White Power Larry. Sheriff Bando too, for that matter. The longer you wait, the grosser it's going to be."

I raised my hand to my mouth, gagged before the semen even touched my lips, and shamefully began licking my hand.

"Yeah!" Dawn said. "Eat that load while it's still warm!"

The unease in my stomach came back with a vengeance.

"Where's the bathroom?" I asked.

"Awww, is widdle Bwadley sick again? Hissum's got such a finicky stomach." Her voice returned to the less patronizing one. "No bathroom. Suck it up."

I dry heaved as covertly as I possibly could. I would have probably thrown up if I hadn't already done so but managed to keep it all down. I imagined if I had thrown up, Dawn would have filmed the entire thing and then filmed me cleaning it up.

Once I recovered, she took me down to the basement where she showed me video footage on a really big screen of everyone who was in my apartment, along with a young black man wearing the uniform of a local pizza place, urinating on me while I slept in the shower. Also Klint taking a massive dump on my floor. Also a few minutes of Taylor Dream getting ass fucked by Klint while Dawn held her mouth open and Barcie spit into it. Then a few minutes of Klint taking it up the ass from Taylor, a huge strap on affixed to her, while he ate out Barcie's ass. By the time she turned it off, I felt uneasy and anxious.

"Let's go to Barcie's," she said.

I could have said I wanted to go home but I wasn't sure I ever really wanted to step foot in there again.

Dawn drove us to a gravel pit on Route 4. The equipment was set up around the unreal blue lake but none of it was running. Dawn wound around the graveled workspace until it narrowed into something resembling a driveway, and took that until she reached a huge but utilitarian looking house in the front of some woods. The house was newer and landscaped perfectly, but there was still something kind of plain and sad and hurried about it.

"Is Barcie's last name Danner?" I asked.

"Yeah. How did you guess?"

"So her dad owns all this?"

"Yep. Danner Gravel and Concrete. Pretty cool, huh?"

I didn't say anything.

We got out of the car and walked up to the house. Dawn didn't bother knocking. She just walked in. I followed her through the house, upstairs, and down a hall. She swung open the last door in the hallway. Barcie sat on her bed wearing a black sports bra and red underwear, hunched over a dinner plate and snorting something with a straw.

"Do you mind?" Dawn asked.

Barcie offered her the plate and she snorted a long fat line of whatever it was.

They didn't offer me any.

"Where is everybody?" Dawn said.

"Makin deliveries," Barcie said. Her eyes were glassy and a trickle of blood ran from one of her nostrils. She snorted and wiped it away with the back of her hand. "Where you guys been?"

Dawn pulled her phone from the waistband of her yoga pants, presumably pulled up the video of me going down on her, and held it in front of Barcie like she couldn't talk about what had happened or possibly didn't even remember.

"Looks fun," Barcie said. "Will you send that to me?"

Dawn retracted the phone, tapped it a couple of times, and said, "Done."

"Guess I should put on some clothes." Barcie stood up and

looked over at me. "Gimme yours."

The demand was so bizarre I didn't really know what she was asking at first. I didn't even know she was addressing me until she kept looking at me, took a couple of steps toward me.

"Huh?" I said.

"She wants your clothes," Dawn said.

"No," I said.

"That word needs to stop coming out of your mouth. At this point, my only debate is whether I hand your friend's phone over to the police and let you deal with the legal system or whether I go ahead and forward those photos to White Power Larry and let you deal with a more vigilante justice."

"What am I going to wear?"

Dawn walked to Barcie's closet, already open, and pulled out a pink and white dress.

"Here." Dawn tossed the dress onto the floor beside me. "Barcie wore this when she was a little chubbier. Maybe it'll fit."

I pulled off my t-shirt and handed it to Barcie. She put it on. She was so skinny she swam in it. I kicked off my shoes and slid my jeans off.

"Underwear too," Barcie said.

I glanced at Dawn who was, of course, now recording.

I handed my underwear to Barcie. She smelled them before stepping into them.

"You can keep the shoes," she said.

"Barcie's real particular about her footwear," Dawn said.

If I hadn't had to give up my underwear I probably wouldn't

have fooled with the dress. I picked it up while Barcie slid my jeans up her pale, bruised legs.

"Think I'm going to need a belt," she said.

"Use this," Dawn grabbed a length of chain draped over a corner of the bed's headboard.

I struggled with the dress while Barcie wrapped the chain around her waist, reached into the top drawer of her nightstand, and pulled out a padlock. She cinched the chain tight and locked it.

I tugged the dress down over my hips.

"Let me zip you up," Barcie said.

She turned me around.

"He's too fat," Dawn said. "No way you're getting that thing zipped."

As we left Barcie's room, Dawn said, "When are you getting a new room?"

"Daddy says now that I'm eighteen, he's gonna have a guest house built out in the woods for me . . . until I decide to move out. Course he wouldn't mind if I lived there forever."

"Cool."

We walked out of the house. The afternoon sunlight was harsh and bright. I liked it. I wished I wasn't wearing a dress. I wished I was someplace else but I didn't have anywhere else to be. At least I wasn't at work doing something I'd done hundreds of times before.

"I need to get something out of my car," Dawn said.

She opened the back door to her car and pulled out three Donald Trump masks lying on the backseat. I hadn't noticed them.

We followed Barcie around the house to a bank of what looked like storage sheds at the perimeter of the woods. There were around ten orange metal doors housed in the cinderblock structure. Barcie stopped at the third door from the left. She wore a green bracelet that looked like one of the old stretchy phone cords.

"Put these on," Dawn said.

I didn't say no. Didn't even ask why. It was going to be for some reason that was either stupid or horrible. I put the mask on. Barcie unlocked the padlock at the side of the door with one of the keys on the bracelet. She bent down and lifted up the door.

"Hurry up." Barcie pushed me inside.

I heard the screams even before the door was all the way down.

The storage room had gray, egg crate-style foam soundproofing on all the walls, including the inside of the door. It made the screams sound weird. It took the edge off in a way. In another way, it made them even more unnerving. Like listening to the essential nature of a scream. Or a defeated scream, something meant to be heard but muffled and deadened.

The screams were coming from Taylor Dream.

She was strapped into what looked like a vintage electric chair, wearing only her bra and underwear.

I was surprised she wasn't gagged but guessed it wasn't really necessary with all the soundproofing. And, for all I knew, Dawn and Barcie liked the sound of her screaming.

"I think you would agree there's a lot of porn out there." I didn't know if Dawn was specifically addressing the general assembly or me so I didn't answer her. Turns out I didn't really need to.

"The real question, from an entrepreneurial point of view, is how to get people to pay for it. Obviously you look for attractive actresses that are on the palette of what guys currently like to jerk off to. Then it helps to have some kind of scenario that's appealing to a lot of people. You want the girl to get fucked by the biggest cock you can find. But it ultimately comes back to the actress. Once you've found a winning actress, the question of getting people to pay for it is, again, the real problem. You can provide a teaser video to lure them in. Long enough to generate interest but not too long. You don't want the guy to be able to satisfy himself. You want to be the first site to feature the actress. And you want her to eventually end up doing everything. But, inevitably, they're going to ask for more money or go to another company who they think is going to treat them better. Or, God forbid, they're going to try to do it themselves with whatever lame ass tiny dicked guy they can find. Then, before you know it, they're all over the internet and people are watching them for free. Suddenly, the little cash cow you worked to build is completely destroyed. So the question is how you can stop them from doing that.

"This is the only thing that works."

Taylor's screams had subsided somewhat but now they came back with a raging fury. Since she was the only one in the room not wearing a mask, she seemed exceptionally naked.

"In this scenario everyone wins. People will pay more for this than any of her fuck videos. The premium rises on her existing videos because she'll never make another one. She'll be free."

Barcie used the key ring around her wrist to unlock the padlock enclosing the chain around her waist. My jeans slid off her hips, taking my underwear with them, and she stepped out of them. She pulled my t-shirt over her head. It was so large the mask didn't pose any problems.

Dawn stood close, filming everything with her camera.

"Want to eat her pussy while we do this?" Dawn said to me.

"No."

"What did I say about that word?"

"I'm not doing it."

She paused. I couldn't read her face. I thought about running but the door was probably locked and I wasn't really sure how well I'd fare running through our conservative small town wearing only a dress.

"Barcie." Dawn jerked her big Trump head at me.

Fuck it.

I turned for the door and at least gave it a shot. I was still giving it a shot when the chain came down between my shoulders.

I had never felt pain like that before.

She hit me again and I dropped to the cold concrete floor.

Barcie, a lot stronger than I would have taken her for, dragged me across the floor to Taylor Dream. Dawn fixed her phone to a tiny tripod and pulled Taylor's hips out to the edge of the chair. Dawn tightened and adjusted some straps.

Barcie yanked off my mask and twisted my face toward the camera. I could feel blood running down my back and it felt like the skin was gouged.

Dawn yanked Taylor's underwear down to her knees and Barcie

shoved my head in between her legs. I would have probably retched again, but I think my body was in some kind of shock. Dawn straddled my back and forced my face against Taylor's crotch while Barcie started working her face with the chain.

Taylor's screams grew even louder and more hysterical as I mechanically licked her vagina. I tried to pull away when her bladder let go but Dawn kept my head held there.

In reality it probably didn't last very long but it felt like the longest few minutes of my life.

This was the exact opposite of the experience I'd had going down on Dawn.

When it was finally over, I couldn't bring myself to look at Taylor. I was well aware of what she might look like. After the third or fourth time the chain had come down, I'd been licking away blood trickling down her stomach. I collapsed onto the floor in a fetal heap and buried my head in my arm.

Dawn said, "At least you didn't piss yourself, pussy. Get up. We're taking this bitch home and going to a party. We're going to have a lot of fun."

I felt like what little spirit I had left had been beaten out of me.

I braced myself against the storage door and stood up. My legs felt weak.

Barcie held Taylor around the upper arms as Dawn lifted the door. Taylor whimpered and sobbed, shaking uncontrollably.

When we got to the car Dawn opened the back door and I crawled in. Barcie shoved the girl in the other back door. She still wore only her bra and was covered in blood. I looked away as quickly as possible. I had never witnessed anything more violent than a fistfight in high school and, other than in movies, the sight of blood sent a feeling of nausea swirling through me. Dawn went around to the trunk, opened it, came back around to my door, and set a twelve-pack of beer on my lap. She and Barcie got in the front and we were headed back through the quarry and out to the road.

It hurt for me to sit back so I had to turn and put most of my weight on my arm. I chose to face the window so I wouldn't even accidentally glance at Taylor.

She was still sobbing. She said, "Can I see?" Her voice sounded weird.

Barcie turned, snapped a picture of her, and turned the phone around so she could see herself. Taylor began crying even harder.

Barcie and Dawn began laughing even harder. I thought maybe even Taylor's cries turned into laughter but I didn't see how that could be possible.

Barcie reached back, tore open the twelve-pack, and grabbed two cans.

Looking at her face, I wondered if Dawn had done something like that to her at one point.

Taylor reached over with a shaky hand and grabbed a beer too.

How could she think about drinking at a time like this?

Then I thought it would probably help with the pain, which I currently had plenty of. Might help with the nerves too. The girls had mentioned going to a party and that sent sharp little jolts of anxiety and dread through me.

I grabbed a beer.

I'd managed to put away three of them by the time we reached what I thought was the same house we'd picked Taylor up from the night before. I wasn't sure if the beer was helping with the anxiety at all, but the pain from my torn up back had receded to a nearly tolerable level.

Dawn pulled into the driveway and began honking the horn.

Klint came to the car wearing only a pair of cargo shorts. He looked mad.

Barcie got out of the car, opened Taylor's door, and dragged the girl out. She fell into a heap on the ground.

"There you go," Barcie said.

"What the fuck am *I* supposed to do with her?" Klint said. "She looks like a fucking monster."

Barcie shrugged and got back into the car.

"Don't be a so fucking insensitive!" Dawn called to Klint before slamming the car in reverse.

I was on my fourth beer and losing my sense of time but it seemed like we pulled up in front of a house only a few minutes later. It looked like we were in East Dayton and I hoped this wasn't where the party was.

"Watch him," Dawn said, getting out of the car.

She walked up to the porch in front of the large two-story house. The paint had completely worn off the house and it didn't have any windows. A large dog snarled at Dawn from the porch. It looked like the dog was covered in tumors. A rail thin man wearing only baggy, dirty denim shorts and covered in tattoos came out to the porch, barking something at the dog.

"Come on in!" he said to Dawn in a thick Appalachian twang.

"Nope," Dawn said. "Bring it to me."

The man glanced at the car, possibly to see if Dawn had anyone else with her. It seemed like a pretty rapey thing to do.

"Fine," he said. "I got it."

He came down the stairs. It looked like he handed Dawn something but Dawn was partially blocking him and I couldn't tell what it was. She pocketed it, handed him something, presumably cash, and came back to the car.

She drove to an alleyway. Barcie ripped up one of the cans, put a clump of something in the bottom of it, and held a lighter up to it.

Dawn uncapped a syringe and filled it up.

It filled with a neon green fluid and I thought about the movie *Re-Animator*.

Then she turned to me. "We're going to shoot you up."

"Please don't." My voice sounded like it came from somewhere else. Flat and robotic.

"Well, we're going to. If you don't put up a fight, I'll take you back home tonight."

"Then will you leave me alone?"

"We'll take you home."

"Will you tell me about Schrodinger's cat?"

"You already know about it."

"I mean . . . how it applies to me." It was already getting hard to think.

"No. We're probably going to put you in a wheelbarrow and let everyone piss on you."

I leaned my head back, felt one of them lift my arm, constricting it lightly above the crook, before feeling the prick of the needle.

Everything after that became a delicious blur.

It felt like my insides melted and became vapor, lifting me up into some sort of nebulous floating godhead located somewhere just before deep space. I let myself go. I let myself drift.

Up and up and up, floating in darkness, losing touch with my surroundings.

When I came to a little or a lot later I was aware enough to know I was in the car. It was dark outside and all the windows were up and I was hot and sweating. I opened the door before I died and spilled out of the car. I tried to stand but my legs didn't work so I made my way off the gravel of the driveway and collapsed in the dewy grass.

This part of Ohio became fairly lush in the summer and I lay in the thick perfume of the night air and looked up at the stars in the clear night sky. I didn't see a moon and there was an abundance of stars. I reached into my pants pocket and fished around in it for my phone. I had a moment of distant, barely felt panic when I didn't feel it. Then I remembered I wasn't wearing pants. I still wore Barcie's dress. Was she wearing my pants? Had she left them back in the torture storage shed? Did she have my phone?

I thought about crawling back to the car to look for it but that seemed like too much work and what did I really need it for anyway?

I continued lying in the grass and looking up at the night sky. Beyond the ringing in my ears, I could hear distant music and the laughter and conversation of a large group of people.

I struggled to stand up. My head was spinning and my throat burned all the way to my sore stomach. I shuffled toward the sounds and the lights, now that I was facing that direction.

I had absolutely no idea where I was. I stopped at a hedgerow on the perimeter of the property, beyond the lights that illuminated the backyard of a large modern looking house. A huge in-ground pool shimmered an ethereal blue and many groups of people in swim trunks and bathing suits stood around it. No one was in the pool. Everyone wore a mask. From this distance I couldn't tell if they were monster masks or masks of famous people. A lot of them had their masks tipped back so they could sip whatever they were drinking.

I stood watching them, thinking I should probably go back to the car.

I looked for Dawn or Barcie but I didn't see them.

I knew I should probably take off walking but I was wearing a dress and had no idea how far away from my apartment I was. I imagined if anybody found me wandering along the side of the road, the outcome wouldn't be good. Even if I could manage to make it back to my apartment, I didn't have any keys.

I barely had the energy to make it back to the car. For the first time, I noticed it was one car in a line of many. I hadn't bothered shutting the door and collapsed into the backseat, reaching over and opening the other door to let a little more air into the car.

There was a single beer on the floorboard and, next to that, amazingly, my pants.

I fished around in the pockets, feeling a slight thrill when I discovered my phone in one and my keys in the other.

I struggled to get the dress over my head and tossed it into the front seat. I slid my pants on and once again lay down on the backseat. I pulled my phone out of my pocket and turned the screen on. There was a text from Travis. It read: "Dude, I'm in the trunk."

I needed to try and get into the trunk.

But I couldn't really think about moving a lot.

The fluid gelatinous feeling previously lubricating my insides felt like it had hardened into something like concrete.

I grabbed the back of the seat to see if they were the kind that folded down and allowed access to the trunk. They weren't. I didn't see how else I was getting in there without a key.

I popped the beer open, took a drink, and ended up dumping the rest of it all over me.

I was pretty sure Dawn had Travis's phone.

It was still possible Travis was in the trunk.

And, I guess, for the moment, he was both alive and dead.

I tugged on the seats again.

Nothing.

I took my keys out of my pocket and tried ripping at the seat.

Remembering the shotgun in the front of the car, I turned to see if it was there.

It wasn't.

The laptop was gone too.

I didn't even know if this was the same car.

I went back to gouging at the seats. I didn't know if there had been something in the beer I'd just partially drank or if it was all the shit from earlier coming back to me or if it was just the heat and anxiety but it didn't take long for me to feel weak and woozy and I eventually had to lie back down—it was all I could think about doing—and close my eyes and let myself drift away.

UNICORNS AND CATS

I woke up in my bed. The wounds on my brutalized back had co-agulated and I had to peel myself from the sheet. I checked my phone and saw I'd received three voicemails from work. It was past noon. I was sure the voicemails were not positive, uplifting things. I couldn't bring myself to listen to them yet. Yesterday evening came back to me in brief snippets and I didn't want to think about it too much. I still wore my dirty jeans, nothing else, an erection straining them. I closed my eyes and unfastened my pants, taking my cock in my hand and thinking about Dawn as I masturbated. I didn't feel good about it but she was at the forefront of my thoughts and sometimes that was just how things happened. Before coming, I rolled onto my side so I could shoot it onto the floor where it could blend in with all the other stains.

Only, when I finished and surveyed the presumably still de-stroyed state of the apartment, I saw that it was immaculately clean. Probably cleaner than it had ever been. I looked down at the floor and noticed I'd ejaculated all over a note written on lined notebook paper in girlish purple lettering. A colorful unicorn made up the background of the paper.

The note said:

I had the apartment cleaned for you. Thought it was the least I could do. Looking SO FORWARD to seeing you again. – Dawn

Something inside of me turned the note's harmless banality into a sinister threat.

I didn't want to see Dawn again. At least, I didn't think I wanted to. I was pretty sure she was dangerous. Until seeing her film her friend mutilating a girl yesterday, I could have told myself she was relatively harmless. Just someone too young for me to relate to. But there was something about her that scared me. I'd been living in a state of dread and fear ever since fucking around with White Power Larry's wife. I should have planned my escape from Gethsemane the morning after that happened. True, we'd met at a bar in Dayton and I was pretty sure there wasn't anyone from Gethsemane around, but we'd ultimately ended up back in my bed, meaning we'd driven through Gethsemane to get there. It had been late and there weren't many people on the streets but it was entirely possible someone had seen us. And, in a drunken, boastful move, I'd apparently sent the photos to Travis. Aside from being a stupid thing to do from a physical safety perspective, it was a sleazy disrespectful thing to do, period. Something I'd never done before and would have never done if I hadn't been extremely drunk. And, of course, her actions were completely out of my hands. What if she started feeling guilty and told White Power Larry about it? She seemed pretty terrified of him so I didn't think she would but I was obviously a terrible judge of character.

As much as I didn't care to see Dawn again, I felt like I'd have to. That's what I told myself anyway.

I at least had to find out if she knew what had happened to Travis or if she was just fucking with me.

The text from Travis's phone came back to me.

He couldn't really be in her trunk, could he?

What if everyone was fucking with me and Travis was in on it?

Should I call his parents and see if he was around? Would that worry them? Shouldn't they be worried? At least a little? If he hadn't been around in a couple of days, wouldn't they already be worried? I was a little surprised they hadn't contacted *me* if they hadn't seen him.

I was starving. And filthy. A little panicky about the voicemails. If I lost this job, I'd probably lose the apartment before I was able to find another one.

I needed to take a shower and clear my head and try to eat something before listening to the voicemails.

I got out of bed and walked through my sparkly apartment, now so clean I wasn't afraid to take a shower without my socks on. The gouge from the chain throbbed with a hot pain.

Cleaning out my wound and slathering it in Neosporin made it feel a little better.

After my shower, I went into the small kitchen area and made coffee and a two-egg omelet with eggs I deemed 'good enough' and cheese I trimmed the mold from. I ate slowly while checking my email and bouncing around a couple of sites on my phone and trying to avoid calling Travis's house. I didn't know why it should make me nervous but I knew I didn't want to. I wasn't sure if it was because I would rouse some suspicion in his parents and put myself in a position of explaining or if I was half afraid he would be there and fine, leaving me with no excuse to never go near Dawn again.

I decided on a far more passive course of action.

I had my truck back. I'd call Ted at work without bothering to listen to his voicemails. We were so short staffed and the other people who worked there were so erratic, I was pretty sure I wouldn't be fired. I'd overcompensate to show how sorry I was. I'd offer to work Saturday and Sunday. I'd offer to do the Dinsmores'. The Dinsmores were a creepy couple, neither of which seemed to have a job. The guy sat around zonked on meds and watching children's programming in the living room while the wife fucked random guys. The husband would occasionally mutter, "We're so happy now. So much happier." One time he cried while writing out a check for his bill. After work, I'd drive back to the field and check to make sure Travis's dead body wasn't lying somewhere in it. If his parents happened to be aware I was there and one or both of them came out to see why, I would tell them he hadn't texted me in a couple of days and I was worried about him. If they asked why I was in the field I would tell them Travis had said he sometimes liked to sit out there and think. This wasn't true at all but I would just hope their son was as much a stranger to them as I had been to my parents.

I was convinced I wouldn't find anything and planned on doing something to clear my head afterward. Maybe go to a bookstore or a record store. It probably wouldn't be a good idea to buy anything, since my next check would be small, given all the hours I'd missed. I needed to call into work, needed to do something before I became melancholy to the point of despondency.

"Renfield, where the heck are you?"

"That's why I'm calling. I'll be in. They didn't get the part they needed for my truck until this morning."

"Good. Only two people showed up this morning. I'm gettin too old to do everything by myself."

"Did Travis come in?"

"Nope. He was a no call no show too."

"I'll go over to his house when I get off. He's not answering his phone either." I didn't mention that a psychopathic teen girl had his phone. I thought my offer would score me some brownie points. Maybe I could even get out of doing the Dinsmores'.

"This whole town's gonna be overgrown if I can't get some people in here. By the way, Joe Dinsmore called and said their pots are filled with trash."

Shit. Neither one of them ever cleaned the place.

"It's because they put the trash there. They're hoarders or something. We're plant and landscape technicians, not maids."

"If it's in the yard or the containers, we gotta take care of it."

"You want me to just go on over there and come in afterward?"

"Just make sure you wear your company shirt. And don't do nothin with that poor man's wife!"

"I haven't!" This was true, but wasn't true for most of the guys I worked with.

"Okay. See you in about an hour or so then?"

"I'll be there."

I took off my black t-shirt and pulled on the green golf shirt with the company logo on the left breast. Beneath the logo was the slogan: "We Care!" It should have said something like "We'll do it because you're too high or lazy!" I typically changed shirts in the bathroom at the office so I'd have something to change into when I left. I didn't want to be seen in my work shirt outside of work. This was southwestern Ohio so everyone dressed like garbage, but wearing a service industry shirt was too loud a declaration of class for me. Gethsemane had a working class suburb and a couple apartment complexes and rentals in town, but for the most part it was made up of people who were pretty comfortable financially and hired landscapers for one or more reasons: they were too drunk or on too many pills, too lazy, had better things to do, or just liked the idea of having people work for them because it soothed some burning desire hearkening back to their slaveholding ancestors.

I went down to the street and got into my truck. I put the keys in the ignition and tried to start it. It wouldn't even turn over.

Fuck.

Part of me had been really grateful Dawn had had the truck fixed. That part died and vanished quickly, the lingering hate for

Dawn swelling to an all-time high.

I didn't know what I was going to do now. I could have walked to the Dinsmores' and removed the trash from their containers but something about that terrified me, like maybe I wouldn't be able to get away fast enough. I could go back up to my apartment and give Billups a call, try not to think about what was happening but, given that my truck was not really repaired, I feared I would find my apartment in its previous demolished state if I did that. Irrational, probably.

A car horn shocked me out of my angry fugue.

A black Mercedes convertible had pulled up next to the truck.

Barcie sat in the driver's seat.

She was alone.

I rolled down my window.

"Need a lift?" Barcie said. She wore a black sun hat that reminded me of something a witch would wear and I wondered how she kept it on her head in the convertible.

"I think I've got it. Thanks, though," I said.

"I know it doesn't run." Barcie's smile seemed warm and friendly and I had to remind myself she had hit me with a chain yesterday, had brutally deformed a girl while I was in the same room trying not to watch.

"Yeah," I said. "I'm gonna check it out."

"Come on. Dawn sent me to pick you up."

"I, uh, don't really want to go. I have to go to work."

"That why you're wearin that stupid fuckin shirt?"

A car honked as it passed Barcie.

"Get outta the middle of the fuckin road!" the driver shouted.

Barcie ignored them. "Awww, widdle Bwad still thinks him has a choice."

Why *didn't* I have a choice?

Soon I would stop asking myself that.

Eventually, I felt like I was going to be more afraid of Dawn and Barcie than whatever would happen to me at the hands of White Power Larry. If that happened the only thing they'd really have as a bargaining chip was Travis's well being, and I didn't know if his safety or fate or whatever was really worth it to me.

For the moment, what was I going to do? Get out of the truck and take off running?

"Come on," she said. "It'll be a lot of fun."

I got out of the truck and slammed the door. I didn't bother locking it. Didn't even bother rolling the window back up. I thought about calling Billups and telling him I wasn't going to make it after all but didn't want to deal with his disappointment.

I hopped in the car. Barcie wore a loose fitting black dress so short it exposed the crotch of her white underwear. It made me kind of nervous. Her skinny legs were covered in bruises, and the sinewy muscles flexed as she took her foot off the brake and pressed the accelerator.

"So where's Dawn?"

"She was in one of her moods. She sent me out to do an errand."

"What's the errand?"

"You'll find out."

"Can't you just tell me?"

"Rather not. It'd sound weird."

"Yeah. We wouldn't want that."

"So you was goin to work?"

"Yeah."

"You work for Billups?"

"Yep."

"He's good friends with Daddy."

"Then maybe he can help me get my job back when I get fired."

"Billups ain't never fired nobody."

"Doesn't really matter. I'm not going to get paid if I don't go to work."

"Don't worry about it. Me and Dawn'll take care of you."

I rolled my eyes. The thought of two mentally defective teenage girls supporting me seemed ludicrous. And emasculating.

Barcie slid her right hand into her underwear and began slowly masturbating.

"You don't mind me doin this, do ya?"

"It makes me a little uncomfortable but I guess I can just look away."

"Or you can watch."

"Is it okay if I don't?"

"Better yet, you could record it. That might cheer Dawn up."

She pulled her hand out of her underwear and grabbed her phone from the console. She tapped the screen a couple of times and said, "There. It's ready."

She handed the phone to me.

"My pussy don't stink today. Sometimes it smells real bad."

I thought about this girl, so stupid she was probably wandering around with about ten undiagnosed STDs.

"Well, sometimes you have to wash it." I didn't know what else to say.

She continued to drive through suburban Gethsemane while playing with herself. I held the phone up, occasionally glancing to make sure she was still in frame but mostly just looking at the town as we drove around. No one was outside and it had the feeling of being slightly abandoned even though it wasn't. The houses were well maintained and the lawns were kept up. Mostly because of Billups. It was like everyone stayed locked up in the air conditioning of their houses, amusing themselves to death or waiting for the apocalypse that, if they'd been paying attention, had been happening for a while.

I kept waiting for Barcie to moan with a climax or something but she never did. She drove around and around in a random pattern. A fairly small orange cat ran across the road and under a car on the curb.

Barcie stopped the car and got out.

"I'm going to stop recording," I said.

"No. Keep goin."

I trained the phone back on her. Standing, the dress did actually cover her underwear. Barely. She must have just had it hiked up for my benefit.

She crouched down beside the truck and called for the cat. The cat cautiously crawled out from under the truck and Barcie began scratching it between the ears.

Who stops the car to pet a cat?

Maybe she really was brain damaged.

She ran her hand along the cat's head and back, pressing harder and harder until the cat was flattened against the road. Then she wrapped her hand around the cat's neck and I watched the muscles in her forearm flex as she squeezed.

"Don't do that!" I called from the car. There wasn't a lot of passion in my request. I felt like I had to say something. I knew what she was about to do was wrong but I didn't really have any feelings one way or the other. Was it possible to feel bad for not feeling bad? The more I tried to get her to stop, the more she would enjoy doing it. And if I tried to get her to stop, I felt like the chain would be in my future. My back throbbed with a reminder of yesterday. That was how I justified not doing anything about it. If you were going to have a loathsome lack of empathy, it was good to have an excuse for it, at least.

"Get out of the car. Get up close on this."

I did what she asked without even thinking about it.

The cat spasmodically jerked against her. The arm holding the cat had a few bloody scratches on it and I thought, *Good.*

I continued holding the phone, trying not to watch even though when I did occasionally glance up I had no sense of anger or repulsion.

She tossed the spent cat into the back floorboard and hopped into the driver's seat.

She snatched the phone out of my hand and scrolled back through the video I'd just shot.

"Were you even fucking watchin? You didn't even get half of it."

"I did my best."

"Sometimes it's not enough to just do what we ask you to do. You gotta at least try. Pull down your pants."

"What?"

"Pull down your fucking pants."

"No."

She punched me on the leg. Hard.

"Do it. Underwear too."

I unbuttoned my pants and pulled them down to my knees.

Barcie began driving. She handed her phone back to me and said, "Record it. Remember what I said about doin a good job."

I pointed the phone at my limp dick.

She reached her bloody hand over and began massaging my cock. It was like the more I didn't want to get hard, the quicker it happened. Barcie was as skilled with her hand as she had been with her mouth. I closed my eyes and leaned my head back against the seat, thinking about Dawn. Barcie's hand squeezed and massaged, moving faster and faster. We were stopped at a red light when I finally came. She continued rubbing my cock, using my semen as lubrication. Since I had clearly finished I thought she would stop but she kept going. It felt pleasant at first, as she milked every drop of come out of me, then it started to feel overly sensitive and slightly painful. My leg throbbed from where she had hit me.

We reached the quarry and drove around the gravel pit. She drove back to her house and farther back to the bank of storage sheds.

She took her hand off my cock and said, "You can pull your pants up now. And give me back my phone."

I handed the phone back to her.

She stopped the car. One of the shed's doors was already open.

Barcie got out of the car and grabbed the dead cat off the floorboard.

"Come on," she said.

I followed her to the shed.

Dawn was already in there. She stood behind the camera, trained on a red X on the floor. Ten men formed a half-circle on the other side of the X. They were all naked save for masks of political figures and famous people and cartoons. Most of them were white. A couple of them were black. Some of them were super ripped and a couple were chubby, but most of them were average. They were all very well endowed, some of them actively stroking their huge cocks.

Barcie held the cat up by the tail and Dawn squealed with delight.

"Let's get this party started!" Barcie yelled.

She tossed off her huge hat, unbuttoned her dress and let it fall to the floor.

Loud electronic music began blaring from no easily discernible source.

Dawn slammed the door of the storage shed down, moved close to me, and said, "I'm going to be watching you. I want to know you're watching. Don't think about leaving. If you fuck up, I'm sending all the photos to White Power Larry. And that's not even the least of it."

I had dropped my head to stare at the floor while she spoke. I heard her spit and felt it spray the top of my head. I raised my hand to wipe it away and she smacked it down. She grabbed the back of my head with her hand and pointed it toward Barcie. I liked it when Dawn touched me. It sent some sort of calming current through me. I took a deep breath of her scent, something airy, like the wind before a storm.

Barcie wasn't wearing a bra, probably because she didn't need to. Her dark nipples dotted her chest. Her torso was streaked with welts and scars and I wondered what had happened to her. She wasn't born looking like that and I again wondered if Dawn had beaten her with the chain or possibly watched while she had some-one else do it. Barcie peeled her white underwear down her legs. She dropped to the concrete floor and the half-circle of men moved in.

Barcie spread her legs and Dawn dropped the cat between them.

The men were down on their knees, a couple of them pinching Barcie's nipples and sucking on them. One man in a Mickey Mouse mask was forcing his huge cock into her mouth. Dawn was now between Barcie's legs, grabbing the dead cat by the head and press-ing it against Barcie's cunt.

I watched.

Dawn, true to her word, periodically glanced back at me.

I watched without really watching. I rationalized it by telling my-self I hated everyone in the room. They were all there by choice, and they all seemed to be loving it. Even Barcie, who just seemed to be undergoing one degradation after another. Who was I to judge?

Once the entire cat was inserted into Barcie, her abdomen was noticeably distended.

Dawn rolled her over, crouching down with her back to Barcie's head. Dawn spread Barcie's ass cheeks.

The guy who had his cock in Barcie's mouth circled around her and struggled to put his cock in her ass. The next guy sat in front of Barcie and she began sucking him off. He wore a Hillary Clinton mask.

One of the men, in a nearly frenzied moment of passion, wearing a Richard Nixon mask, stood in front of Dawn.

I almost expected her to take him in her mouth—maybe even wanted to see that—but she slapped him away.

The first man who had fucked Barcie in the ass grabbed the man and dragged him outside. Once they disappeared, the only thing I could really think was that somewhere, there were two naked men wearing Mickey Mouse and Richard Nixon masks and fighting.

Dawn eventually stood back up and took her place behind the camera, taking it off the tripod and moving it in for various close-ups. Sometimes she focused it on me. It made me uncomfortable but I was afraid to look away. The remaining men continued to use Barcie like a battered, skinny toy, positioning her however they wanted in order to accommodate every sexual penetration. She moaned and said everything she was supposed to say but her eyes looked completely dead. I wondered who these men were. Had they been like me at one point? Were they getting paid for this or was it something they were doing because they enjoyed it? I imagined them having no faces beneath the masks. And when they finished here I imagined them disappearing into dark rooms and sitting on the floor until they were called to participate in something else. Was this what Dawn and Barcie were grooming me for? It didn't seem likely. I was way too old and my cock wasn't nearly big enough.

Dawn didn't offer any instruction. It was almost mechanical the way the men switched positions, rammed Barcie as hard as they could, before once again swapping. Eventually Barcie was covered in sweat and gag juice, blood trickling from her cunt. I didn't know if that was from being stretched too far or if it was from the cat inside her.

By the time the last man, wearing a Jack Nicholson mask, had shot his load onto Barcie I felt tense, a little bored, and relieved that I hadn't been forced to take part.

The men continued to awkwardly stand around.

Dawn shut off the camera and the music.

A few of the men were engaged in muffled conversations.

Barcie stood up. She seemed shaken and even paler than usual. Her hipbones were bloodied from where she'd been driven into the floor over the last hour or so. Her knees and elbows were red.

She pulled her underwear and dress back on.

Dawn opened the storage shed door and the men filed out, some of them lifting up their masks, producing cigarettes and lighters from their clothes that I now noticed were piled up beside the door.

The man who'd been escorted out earlier lay in a bloody heap on the gravel drive. There was no sign of the other man.

Spotting the fallen man, Dawn said, "Will one of you guys check to make sure he's still alive?"

One of the nude men who was not smoking but still wearing a Bart Simpson mask walked over to the downed man and crouched beside him. He nudged him. He felt for a pulse at the neck and wrist. Nudged him again. Gave him a few rough shakes.

The man on the ground flinched into consciousness and craned his head around to look up at everyone staring down at him. His mask had been split down the middle and the man who'd helped him pulled it off. The downed man stood up and began dancing exuberantly to music that wasn't there, his flaccid penis bouncing from thigh to thigh.

Dawn turned to a large black man wearing a Prince mask and said, "You need to get him out of here."

The black guy approached the dancing man. He made a grab for the dancing man but couldn't get hold before he started half-running, half-dancing away. The black man continued trying to catch him but it looked like the gravel driveway was rough on his feet so he was a couple of steps behind at all times. The black man bent and scooped up some rocks from the driveway. He began chucking them at the dancing man before he disappeared around a bend in the driveway.

"We ready to go back to the house?" Dawn said.

"Yeah. I think the DJs are setting up," Barcie said.

"How'd you get those guys?"

"Paid a lot of money."

"This is gonna be so cool."

I followed them up to Barcie's house. The sun was going down and the large pine trees around the house cast long shadows over the grounds. The remaining naked men followed along behind us.

There was a huge pool in the backyard. I briefly wondered if this was where we had been last night but didn't think it felt the same. Similar, definitely. I imagined there were very slight differences in the abodes of rich people with no taste. They were all still buying the same shit from the same places.

A small stage was set up near the house. There were four guys who looked about the same except for the colors of their shoes and ties. Otherwise they wore all black. At the back of the stage was a rainbow lighted sign announcing them as Team Klaus. I'd never heard of them.

The smell of food made my stomach grumble.

There were banks of food to the left of the stage. People who were dressed really well, couples mostly, began coming through the large French doors leading to the backyard. Some of them came from around the house. I began feeling really self-conscious about my jeans and work shirt. All the naked men seemed to have vanished.

Most of the people arriving seemed older than Dawn and Barcie. Most of them looked old enough to be my parents.

How had I been witnessing what I'd seen only a short time ago and was now at some party that seemed like it was for the cultural elite?

"What is this?" I said.

"It's a Democratic fundraiser," Dawn said.

"And these people are . . .?"

"Backers, I guess. Contributors. It's kind of Barcie's thing. Or her dad's. One of them paid for what you just watched back there."

People mingled with drinks, engaging in bright-eyed conversations.

Team Klaus began playing, the music soft and low. They had no instruments. Just four laptops. I imagined it would get louder as the night wore on.

"Why am I here?" I said.

"I don't know," Dawn said. "You can leave if you want."

"I don't have a car."

"Walk then. Or go grab a drink or something. I'll take one too. It's all free."

I went to the bar area and got a couple of beers. I noticed an already overflowing tip jar but didn't have any cash so I feigned ignorance of the jar and offered a quick smile instead.

I found Dawn sitting on the edge of the pool with her feet hidden in the water. I handed her the beer and pulled a wooden deck chair up next to her.

"Why are *you* here?" I said.

"I'm providing the entertainment . . . for later. I have really good organizational skills."

"Entertainment?"

"If you want to find out, you're more than welcome to take part. But you've been pretty resistant to things so far."

"Is it like . . . a sex club or something?"

"Not always sex. These are people who can afford to indulge their fantasies. Let's just say that. Like I said, if you're interested in taking part, I'm sure I can find something for you to do. See, these people need some incentive to be here. They're never going to show up to eat free shitty food with people they spend their daily lives dealing with."

"Is that Dr. Weishaupt?" His was the only face I recognized.

"It is. You don't recognize anyone else? This is the Gethsemane elite."

"I don't really pay much attention to what's happening in town."

"Well, that's apparent."

"So do people work for you by choice or are you blackmailing all of them?"

She pulled her feet out of the water and stood up. "You're boring me," she said.

I watched her join a group of older men and begin talking to them. I found myself slightly jealous. I saw no sign of Barcie. I became overly conscious of the well-dressed people passing me and either looking at me for too long or quickly looking away.

I pulled my chair to a somewhat darkened area on the perimeter of the pool patio. I kept going back to the bar for more beer. The music settled into a tight groove and I locked into it. Once it was fully dark I noticed there was a massive movie screen above the stage and images began flickering across it. I wasn't overly surprised when I appeared on it. It was the scene of me vomiting out of the car, looped continuously and hilariously, syncing perfectly to the music. There were a number of other loops similar in theme and with similar men.

I also couldn't say I was incredibly surprised to see Travis in one of them. He looked sloppy and passed out and was getting urinated on by several dogs at the same time. Of course he'd never told me that happened but it reaffirmed my suspicion his connection with Dawn was maybe not a completely random thing.

Deeper into the night, deeper into the beer, there seemed to be a lot fewer people milling around. If this were a Democratic fundraiser, and I still wasn't really sure it was, maybe everyone was off listening to political speeches or something while the bored people they had brought with them were out here watching humiliation reels of poor people. But I thought Democrats liked poor people.

A scream startled me and I turned to see a very young nude girl running beside the pool, an old man wearing boxer shorts emblazoned with Satan heads and tented with an erection chasing her.

Dawn came through the steamy darkness.

"Get up," she said.

I stood up. I was a lot drunker than I thought I was.

"Can you drive?" she said.

"Sure." I could drive. I probably couldn't drive very well.

"Barcie needs to go to the hospital. She's not feeling well."

I then said something I was pretty sure I'd never contemplated saying before.

"Did you take the cat out of her?"

"I couldn't get it."

"I'm not taking her to the hospital with a cat shoved into her vagina."

"I don't know what else to do."

"Where is she?"

"In her room."

"Let's go look for tongs or something."

I followed Dawn into the house.

We found some tongs in the kitchen. I followed Dawn upstairs and down the hall to Barcie's room. Barcie lay on her bed in a state of semi-consciousness. I handed the tongs to Dawn.

"What am I supposed to do with these?" she asked.

"Get the cat out."

"Ew. I don't want to do that."

"You put it there!"

"It's so gross."

"Look, I'm not taking her to the hospital if that's still there. I don't really care what you do. I should have stopped her from killing it in the first place."

"Fine," she said. "But I'm only doing this because it's Barcie. Not because you're telling me to."

She got down on her knees like the world's youngest gynecologist.

"We should really be capturing this," she said.

"Come on."

"It's happening anyway. It seems like a waste if we don't."

She produced her phone from somewhere in her dress and held it in her left hand while she snapped the metal tongs a couple of times with her right.

"Might be easier if you try to hold her open."

Barcie's legs were hanging over the edge of the bed. I sat next to her and leaned over, spreading her open as much as I could. The smell wafting up from her was revolting and I had to struggle to keep the beers down.

Dawn closed the tongs and slid them into Barcie until she couldn't push them in anymore. She dug around, opening and closing the tongs.

"Do you have your phone on you?" Dawn said.

"Yeah."

"Can you turn the flashlight thing on? I can't see what I'm doing. You're probably okay to let go of her pussy."

I took my hands off Barcie and found myself hesitant to touch anything with them.

I fished my phone out of my pocket and turned the screen on.

There was a text from a number that didn't have a contact associated with it.

I tried reading it without acknowledging it so Dawn couldn't tell what I was doing.

The message read:

RUN FUCKER RUN

My heart began racing as I accessed the flashlight.

"You're going to have to shine it up in there," Dawn said. "My hands are full."

I got down on my knees beside her and shone the flashlight up Barcie's vagina.

"I think . . ." Dawn said.

Her forearm muscles strained and she began retracting the tongs until I could see some wet fur in the opening of Barcie's vagina.

"Got it!" Dawn beamed with excitement. "Grab that trashcan over there."

There was a black plastic trashcan next to a small desk near the foot of the bed. I grabbed the trashcan and came back.

Dawn finished pulling the cat out and dropped it into the trashcan.

I fought to steady my heartbeat and establish some sort of clarity. Upon seeing the text, my first impulse was to just take off running, but I stopped myself. I didn't think I'd get far. If I was taking Barcie to the hospital, I might be able to get away. At least I'd have a car. I wondered if Dawn was coming with us.

I was going to ask Barcie if she could walk but I figured she'd be so light I could probably actually carry her. Besides, she still seemed mostly unconscious.

I picked her up, one arm behind her knees, the other behind her neck.

"Are you coming with us?" I said.

"I can't. I have things I need to tend to."

A small purse sat on the nightstand beside the bed. Dawn picked it up, fished out the keys and placed the keys on top of the purse on top of Barcie's stomach.

"Is there anything else I need to tell them?"

Dawn shrugged. "Maybe she's had a little heroin too."

"Jesus. Okay."

I walked sideways down the hall and the stairs. A soft rain fell outside, almost more of a mist, and I found Barcie's black Mercedes.

Dawn was gone.

I struggled to open the passenger door and placed Barcie on the seat, fastened the seatbelt around her, and reclined it slightly.

I got behind the wheel.

Barcie's purse rested on her lap.

She still seemed mostly out of it.

I grabbed the purse and rifled through it.

There was two hundred dollars in cash and a wallet with some credit cards in it.

I pocketed the cash, started the car, and thought about how I was going to get away.

As a kid I remember watching horror movies about haunted houses and wondering why the family didn't just move out. Once I reached adulthood, I realized it wasn't that simple. While it may not be true money is the root of all evil it is possible the lack of it is the reason why many people stick around to have evil things done to them. It may also be the reason many people do evil things which possibly just verifies that money *is* the root of all evil. Still, I think a person has to have evil in them to perform evil acts. For those people, money is just a bonus. Maybe even just a diversion. It's socially acceptable for a businessperson to do evil things to people if it's under the auspices of buying a better life for themselves and their family. But they're probably still sociopaths.

Maybe I'm getting ahead of myself.

I could have pulled a map up on my phone to find a hospital but knew if I just drove to Dayton I'd eventually start seeing signs for at least one of them. It seemed like the medical industry had gradually replaced the manufacturing industry as Dayton's leading cash cow. Corporate America puffed the baby boomers up with a flourishing economy and cheap and abundant food and now they were getting rich by treating their diabetes, depression, and various cancers.

I didn't know exactly what Dawn and Barcie were involved in. I didn't even really know the extent of their involvement. But I knew I didn't really want to be a part of it. It made me nervous, uncomfortable, humiliated, and I found it a little terrifying. I didn't know how I could get away from it, though. I didn't have the money to just disappear. If I stuck around Gethsemane, I either had to do what Dawn wanted me to do or she was going to send the photos to White Power Larry. I didn't want to be around for that. I could man up and just fight the guy if it came to that but I wasn't going to fool myself. I wasn't a fighter. White Power Larry was legendarily violent. Since there weren't enough minorities in Gethsemane for him to take his aggression out on, this was one area of his life where he didn't discriminate.

I didn't have a lot of options. I didn't have any siblings and my parents had been dead for years. They'd left me a tiny inheritance that afforded me the luxury of not working for about a year afterward and then to be able to scrape by with shit jobs. I wasn't going to be able to go far on two hundred dollars and I didn't even have that much in my checking account until I got paid again.

My plan was to drop Barcie off at the hospital, drive somewhere

near the airport where there were a lot of hotels, ditch the car, and
. . . what?

I didn't know.

Travis was my only friend. He was missing. I didn't know if
Dawn had anything to do with that or if she'd just found his phone
and was fucking with me.

"What the fuck should I do?"

I glanced over at Barcie, who seemed mostly unavailable for
comment.

I pulled my phone out and re-read the text:

RUN FUCKER RUN

I called the number back, my pulse ticking up.

Barcie's purse began vibrating.

In a state of near hypnosis she reached into her purse and ex-
tracted her phone. She opened her eyes just long enough to glance
at the screen and mumbled, "Why are you callin me?"

I ended the call and sighed.

I didn't think Barcie had sent the message to me. I didn't think
she had been in any condition to. I was pretty sure it was just
Dawn testing me to see what I would do.

Did she think I would actually try to run away?

My only other option was to return to Gethsemane and try to lay
low.

Or not.

If I just went back to my apartment I knew Dawn would come
around again. I'd probably be disappointed if she didn't. What
would be the harm in joining them? What else was I really doing?

Barcie had said not to worry about money but, being perpetually broke, I found that impossible. Was what Dawn doing actually criminal or just creepy?

I thought about Taylor Dream howling as Barcie beat her savagely with a chain.

Okay, so a lot of what they were doing was definitely not legal and more horrifying than creepy.

I turned onto Route 35 from Route 4.

The highway was virtually empty. The windshield wipers swept back and forth on the lowest setting. After only a couple of minutes, a hospital loomed like a giant beacon in the darkness.

A lighted amber sign hanging from an overpass announced:

THE POINT CENTER FOR MEDICAL TREATMENT AND
RESEARCH NUMBER THREE
NEXT EXIT

I took the next exit and wondered when even hospitals had become gross and overly corporate. Did they even refer to people as patients anymore? Or were we just test subjects for their medical products?

Getting anywhere near a hospital filled me with dread and anxiety. I momentarily resolved to again quit smoking, drinking, and having sex with strange women, to try eating better once I could achieve a more stable life, and maybe even exercise more often.

I followed the signs to the 'Patient Drop Off,' feeling a little relieved it wasn't called something like 'Subject Deposit,' and knew I wasn't going to be able to go into the hospital, if I'd ever planned to in the first place.

There was a pull around under an awning and it felt not unlike a large hotel or an airport. The entrance was brightly lit and it was overall a lot calmer than I thought it would be. A couple of women sat on a bench to the right of the entrance, smoking. I couldn't tell if they were nurses or janitors.

I pulled to the far side of the doors and stopped the car.

I took a deep breath.

I told myself I wasn't a terrible person but knew, at the end of my life, I'd probably have to look back and make that decision based on my actions rather than my actual thoughts.

I got out of the car, crossed around the front of it, opened Barcie's door, tugged her out, and placed her on the curb. Then I hurried back to the car, slammed the door, and drove away.

I glanced into the rearview mirror before pulling onto the road and was pretty sure Barcie was now standing, one of the nurses or janitors approaching her.

Had the whole thing been a put on? What would have happened if I'd gone into the hospital with her?

I pulled onto the road, devoid of traffic, and my phone vibrated.

I slid it out of my pocket.

A text message lit up the screen.

It was from Barcie.

It said: DICK.

I should have turned around but felt like I'd already committed to something, although I wasn't sure what that something was.

Maybe it was fatigue or lingering drunkenness or just burgeoning insanity, but I felt a whole swirl of emotions. I felt bad for just dumping Barcie at the hospital but felt a little better knowing she was alive and well, or at least well enough to stand up on her own. I told myself that, since there had been onlookers, it would actually look worse if I went back to pick her up. Barcie may not have been the smartest girl on the planet but she seemed to have some kind of survival instinct, and a phone, and I felt like she'd be fine in the long run. Plus there was that thing with the cat, so she deserved whatever happened to her.

My panic ramped up considerably. Technically, I was now driving a stolen car. I should have disabled Barcie's phone before dropping her off. I hoped her first call wasn't to the police. I needed to get rid of the car as quickly as possible.

I still had trouble wrapping my head around the situation I was in. It made me nervous and I struggled to find the tiniest sliver of hope. There were a couple of scenarios I had worked out in my head. The first was that Barcie knew something I didn't, had some genuine concern for me, and sent the text before blacking out or whatever. I didn't think it was likely but it *was* possible. That made me feel even worse for dumping her but I was ultimately doing what she had told me to do in the most efficient way possible. The second scenario was that everything had been staged and planned. Was it possible Barcie wanted us to escape together for some reason? Maybe she hadn't really blacked out at all. Maybe she had sent the text and faked the blackout, knowing how Dawn would react. But that didn't make a lot of sense. We'd been alone all afternoon.

We could have gotten away then. Or if she'd faked the blackout, why hadn't she miraculously come to the second we were away from the party and filled me in on the plan. Another possibility was that it was just another scene in whatever bizarre document of my humiliation Dawn was making and this was all constructed by her, the whole thing some kind of ruse to get me to the hospital for some heinous reason. I'd need to check the car for cameras before abandoning it. If there were a reason for them trying to lure me to the hospital, Dawn would have surely wanted to capture it.

I needed to sleep.

I pulled the car into the parking lot of a Holiday Inn.

I wouldn't be able to walk too far but I didn't want to stay in the same hotel I left the car in. I didn't know if they'd come looking for me or not but it seemed like that would make things a little too easy for them.

I quickly glanced and felt around the interior of the car, looking for any little lights or some gadget that looked like it didn't belong there.

I pulled out my phone and brought up a map.

There was a motel called the Pine Sweat Lodge about a half-mile down the road. It was kind of a weird name and sounded horrible. It had a one-star average review. The first three I scanned through said they wished they could give it no stars or negative stars. I was sure it would be really cheap and hoped they had rooms available.

I began walking through the drizzle. The sky had lightened to a dark gray and I figured the sun would be up within the hour. Since a lot of the terrible things I'd witnessed over the past couple of days had taken place while the sun was up, this didn't offer me a lot of comfort. I half expected a series of texts from Dawn and Barcie and was a little surprised to not get anything.

By the time I reached the Pine Sweat Lodge, I was beyond damp.

The main building looked like a dilapidated halfway house with a couple of low cinderblock buildings behind it. Just when I started to wonder if they were still in business or not, I noticed the neon sign hanging below the hand painted plywood sign. The neon sign was struggling to be lit up and it looked like they had vacancies or, at least, 'V----C-.'

I walked up onto the front porch, all gray wood with no paint. The front door was covered in bars. A window to the right of the door that looked like it had been cut poorly out of the house had a cardboard sign in the corner that said: OFFICE.

A bell had been drilled into the boards of the house.

I tapped the bell. It didn't chime, just emitted a muted sound of metal striking metal.

The window slid up, filled by a man or a woman, I couldn't really be sure. He or she was enormous, pale, and wet looking. With greasy stringy hair hanging down to the shoulders.

"Yeah," he or she asked through speech unencumbered by teeth.

"Do you have a room?"

"I guess."

"I'd like to, uh, rent it."

"Fifty bucks."

I pulled the modest wad out of my pocket and handed the money to the creature in the window.

He or she jerked a meaty hand over its shoulder and said, "Room six. All the way in back. Checkout's at noon."

"Do I need a key?"

"It's unlocked."

I felt like I'd made a bad mistake but imagined I could sleep anywhere at this point.

I walked around the main house and into what I supposed could have been a courtyard under different maintenance. As it was it was just a yellow security lamp in a wasteland of liquor bottles, cigarette butts, trash, and used tires. There was some mostly dilapidated lawn furniture in various states of decay scattered around. A skinny old man wearing only underwear sat in a lawn chair, smoking and looking up at the sky. Birds were chirping and I heard a plane rumble, coming from or going to the airport or the air force base.

I found my room and opened the door, feeling a moment of panic. Given the area this place was in and the fact that the door was unlocked, I would have been amazed to find the room unoccupied.

It wasn't.

Two men who looked like FBI agents sat on the edge of the bed, staring at a blank television screen. They wore identical black suits and had identical haircuts. They didn't look like people you typically saw around here.

I didn't want a confrontation.

"I guess you've rented the room?" the man on the left said.

"Yeah," I said.

"We'll vacate," he said.

"Let's vacate now," the man on the right said.

They stood robotically, each bending to retrieve a metal brief-case, and left the room, trailing an odd chemical scent behind them.

I locked the door, somewhat surprised it even had a lock.

The bed looked reasonably clean. I went to the bathroom to take a piss. The bathtub was covered in a blackened green substance and, while I don't think it was smoking, there was something in the room making my eyes and lungs burn. When finished, I zipped up and looked for a switch to an exhaust fan. There wasn't one. Nor was there a window in the bathroom so I grabbed the roll of toilet paper, shut the door, and crammed a bunch of it in the crack.

I checked my phone before lying down.

No messages.

My clothes were still damp but I didn't even think about taking them off.

I was asleep within seconds.

I coughed myself awake, rattled by the momentary disorientation of where I was. Once I placed myself at the seedy motel in North Dayton I had a moment of panic I'd slept well past check out time. Not that it really mattered. I hadn't given the clerk a credit card or any ID so I imagined all they could really do was ask me to leave.

I grabbed my phone from the upturned cardboard box serving as a nightstand and noticed there were a couple of texts with attached images from Dawn. The first was a picture of Barcie's car in the parking lot of the Holiday Inn. The time stamp on that one was

6:52 a.m. It was currently 11:38. The next picture was a photo of the front door of my motel room. The time stamp was 8:30. The two well-dressed men stood to the left of the door, almost like guards.

I went to take a piss and my phone vibrated again.

The bathroom still smelled horrible. I shook myself off and got out of there as quickly as possible.

The message read: "You get one more chance."

It was from Dawn.

I didn't know if I wanted one more chance.

I was pretty sure I just wanted to get away.

I could find a bus station and buy a ticket to get as far away as I possibly could.

But what then?

Finding some kind of homeless shelter to check into until I could get a job and save up enough for an apartment? I felt like I'd been through this before. Not to that extreme. I'd be substituting a homeless shelter for my parents' house. I'd started the cycle when moving out of their house after high school and repeated it every three-to-five years since, usually following the break up of a long term relationship. I took what I needed, usually had no money in my bank account, and moved back in with my parents. Then I found a job, had to save for nearly a year before getting enough money for a deposit, first month's rent, and deposits for the utilities. Having a job and a place of my own led to me getting into another relationship. Things went well for a while. Then they either exploded or just fizzled out and I was left alone, empty, and sometimes without a place to live. I'd never really moved far away so my parents' had been the cheapest and most convenient place to go back to. But they weren't around anymore and I felt like if I left without Dawn's permission, I probably wouldn't be able to return to Gethsemane.

But why would I *want* to return to Gethsemane?

Couldn't I live in squalor practically anywhere?

At least in some other town in some other state I wouldn't feel that anxious fear I'd felt since sleeping with Stasia Warner. But, let's face it, that was just a heightened sense of the anxious fear I'd felt every day before that.

Going back to my rinse and repeat life seemed soul deadening. At least Dawn represented change. Actually, if I looked back at my life, Dawn was the most exciting thing to happen to it since losing my virginity as a teenager. Scary, sure, but avoiding things I was afraid of had gotten me exactly nowhere.

It had kept me alive and out of any trouble that could be considered too serious, but that was about it.

Then again, doing things against my better judgment was what got me into the whole White Power Larry situation and was ultimately why I wanted to get away.

It wasn't really Dawn's fault at all. She was just a physical manifestation of my conscience. I could tell myself she was evil but I'd been right there with her the past couple of days. How was she any worse than me?

I didn't really know what to do, but then again I never really had.

I stepped outside into a hot, humid day.

The two well-dressed men still stood outside the room. Before I could even shut the door, they'd pressed back into it and shut the door behind them.

The man in the chair I'd seen smoking last night was still there.

He wasn't smoking now.

He may not have even been alive.

His head was craned toward the sky, his face frozen in a kind of twisted terror. A series of vicious cigarette burns and bruises covered his torso and it looked like his left arm had turned to rust.

Part of me felt like screaming.

Part of me felt like calling the police.

I did neither.

Some grim part of my brain looked at that man and thought, *This could be you.* And I could see it clearly. Twenty more years of desperate scrabbling, shit jobs, loneliness, and self-abuse. What if this motel were not a way station but my final destination?

I shuddered and forced myself to move on.

I walked out to the busy main road, already sweating. I felt like shit. Following through on any of my planned journey seemed absolutely absurd.

Maybe I needed to eat.

I wasn't particularly hungry but felt like it would supply a bit of clarity.

I saw a sign up ahead for a place announcing itself as AIRPORT BUFFET AND GENTLEMENS CLUB and thought it sounded not only weird but probably too expensive. I wondered how a woman could work there and not feel like food.

A little beyond that was a Denny's and I made that my destination.

I was nearly there, drenched in sweat, when Dawn's car pulled up to the curb and crept slowly beside me. It was a busy, four-lane road and cars flew past in either direction so I thought I was safe and just kept walking.

"Hey!" Barcie shouted from the passenger side. "Get in the car."

I ignored them and kept walking.

I heard a familiar sound I couldn't immediately place and then felt a sharp painful sting in my hand.

I heard the sound again and now recognized it.

Barcie was pumping a BB gun.

I felt another sting on my neck, loud derisive laughter accompanying the pumping of the gun.

The next BB hit me in the middle of the back, my shirt taking a lot of the sting out of it.

If I just ignored them, maybe somebody would stop it. Hell, we weren't in Gethsemane anymore. I could probably just call the cops.

Or at least threaten to.

I pulled my phone out of my pocket.

"Who you callin?" Barcie mocked.

I stopped. "I'm calling the cops, okay? Two psychopaths are in a car shooting me with a BB gun."

I glanced at my screen just in time to see the BB strike it and spread a crack through it. The left side went black.

"Dawn says you don't wanna do that."

"Why the fuck not?" I wasn't sure I could do it if I wanted to.

"She says White Power Larry could be here in about fifteen minutes and that we'll keep tabs on you for him. She also says to make sure you tell em about stealin two hundred dollars and my car from me."

I put my phone back in my pocket and approached the car. I bent down and looked across Barcie, at Dawn.

"What do you want from me?"

"I want you to get in the car."

"Look, I just want to get away, okay? I don't want to get mixed up in anything else."

"Maybe you should have thought about that before."

"So . . . what? White Power Larry's going to beat me up? Kill me? Maybe that would be better than living like this."

"Just get in the car. We'll take you home. You're being ridiculous."

Was I, though?

I didn't really know but just her saying that made me feel like I *was* being a little ridiculous.

"I just need some time to clear my head, okay? That's all I want."

"You can probably do that in your apartment just as well as you can . . . Where were you going anyway? The strip bar buffet?"

"I wasn't going to the strip bar buffet."

"I bet you were. Come on. Get in the car. Barcie'll suck your cock for you."

"I don't . . ."

Barcie shot me in the forehead. I think the range was so close it actually broke skin.

"Get the fuck in the car," Dawn said.

I sighed and opened the back door, throwing myself in and pouting like a bratty child.

"How can I get out of this?" I asked.

"Maybe you don't want out of it."

She pulled back into traffic.

"I definitely do."

"Why? Izzum scared?" Dawn said with a mocking baby voice.

"A little, maybe."

"Aren't you tired of being poor? Of being powerless?"

Of course I was. Who liked being poor and powerless? But I definitely didn't want to tell her that.

"It suits me," I said.

"That sounds defeatist."

"Then . . ." I threw my hands up in the air. "Tell me how I can stop being poor."

"The real question is not how you can stop being poor, it's how you can start making money. You gotta think positive."

"Okay, whatever, I'm listening."

"You should go home and rest first."

The trip back to my apartment was mercifully silent.

BILLUPS' INTERIOR AND EXTERIOR LANDSCAPING

Dawn didn't contact me for nearly a week.

After my brief escape I'd gone home and slept for nearly twenty-four hours. I awoke the next afternoon. I hadn't received any texts or calls. My phone was fucked but functional. Except for the itching, my back felt a lot better but there was a large knot on my forehead from where Barcie had shot me with the BB gun. I ate some old chips and made some coffee. I needed to try and get a handle on what I was going to do. I felt like I was ultimately going to take part in whatever Dawn wanted me to take part in. At least for a while.

The good thing about doing the type of work I did was that it provided ample time to think, which I needed. I finished my coffee and called Billups.

"This better be good," he said.

"Look, I'm sorry I didn't call yesterday."

"And you didn't do the Dinsmores' like you said you was the day before. He called me again this morning to complain about all the trash. Said his wife's bad sick and the trash is really depressing him. Pretty sure he was cryin."

"This is embarrassing . . . My truck still isn't fixed. I took it in to get the estimate and thought I'd have enough but then my rent was due and I had to pay utilities and . . . anyway the guy at the car place had it towed back to my apartment and told me to stop wasting their time so . . . I guess what I'm asking is do you think you'd be able to send somebody to pick me up?"

He paused and gave a sarcastic little laugh that was really more of an exhalation. "I guess I don't got much of a choice, do I? Donnie was the only one who came in this morning and he says he thinks he's concussed."

"Concussed?"

"Yeah, he hit his head real hard yesterday."

"Doing what?"

"I don't know. Probably somethin stupid. You know Donnie ain't right."

More and more, it didn't seem like anybody was right.

"So . . ."

"Yeah, I'll be there in about ten minutes. I'll need to get back."

"Thanks, Mr. Billups."

"Be ready when I get there."

I dug out my laptop to look at my bank account and try to do some more research on Dawn.

I pulled up the account for my apartment on the realtor's website. Even with the money I'd stolen from Barcie, I still wouldn't have enough to cover the rent but I felt like it would be good to know how short I was. I could have researched tenants' rights, eviction, and all that, but figured I could count on at least one free month, although it may consist of avoiding a lot of calls from the landlord.

The rent for July would be due by the first.

Surprisingly, it had already been paid.

While I knew this would come with dire consequences, I felt a momentary sense of relief.

It had to have been Dawn who'd paid it.

I typed the name 'Dawn Bando' into Google and it brought up the same links it had before.

I noticed again that she was in the graduating class of 2017. There was a link to buy the digital yearbook for five dollars. So that was a thing. I supposed it was for people who'd lost theirs to relive the memories but there was a part of me that felt like the only people who would use it would be pedophiles.

I waited for it to download and scrolled through the senior class until I got to the 'B's. There she was. She looked pretty, a broad smile with a devious glint in her eyes. She didn't seem to be a member of anything.

I paid for the yearbook from the previous year. I told myself it was for research. I didn't want to think it might have been to see another picture of Dawn. The memory of me down on my knees, licking her cunt, came back to me and I was suddenly hard. She had filmed that. I wondered if she'd send it to me if I asked. I wondered if she'd ever let me do it again. I nearly salivated at the thought.

I found the 'B's in that year's junior class and scrolled down.

She wasn't there.

The classes of Get High were pretty small. A little larger than when I'd graduated nearly two decades ago, but not by much. Fewer than a hundred students per class.

I continued scrolling through the images until I eventually found her again.

Under the 'R's.

Dawn Rosen.

Oh fuck.

My erection wilted and my sense of panic came back with a vengeance.

I went to the tab with the Google search still open.

I continued scrolling down, finding nothing of real interest.

I clicked to the second page of search results and found what I was afraid of.

The marriage announcement of Sheriff Charles "Chuck" Bando and Dawn Rosen.

Not his daughter.

His fucking *wife*.

I now wished the video of me eating Dawn's pussy was nowhere in existence.

Dread and worry.

I really really needed to get the fuck out of Gethsemane. I immediately regretted getting in the car with Dawn and Barcie. I should have just kept running. Why did I ever think something good could come from this?

I began adding up the value of everything in my apartment and realized I was worth nothing. Even the laptop I was using was five years old and had a number of keys that had to be struck repeatedly to work.

What I would be able to come up with, along with what I already had, would maybe afford me a cab ride to a train station and a train ride to some place not super far away like Chicago. But I couldn't do that only to show up with nothing. I was tired of starting from scratch. I'd rather just stick around and deal with the fear and humiliation than do that again.

As something of a last resort, I went to Career Giant and uploaded a resume that permanently sat on my desktop. It was seventy-five percent made up so there was never any need to update it. I didn't put in a specific location. I wasn't particularly qualified to do anything. I would entertain offers from anywhere. The farther away, the better.

I moved over to the window of my apartment and looked out, my sense of dread mingling with the thought of Dawn's pussy.

I was super fucked.

At least if White Power Larry came after me, I could fool myself into thinking the law would provide some level of protection. But Sheriff Bando *was* the law, and a recording existed of me going down on his beautiful teenage bride.

I was an idiot.

I saw Billups pull in front of my building and headed down.

There was another flyer for a missing dog taped beside the bank of mailboxes, most of which were open, like the mail person was too exhausted to shut them.

A sweaty Mr. Dinsmore answered the door.

"I'm so glad you're here." He stepped away from the door and motioned me inside.

It was easy to figure out why he was so sweaty. The house was stifling.

"As you can see," he said, "all the flowerpots are filled with trash."

"That's what I'm here to take care of."

"Good. Real good."

He patted me on the shoulder and smiled. His eyes were glazed over like he had been crying or was super stoned.

I went to the large areca palm by the TV. I pulled a trash bag from my pocket and set about removing the trash from the container. I quickly broke out in a sweat. The pot contained common trash—things like snack wrappers and soda cans—and I didn't know why they didn't just throw it in a trashcan. Maybe it was too far away or full and they were just too lazy to take it out. The way the house smelled it was easy to imagine the trash hadn't been removed in a very long time. I also wasn't sure why they paid a hefty amount to have people take care of their landscaping and houseplants when the money could have gone for a maid. Maybe they did have a maid and they were just able to trash the place that quickly. It was like they wanted nice things—could certainly afford nice things—but were repeatedly transformed into some wild animal lurking inside of them.

I moved away from the plant and Dinsmore scampered over to peer into the container.

"Yeah." He beamed. "That looks real good."

I moved into the kitchen. A large pothos climbed a stake in an 18-inch pot. This one was also filled with trash. Some of this looked grosser, more like kitchen trash, and I wished I'd brought my gloves.

Mr. Dinsmore stood over me while I crouched down to get to work.

"This one's real bad," he said.

"I'll take care of it."

"Oh, I know you will. I know you will. I was just saying . . . it's pretty bad."

I plucked out all the dry paper trash and put it in the bag. That left three hot dogs, some moldy bread, a perfectly preserved fast food hamburger, and a spent condom. Since the rest of the house was covered in trash too, I picked up an empty chip bag from the floor to use it in lieu of gloves.

"Oh, don't do that," Dinsmore said.

Since I was already holding the bag, I started to put it in my trash bag and Dinsmore said, "Just . . . put it back where you got it. The cleaning lady'll take care of it."

I put it back relatively close to where I'd gotten it from and reached into my trash bag to find something else to use.

I stood up to move to the next one.

Dinsmore followed me through the kitchen to a really nice sunroom they had on the back of their house. Because of all the glass and not a single open window, this room was even more stifling. My shirt was already damp. This was where most of the plants were located. I shuffled through the trash on the floor to get to the first container. All the containers brimmed with trash but most of this looked like beer bottles, cans, and cigarette butts. Party trash. It was going to take a while. Hopefully I could get through it without passing out.

"I ate so much I threw up last night," Dinsmore said. "I had a five pound hamburger. No bun. I do the low carb thing so I can eat as much as I want, as long as it's mostly meat or eggs. It's great. Doc says it's okay as long as I stay active. So I had to work out for like an hour this morning to make up for it. I feel great now. Really good. And I lost two pounds."

He surveyed all the empty booze bottles in the room as if seeing them for the first time.

"Man, it looks like I drink a lot, doesn't it?"

I just shrugged.

"Oh well. If it gets to be too much of a problem, I'll just go back to rehab."

I pulled my wet shirt away from my skin and wiped my dripping face on my sleeve before moving on to the next container.

"It's really hot in here. I'm gonna go cool down."

I felt relieved when Dinsmore left the room, trying to move as quickly as possible before he came back, moving on to the next container, kneeling in trash to remove the trash from the container. I heard water running and splashing from the kitchen. When

Dinsmore came back, he was dripping with water, all of his clothes drenched.

"That's a lot better," he said.

I had a brief image of him standing at the kitchen sink and spraying himself with the hose attachment.

In one of the containers I found a pair of small blue women's underwear.

I held them up and said, "Trash?"

He snatched them out of my hand and said, "I'd better hang on to these."

By the time I was finished in that room, my trash bag was bulging. Standing made me lightheaded.

There was only one more left. A large black olive tree in the master bedroom. I hoped Mrs. Dinsmore didn't have a man in there with her, which she had on at least two occasions. She was an attractive woman but being in the same room with a couple who are having sex while trying to do my job made me uncomfortable. It didn't help that Mr. Dinsmore had been in the living room sobbing while this happened. Mr. Billups wouldn't let us complain about anything because he was afraid of losing an account.

Mr. Dinsmore led the way. He tapped gently on the door and cracked it.

"Sweetie?" he said softly. "The plant guy's here."

He opened the door and followed me into the room.

Mrs. Dinsmore was in the bed, nude and uncovered.

I tried not to look at her.

This was the largest container, filled with a lot of used Kleenex and other stuff I couldn't really make out because it was all covered in a greenish substance that reminded me a little of what I'd seen back at the motel. It smelled like vomit with a more chemical undertone and I had to try really hard to keep from throwing up myself as I used a discarded red cup from the sunroom to scoop out the pulpy waste. I breathed through my mouth and worked as quickly as possible.

When I was finished, I stood up, staggered, and said, "I think that's it."

"Beautiful." Mr. Dinsmore smiled like a lunatic. "Can I get you to look at one more thing?"

"Sure."

I expected him to take off walking to another room or maybe even outside but he just motioned me to where he stood by the bed and said, "Come here."

I set the bulging trash bag down and went over to him.

He motioned down to his wife.

"I don't know what's happening to her."

He reached down and scraped his fingers along her arm that looked different than the rest of her body. He held his fingertips up. They were covered in a reddish brown dust.

"It's like she's turning to rust," he said. "Do you think it's an STD?"

"I'm sorry," I said. "I'm not a doctor."

He looked sad, the lunatic gleam in his eyes turning to an equally barbed gleam of fear.

"You're right," he said. "You're right."

I just wanted to get out. Looking at Mrs. Dinsmore, I wasn't even sure she was alive but I didn't want to ask any questions because I didn't want to implicate myself any further. I took a couple steps back to grab my bag.

"Call us if you need anything else."

I left the house as quickly as possible, taking a deep breath once outside. It was a warm day and still felt cool compared to the inside of the Dinsmores'.

Thankfully I only had two more stops for the day. The Tewksburys' and the Farleys'—and those were both outside jobs.

I got back to the shop just after sundown.

Billups was in his office, drinking coffee and watching a *Highway to Heaven* rerun on a small television.

"How was it?" He didn't look away from the TV.

"I think the Dinsmores' gave me PTSD."

"It's unsavory the way he just rents his wife out like that. I mean, I don't think any money changes hands but still . . . Anyway, Donnie says Mr. Dinsmore's had another girl around the place himself so I guess everything's even. Was she there?"

"Didn't see anyone."

"Donnie says she couldn't be more than fourteen or fifteen. Real pretty though."

I thought about the blue underwear I'd found in the plant container.

"I don't know what's happenin to this country," Billups mused.

I absently checked my phone but hadn't missed anything. Maybe Billups had forgotten I needed a ride. I didn't want to stick around and listen to him talk about the moral failings of America.

"So . . ." I said.

"Right!" he said. "You don't have your car. Tell ya what . . . we're so short staffed right now that I don't really have the time to be runnin you all over the place. You can borrow one of the company trucks, just make sure all the equipment's locked down."

"Okay. Thanks. Um, see you in the morning, I guess."

"No excuses now."

I left the shop and got back into the truck, feeling a small sliver of freedom. I drove out to Travis's place, not knowing what I expected to find. I thought about Dawn the entire way there. I didn't know what it was about her. I wasn't the type of guy who gets smitten with people. I wondered if she was waiting for me to contact her. Hadn't I told myself I never wanted to see her again? And now I was freaking out that she hadn't contacted me and it hadn't even been two days? Was I just thinking about her because I'd had to go back to work today? I felt like Dawn was doing her best to humiliate me and make me feel uncomfortable but, really, how much more humiliating could it get than working for Billups?

I sighed. I should have gone to college. The things I'd been able to laugh off with the optimism of youth were the very things making middle age nightmarish.

I flipped my brights on and turned onto the access road leading to the field. I stopped the truck and let the headlights illuminate as much of the field as possible. I didn't see anything out of the ordinary. I got out of the truck and walked over to the fire pit. No evidence of recent fires. The insects made rhythmic humming noises around me. I walked a little farther back in the field and came to a wooden cross stuck into a mound of dirt. It looked like the kind of grave people created for pets.

I turned the flashlight of my phone on and shone it on the cross.

Printed on it was this:

HEAR LAYS TARVIS STANELY

I took a photo of it and shook my head.

Did Dawn actually expect me to believe Travis was buried here?

I sent the photo to her with the message "Ha ha."

I pulled back onto the road and around to Travis's parents' old farmhouse. Even though Travis and I had been friends since high school, and I had been over there a lot during that time, I probably hadn't seen his parents in over a decade. I was a completely forgettable person and hoped knocking on their door wasn't going to get me shot by his dad.

The porch light flipped on and his mother opened the door.

She hadn't aged well.

Her thin hair was puffed around her deeply lined face, watery light blue eyes peering out from what looked like a melted mask of the woman I remembered.

"Can I hep ya?" There was no recognition.

"Hey Ruthie, it's Brad."

I thought this would help, maybe even elicit a smile of recognition. But it did nothing.

"Travis's friend," I elaborated.

"Travis ain't here," she said.

"Do you know where he is? I haven't heard from him in a few days."

"Travis does what he wants. He ain't here."

I decided not to press it any further. It was like whatever life force Ruthie had had been drained completely.

I went back to the apartment, masturbated to the thought of licking Dawn's pussy, and went to bed after reading for a few minutes.

The next morning I made coffee, watched a beheading video on MeTube, and went to the first stop on the route. I didn't know if I should be worried about Travis or not. Dawn had never responded to my text and, frankly, I was more worried about that. Maybe it was just because the couple of nights I'd spent around her were juxtaposed with returning to work. If given the choice to be with Dawn—or just part of whatever it was she was doing—or getting up and going to work everyday, I would choose being with Dawn. What would that make me? An employee? A servant? A sycophant? You could say it would mean giving up my freedom—having to do whatever she asked me to—but I'd never really seen having a job as a major hallmark of freedom. All it meant was making barely enough to keep myself alive. That's the big, cruel joke of a capitalist country. They tell you you have the freedom to do whatever you want to do but you have to have the money to do it.

I mowed three lawns on Main Street. I remained unmolested on the first two stops. The third stop I made it all the way to getting everything loaded back up on the truck before Mrs. Evans came stalking out of the house. Like many Midwestern women her age, she was built like a man, had a man's haircut, and a dour humorless demeanor.

She didn't say hi or thanks or anything, just, "Will you come and look at something?"

"Sure."

I followed her to a flowerbed at the front of the house.

"There," she said, pointing down between two boxwood bushes.

I looked, not really knowing what I was supposed to be seeing.

I smiled and confusedly shook my head. "I'm sorry," I said.

"You don't see?"

"What am I . . . supposed to be seeing?"

"Grass," she said. "There is grass in the flowerbeds."

Her severe expression turned to something closer to fear or maybe just utter, soul crushing disappointment.

I got down on my knees and scrambled between the two bushes. Ultimately, I thought, they really just wanted to see you down on your knees so they could lord over you. It must have righted some balance of class they felt entitled to. I had a quick thought of being on my knees between Dawn's legs. Why hadn't she contacted me?

I managed to find one blade of grass about an inch long.

"This it?" I held it pinched between my fingers.

Her look of disappointment turned to one of relieved joy.

She placed a hand over her chest and said, "You got it."

I was afraid she'd cry if I dropped it onto the lawn so I slid it into my pocket, patted it, and said, "I'll make sure it goes where it needs to."

But she was already gone, back into her closed up house. I watched the door shut and noticed a security camera above the front door. A quick perusal of the front of the house revealed two more cameras on either corner. I'd lived in Gethsemane my entire life and never really got the feeling crime was rampant. Something else for rich people to spend money on. I was going to drop the blade of grass on her lawn before getting back into the truck but I imagined her watching me from some darkened room of her house and was afraid it would bring her running back out.

I mowed the grass and trimmed some shrubs for the Baptist church in town, the Presbyterian church on the opposite side of the street, and went to one of the two bars in town to trim and water the ferns surrounding their party patio.

After that I went to my last stop, the Gundersons', an indoor one.

I parked on the street since Roberta was in the driveway. I'd met her coming and going on a number of occasions. Roberta was a type of light nurse who bathed them and turned them.

She emerged from the house as I was on my way up to it.

She smiled a little and said, "Well, it should smell a little better anyway. I got em all washed up."

"Yikes."

"And I passed the maid on my way in."

"Makes my job sound too easy."

"Yeah, put in a good word for me, would you? I'd love to stop doing this shit."

"You know . . . come by and fill out an application. I'm not exactly a model employee but I'll do what I can. We're really short handed right now."

Roberta let out a little laugh and said, "*Okay.* See ya around, Brad."

"See ya."

We both knew she wouldn't bother asking for an application from Billups. Roberta had a vagina and was probably too brown to work for Billups, even though those things would never come from his mouth. They didn't have to. Like a lot of guys his age and socioeconomic status, he said it by what kind of radio shows he listened to and television shows he watched, how he dressed, the bumper stickers he chose to put on his car, the slogans he decided to wear on his t-shirts or hats.

I waved to Roberta as she pulled away, wondering why I'd never found myself with someone like her. Someone who seemed nice and genuine. Of course, I knew Roberta already had two kids and had to take a second job because her husband was too busy battling alcoholism and drug addiction to really be present. The nice ones got chewed up young and just kept getting gnawed on until there wasn't anything left.

I knocked on the Gundersons' door and waited for the faint click of the automatic lock, my cue to enter.

Unlike the crushing heat of the Dinsmores', the Gundersons' was like walking into a meat locker.

There were four of them—two parents and two kids—all so morbidly obese they were virtually bedridden. The good thing was—since they were virtually immobile—they couldn't follow me around the house. The bad thing was that they always had a laundry list of things for me to do. Like they spent a good amount of their lying around time, which was all the time, thinking about the plants in their house, most of which they were too fat to get up and actually look at.

Mrs. Gunderson lay in a trundle bed in the living room, wearing the bare minimum of clothes stretched over her pale, doughy flesh. She and Mr. Gunderson were nearly indistinguishable from one another. I waved to her but it didn't elicit any kind of response. I typically dealt with Mr. Gunderson, who was one of those fat men who'd developed a lady's voice, possibly because of all the weight on his trachea or vocal cords or whatever. The first time I'd heard him speak, I'd had to stifle my laughter for the rest of the conversation, feeling like a jerk the entire time.

I walked through the house and to the large master bedroom in the back.

The door was open and I leaned in.

"Hey, Mr. Gunderson. I'm here to take care of the plants."

"Oh, hey, Brad." Man, that voice. It got me every time. I ducked back out of the doorway for just a moment so I could compose myself.

"Could you come here a minute?" he asked.

I took a deep breath. At least Mr. Gunderson never talked long. It seemed like, as I'm sure with most things that weren't eating or watching TV, it took too much effort. I wasn't sure how he and Mrs. Gunderson had ever managed to work up the energy to fuck and have children. But they hadn't always been morbidly obese.

Somewhere along the way they'd simply chosen to pick their poison. What was it Charles Bukowski said? "Find what you love and do it until it kills you." Something like that.

I went into the room and got to within three feet of the bed. Roberta was right. It didn't smell like it did on a lot of other days— sort of dank and musty, maybe a little cheesy or yeasty. I'd have to remember to try and time it like this. After the humiliations suffered at the hands of a lot of my other clients, the Gundersons' would be just about the easiest on my route.

I leaned in so I could hear Mr. Gunderson.

He held out his phone. "Will you do me a big favor and take a photo of the plants when you're finished with them? I haven't seen them in a while and I'd love to look at them, but I don't think I'm going to be getting up any time soon."

He moved his eyes toward the foot of the bed.

I hadn't even noticed his left foot had been removed, the leg above its absence covered in purple knots and suppurating wounds. The other leg didn't look that much better and I imagined that foot probably wasn't far behind.

"Sure." I took the phone. "You just want pictures or you want me to shoot some video?"

"Yeah," he said. "Video would be really nice."

"Sure thing."

I dropped his phone in the same pocket as mine. On the way to the first container, I felt a vibration and got momentarily excited. Maybe Dawn had decided to text me.

I pulled out both phones and turned the screen on mine on.

They were both the same, but mine was the broken one.

Nothing.

I put my phone back in my pocket, now holding Mr. Gunderson's. I turned the screen on, telling myself I'd have to do it to shoot the video anyway.

The text was from Patty Gunderson, his wife. It read: "I want that fat horse cock inside of me, Mr. G."

I felt myself blush a little. Not because of the content of the text, but because I was reading something meant to be private.

I put the phone in my pocket and pruned and watered and dusted the plant until there was no more brown and it was a shiny, healthy green. The phone vibrated a few more times before I was finished with the plant.

Of course, I read the messages.

"I'm gonna suck that fat cock halfway down my throat."

"I wanna gag on it."

"I want you to pull my hair while you fuck my tight asshole."

I tried to imagine this happening. I wouldn't mind watching it. I'd have to Google 'morbidly obese people having sex' when I went home. It wasn't something I'd ever done but found myself becoming more and more obsessed with it as I wandered through the Gundersons' frigid house taking care of their plants and reading her filthy texts. Was this how they spent every day? Would Mr. Gunderson be in his room jerking off right now if he were actually getting these?

I knew he'd been a lawyer at one point but couldn't really imagine him doing much in the way of working right now. I could tell by the pictures hanging around the house they'd lived a full life at one point. There were tons of pictures of he and Mrs. Gunderson standing in exotic looking places from around the world. Sometimes it looked like they were surrounded by family and friends but mostly it was just them. It made me a little sad. They clearly still had passion for one another and had had a passion for life, at some point. Now everything was all virtual. Sex via text. Videos of the plants that had been in his house for years and that he clearly enjoyed looking at.

Sometimes I felt fortunate to have been poor my entire life. While my parents had never been as poor as I was, my dad was a major tightwad who put everything except the bare minimum into savings so he and my mother could have a good retirement. I guess he had to. And they did have a good few years before they were both diagnosed with cancer and died within months of each other, the considerable savings mostly depleted by their treatments and eventual hospice care. I'd never had the money to develop a thirst for anything. Therefore I'd never had to experience the sad turn that thirst could have taken when something threw a wrench in my life. For the Gundersons, I was assuming that wrench was their children.

Oh God, their children . . .

I saved the plant in their room for last, hoping it wouldn't throw a pall over the rest of my evening.

Twin boys. I didn't know their names. Both around age twelve and a little over 400 pounds each. They were mobile, but never moved from in front of their massive TV where they sat in big recliners and played video games and drank soda and ate snacks and occasionally shit themselves.

It was this last thing that always brought me down.

But, I assumed, if Roberta had been there only a few minutes ago, I might be safe.

She would have emptied what I'd dubbed 'the shit hamper,' a chest-size container where they disposed of their soiled diapers.

I slid into their room trying not to be noticed. I quickly took care of the plant, which seemed fairly traumatized. I imagined one of the boys slapping out his frustrations on the leaves. Since they hadn't acknowledged me yet, I thought about slipping out without shooting the video but knew I probably wouldn't get away with it. It would have ended up being the one thing Mr. Gunderson actually wanted to see.

I pulled the phone out and read the last message.

"I want to gargle with your cum."

I filmed the plant before focusing the camera on the broad backs of the two boys.

The one on the right turned and stared directly into the camera.

"Nyah!" he barked.

The other boy turned.

"Blub," he garbled. "Blub."

"Nyah!"

I left the room to the chorus of 'blub's and 'nyah's.

I handed the phone back to Gunderson and he said softly, "See ya next week."

A lot of the clients closed this way and, since starting there, I'd always fantasized about how nice it would be to say, "Actually, this is my last week."

Instead I said, "Yeah, see ya. Hope you like the videos."

I felt pretty sure I'd be back the next week.

And because of *that* feeling, I felt pretty sure I'd do whatever Dawn asked if she even bothered contacting me again.

I went down to check the mail while the coffee brewed. Most everything I did was online and I didn't have money to order things so I'd often go days without checking my mail. There was yet another flyer for a missing dog and I found myself slightly annoyed by this. What had happened to the other dogs? Why didn't they ever put up a dog found flyer if that happened? If one were worried about the missing dog, it seemed like it would be a great relief.

I threw the small stack of mail on the table in the kitchen, poured some coffee, and sifted through it.

Most of it was junk mail from The Point Medical Center, soliciting me to engage in procedures for everything from pain management to weight loss. I threw it in the trash. There was a handwritten envelope addressed generally to 'Our Neighbor' with no return address. I opened it up and three teeth fell out. They looked human. I threw those in the trash, as well.

I drank my coffee and watched a few videos of teenage girls modeling newly purchased swimsuits on MeTube. One of them reminded me a little of Dawn so I started it from the beginning and jerked off to it. I tossed the soiled paper towel in the trash, washed my hands, pounded the rest of my coffee, and headed to the shop.

Today was Friday, one of our busiest days. Everyone wanted their lawn to look good for the weekend but nobody wanted us there on the actual weekend when they were to have their theoretical barbeques or get-togethers. I didn't spend a lot of time wandering around Gethsemane on the weekends, but I rarely saw anyone out when on my route. I'd always found it slightly odd these people lived in awesome houses with awesome yards in a not bad town, and never seemed to go outside. Friday was also the day with the most new clients.

I got to the shop a few minutes late.

Donnie was there, drinking Mountain Dew from a two liter.

"Hey, Donnie," I said.

"I can't open my left eye," he said. "At all."

"How's the concussion?"

"Not good."

Mr. Billups came out of the office and handed me the route sheet. It was very robust.

"There's a lot to do today," he said. "I want you guys to go out together. Have Donnie help you out. He's hampered what with the eye thing and concussion. Not sure he's okay to drive."

"Okay." I wasn't incredibly happy about it. Donnie didn't talk a lot so it wouldn't be that bad but the general solitude of the job was one of the only redeeming things about it.

I looked over the route sheet. Thankfully, the Bachmans' was still the only indoor stop on the list but my stomach clenched a little when I saw the name Larry Warner. It was, of course, missing the 'White Power' in front of it. Maybe I'd just drop Donnie off there and pick him up after I did the next one on the list.

"You guys should probably get movin. It's supposed to storm this afternoon so you're really gonna have to bust yer butts." Billups' voice broke Donnie and me from our impending workload stupor.

Donnie chugged the rest of his Mountain Dew and looked like he was going to vomit for a second.

"You ever happen to hear from Travis?" I asked Mr. Billups.

"Funny you should ask that. I tried callin him again this morning but all I got was sex noises."

"I think someone's hijacked his phone. I can't get ahold of him either."

"Well, there'll be plenty work for him if he comes back."

"I'm a little worried."

"No sweat. Happens all the time. He'll turn up somewhere."

I turned to Donnie. "You ready?"

"I guess," he said.

On the way to the first stop, Donnie packed a little bowl with weed and took a deep drag, offering me some.

"No thanks," I said.

He took another drag, tapped it out on the outside door of the truck and put it in his pocket.

"So how are things?" I asked.

"Not good," he said.

"I mean, like, besides the eye thing and the concussion?"

"All right, I guess. I think my parents are getting divorced or something."

"Aw, man, that sucks. You still live at home?" I didn't have any idea how old Donnie was. He could have been anywhere from nineteen to forty. He was painfully skinny, with a tightly drawn and lined face that looked like he'd been living rough for a number of years.

"Yeah."

"Where do you live?"

"Up on Cooper Place."

Gethsemane didn't really have many bad areas, but every house on Cooper Place was a Victorian mansion. There were only about eight of them on the entire street. It was probably the most sought after and expensive area in Gethsemane.

"Damn, man, that's nice," I said. "Why do you work here?"

"It's one of the only places in town to work. And I like being outside."

"Did you go to college or anything?"

"I tried but I didn't do so good. And I missed being here."

"In Gethsemane?"

"Yeah. I don't know why."

"What do your folks do?"

"They're both professors in Twin Springs . . . at, uh, Shrine College. But now that it's summer I think they're just spending most of their time fucking other people."

"Oh shit."

"It's kinda creepy. These two girls started hangin around . . . I mean, they're younger than me. And . . . I guess they're kinda hot and all but, fuck, man, I'm still a virgin and my old ass parents are getting more pussy than me."

I thought this was probably what was upsetting him more than anything.

"Well, I mean I guess that's another reason I had to get a job too. Cause they were fine with me just staying home and shit until they got little fuck buddies then it was like, 'You need to pay us rent, Donnie.' I think those bitches are like little fucking leeches, if you ask me."

"Sounds like maybe you should go back to school."

He laughed a little and lit a cigarette. "Not an option, man. I feel too old and I know my parents wouldn't pay for it now."

"How old are you?"

"I turn thirty next month."

"That's not too old. Do community college or something."

"Fuck that. It's not my thing. My brain feels too full as it is."

"That's probably just the concussion."

We powered through the first few stops. After the fourth one, Donnie said he was tired and needed to take a nap. I'd heard that thing about not letting people sleep if you thought they had a concussion and encouraged him to stay awake. I even offered to go to the Snack Barn and get him more Mountain Dew but he said his head was going to explode if he didn't shut his one remaining eye for a few minutes.

I did the next couple of stops and woke him up when we got to the Bachmans'.

"You want to do the outside and I'll get the inside?" I said.

"I wouldn't mind doing the inside," he said. "The lady here is

. . .”

"Mean." I knew he was probably going to say 'hot' but she was savage.

"I'll come in and help."

I shrugged. "It's up to you, man."

We approached the house. I knocked on the door. Alan Bachman answered it. He was probably in his early thirties, chiseled jaw currently covered with a bit of black shadow, piercing blue eyes, and well-coiffed black hair. He wore a blue oxford shirt, completely unbuttoned, and khaki shorts. His body was cut and sinewy and covered in a bright red rash.

Other than opening the door, he gave us no acknowledgement. He was on the phone, shouting, "I'm really excited about healthcare!"

I quickly moved onto the first plant while Donnie stood and stared at the Bachmans' expensively minimal decorations.

Mr. Bachman continued to rant. "I don't care if you're tired of hearing about my rash! It keeps getting worse! And I think it's your fault. I don't care if this isn't your department! If I want to talk about healthcare you're going to talk about healthcare."

I leaned into working on the plant while Donnie dazedly wandered toward the back of the house, presumably to find Kimmy Bachman and hoping there was a plant in the room she occupied. I knew there probably was because she was probably in their home gym, which had a row of mirrors on two walls. One of the mirrored walls was lined with plants, the other with exercise equipment. Despite Mrs. Bachman's abuse, this had always been one of my favorite stops. The way the exercise room was arranged allowed me to tend to the plants while looking at the mirror in front of me, affording me a nice view of Mrs. Bachman on the treadmill or stretching out on the yoga mat. She was a young, lithe blond woman who kept her hair pulled back into a ponytail and wore a sports bra and athletic shorts that were really just thicker underwear. After servicing their house, I'd masturbated in the truck at least three times, the image of a sweated up, rosy-cheeked Mrs. Bachman still fresh in my head. I didn't feel good about it at first but resolved that she must have been aware of what she was doing to me in there. Unless she thought I was gay. I resented Donnie somewhat.

I moved on to the next plant.

"I need to get this taken care of by July!" Mr. Bachman shouted. "My wife and I need to visit every country in the world before September. I need to be in peak health! Then when I come back I have to get started on the Wild Times account! It's gonna be *huge* and I'm gonna be really busy. Then we've got the rally to attend and then Kimmy wants to get pregnant with three kids so we can get that all out of the way at one time and then we're going to have to start interviewing nannies and looking for private schools. And I can't do ANY of this if I'm covered in a fucking itchy rash. I can't even concentrate on my grooming! I look like a monster!"

I hoped whatever Mr. Bachman had wasn't contagious.

I quickly took care of the other plants to see if I still had time to join Donnie in the exercise room. Of course I would. He was probably working at a snail's pace so he could spend as much time in that room as possible.

When I peeked into the exercise room, Kimmy Bachman stood on the yoga mat, her sinewy legs flexing as she bent from the waist, her hands wrapped around her Achilles' tendons. I could see the line between her buttocks and her legs that her shorts had risen slightly to reveal. Also, the shorts were so tight and the lights in here so bright I could make out the outline of her cunt. I immediately felt myself growing hard.

"Need some help?" I asked Donnie.

His one eye was plastered to the mirror. It looked like he was still working on the first plant.

"Nah. I think I got it."

"I'm done with the rest. We need to finish up here so we can get outside. Storm's coming." I didn't know if this was true or not but I thought it might throw him into a higher, slightly less voyeuristic gear.

"You guys need to shut the fuck up and get to work." Mrs. Bachman had pulled out of her bent over position and now stood with her back arched and both of her arms pulled over her head, her perfect breasts straining against the sports bra. "When stupid, poor people talk it makes me feel stupid and poor."

I went to work on the far plant, figuring we'd meet somewhere in the middle. I occasionally glanced up at Mrs. Bachman to see what new, alluring position she had struck. I thought yoga was supposed to calm the mind or something. Make people more peaceful. If Mrs. Bachman was this mean and rabid while actually doing yoga, I could only imagine what she was like most of the other time. Maybe that was the source of Mr. Bachman's rash.

I did nearly the whole row of plants and Donnie had just moved on to his second one.

Mrs. Bachman had finished her yoga and wiped her sweat off with a white towel.

She was perfectly toned, her cheeks pink with exertion.

"You guys get enough of an eyeful?"

Neither one of us answered her.

"Are you both fucking mute? I asked a question."

"I don't know what you're talking about," I said.

"I know you guys were both looking at me. I wanted to know if you got enough?"

"I don't know how to answer that."

"Well, idiot, as with most things, you should answer with a yes or a no."

"Then . . . no?"

"So you want to look some more?"

"Uh . . . sure?"

"You guys are so fucking sad. You should feel lucky you got to see as much as you did, so show some fucking gratitude."

"Okay." I felt really uncomfortable. I went back to lightly wiping down a plant I'd already wiped down.

"Stop ignoring me. I already saw you take care of that one. What's wrong with his eye?"

"He's concussed," I said.

"Do you even know what that means?"

"Yeah."

"How can you guys do this? This is like something you don't do unless you're like eighteen. Or Mexican. Are either of you illegals?"

"Come on," I said.

She moved closer to me, aggressive. "What did you say?"

I threw up a placatory hand. "You know . . . just . . . don't be like that." I thought about how I was going to defend myself if she called to complain to Billups.

"Like what? A *bitch*. You think I'm being a *bitch*? Just say it. Call it like you see it. Call me a bitch!"

I wasn't good at confrontation and didn't think I'd ever called a woman a bitch before. I was shaking and my mouth was dry. I felt like the biggest pussy in the world.

"Look, that's not what I meant. It was just a little . . . maybe racist?"

"Oh that's fucking priceless. I show an ounce of pride in my *country* of *birth* and you call me a fucking racist when you're just some *dirty pervert* who's spent the last half hour watching this American girl's ass! Is that why you like looking at me so much, loser? Because you go home to your brown wife and your four fucking welfare kids."

"Come on, Donnie. Let's go."

"No. Old One-eye's finishing what he's doing. You can't come in here, fuck me with your eyes, call me a racist, and then just leave!"

"Just stop yelling at us." I tried to sound calm but I was sure my voice was quivering.

"I will *not* stop yelling, you fucking little pussy!"

She was so close to me her breasts were nearly touching my chest. I was shaking with anger but my cock was even harder than before. What was happening?

"I don't know what you want me to say."

"I want you to admit to me that you think about fucking me every time you come here. I want you to tell me I'm better than you. Tell me you want to be just like us."

"Okay," I said.

"Okay what?"

"All of that."

"Say it."

I swallowed through my dry mouth. She had been staring hatefully into my eyes, but now her gaze dropped to my crotch, where there was undoubtedly a considerable bulge in my khaki workpants.

"I . . . think about having sex with you every time I come here. You are a better person than me. I would *love* to be just like you."

She smirked and backed away.

"I'd probably let both of you fuck me if you were better looking." She pointed at Donnie. "I bet that one's never had sex before and you probably only fuck fat girls and unwed mothers."

Donnie stood up, as though completely unaware of the situation.

"Finished," he said.

Mr. Bachman stood in the doorway, looking forlorn.

"The rash," he said, "it's worse."

"Nobody wants to hear about your fucking rash," she said.

"We'd better hit the yard." I clapped Donnie on the back and we scooted out of the house as quickly as possible.

"That was intense," Donnie said.

We quickly finished up in the yard and drove to the McDonald's out on Route 4 to grab some lunch. The sky darkened while we were en route to our next stop. We parked on the curb in front of the house as the storm broke and waited for it to pass. Donnie smoked a cigarette and I drank some of the shitty McDonald's coffee. I looked over at the house across the street and saw a child standing in the yard, completely expressionless as the rain pounded down on him.

"What's wrong with people?" I said.

"Whaddya mean?" Donnie absently scrolled through his phone.

"Fuck," I said. "I don't know. Maybe I'm just getting old."

He shrugged. "My parents think we're, like, a test area."

"A test area?"

"Yeah. You know, like market research or something."

"Are they conspiracy nuts?"

"I don't know. They have a point. You ever hear of a rade?"

"Like a drug raid or something?"

"No, uh, a rade. Like spelled r-a-d-e, I think. Short for radiation victim. Most people think it's some kind of urban legend but I know people who swear they've seen em."

I thought about what I'd seen the one night I went to Travis's, the night I'd gone off the road.

"I don't think I have," I said.

"You know, it was rumored the aliens and parts of the spaceship that crashed in Roswell were transported to Wright-Patt for further research."

"I've heard that."

"Other people have other theories, of course. My folks say if that's true about us bein test subjects that it's probably the biggest experiment the government has ever done. I mean, you've heard of The Point, right?"

"Sure."

"Well then you know they're everywhere. But they're a corporation. Not a government entity. And they have their hand in everything from space research down to breakfast cereal. Not to mention all the hospitals and medical shit. Anyway, the story is that the rades came from their chemical plant closer to Dayton. They started as normal humans but something changed them. They lost their hair. Their skin turned a glowing green. They sprouted needles from the tips of their fingertips that they plunged into people to drain them of their life force. Like vampires or something. Some people said it was chemicals. Other people said they'd somehow been given some biologically altering agent derived from the original Roswell aliens. My dad says he thinks they're some sort of weapons experiment that went haywire. He says the government or The Point or whatever is tryin to get them to evolve to the point to where people can't tell if they're humans or not. He says they could be used to fight wars in other countries but would probably just end up being toys for rich people. In fact, he says the world is run by rich people and, once we're all rades, the rich people will have achieved what they want. The ultimate consumers. People who'll make things and then buy and consume the things they make without putting up any fuss."

He laughed a little and took another drag from his cigarette. "I'm just repeating what they said. I'm not sayin I believe any of it."

"Yeah, right? You could waste your entire life thinking about that shit and it's not going to make anything any better. If there is some kind of truth, we're never going to know what it is. It's probably closer to chaos than it is a conspiracy. I don't think humans are capable of that kind of organization, no matter how much money they have."

"You know when I said I came back because I missed this place?"

"Yeah."

"It was pretty bad. I had to go see a doctor when I came back. He said I was having withdrawal symptoms. He was convinced I got hooked on booze or some drug when I went away. But I think it was this town."

"Withdrawal symptoms from a place?"

"Yeah, man, he put me on meds and everything. I've been on em ever since and, man, I didn't do *nothin* when I went to school. Personally, I think it's the air or the water or something. Dad says it could have been chemtrails from the military aircraft."

"Is your doctor here in town?"

"Yeah. Weishaupt. I think he's the only one."

"Can I bum a smoke?"

"Sure, man." He dug his cigarettes from his pocket and handed me the pack.

I pulled one out and lit up. It made the shitty coffee better, at least.

I pulled my phone from my pocket and brought up a weather app to see how long it was going to storm for. If it was supposed to last the rest of the afternoon then we might as well call it a day. From what I could make out from the half of my screen I could see, it looked like it was supposed to be over soon. It had been pretty warm and hadn't rained a lot so the ground would probably drink it up.

The rain stopped by the time I was finished with my cigarette.

The boy I'd been watching turned and went back into his house like he'd only been out there to absorb the energy of the storm.

We got out of the truck and took care of the lawn. By the time we were finished the sidewalk and driveway were already dry enough for us to blow the grass away.

We collaborated on the next two stops. The storm had put us behind by about an hour.

The next stop was White Power Larry's. After the incident at the Bachmans', I didn't think my nerves could take it. I decided to use the storm as an excuse.

"Hey," I said, "you wanna hit this one and I'll move on to the next one so maybe we can get done by dark? We're running a little behind."

"Sure, man. You ever hang out at Larry's?"

"Uh, no. Do you?"

"I have a couple times. He stopped inviting me though. He throws good parties. Good music. And the girls are awesome."

It occurred to me Donnie might have been too stupid to realize White Power Larry threw neo-Nazi rallies, not really parties.

"Not my scene," I said.

I drove up the long gravel driveway on Pence Road, leaving

Donnie in front of White Power Larry's trailer with a riding lawnmower and a leaf blower. I went ahead and did the next two stops before doubling back to pick him up. It was already after six. That would leave one more stop and put us back at the shop around eight.

I pulled up in front of White Power Larry's trailer. He and a couple other bubbas were sitting on chairs in front of the trailer. I quickly scanned around for Stasia but didn't see her. I pretended to look at my phone so I'd appear busy. Donnie drove the lawnmower up onto the bed of the truck and tossed the leaf blower in.

He hopped in next to me.

He was bald.

I pulled away as quickly as I could without being too obvious.

"You're bald."

"Yeah, man, Larry shaved my head."

"Did he make you let him do it?"

"Um . . ." He pulled out a cigarette and lit it. "It's kind of embarrassing."

"It's fine if you don't want to talk about it."

"No . . . Larry's all right. It's just . . . Okay, you won't tell Billups, will you?"

"What? Tell him you shaved your head? I think he's going to notice."

"Well . . . okay, so Larry's got this smokin hot wife. She's way younger than he is."

"Um, yeah." I tried to feign ignorance. "I think I've seen her around. I don't remember her name."

"It's Stasia. Anyway, I was mowin the grass and she's out there in like a bikini top and cut-offs and I couldn't help lookin. So Larry catches me and says, 'You like what you see?' and I say, 'I'm so sorry, sir' cause Larry's a big fuckin guy and I've heard about what he does to people. And he says, 'No, man, it's okay. I'd think you was a fag if you didn't look and that's *not* okay. Bein a fag.' So I told him I wasn't a fag and he says if he and his friends can shave my head, he'll let me look all I want so I go into his garage and they sit me down in a chair and start shavin my head and Stasia comes in and starts takin off her clothes. Then he tells me I can jerk off if I want to. I don't know, I kind of thought it would be insulting if I didn't so I did. Anyway, I did somethin right away and as soon as that happened Stasia was gone. She didn't even take off her under-wear, man."

"It, uh, sounds like you had a good time."

"I guess." He seemed shaken and I got the feeling he wasn't telling me everything.

"What else happened?"

He was nearly crying. "They pushed me down and made me lick up my jizz. Then Stasia came back and all these other hot girls and everyone else who was there and there was hair in the jizz and I couldn't get it down without gagging and a bunch of them had their phones out recording me and just . . . just . . . I don't want to talk about it anymore. But maybe I didn't embarrass myself too much because they invited me to a party next Friday."

"Dude, Larry and his friends are neo-Nazi racist assholes. Stay away from them. Even if you're bored. They're just going to make you do shit you don't want to do." I felt like a hypocrite saying it, especially while we were driving around in a company truck wearing company uniforms, especially when I still had Dawn on the brain, especially when I'd fucked White Power Larry's wife, even after noticing the swastika tramp stamp.

"No, man, I think they're all right."

"Dude, are *you* a fucking racist asshole?"

"I just . . . I agree with a lot of what they have to say."

I held up a hand. "Just stop talking, okay?"

"I just . . ."

"You just what?"

"Thought you'd be okay with it too."

"Why would you think I'm okay with it?"

"Well, I mean, you work for Billups. You ever see any minorities workin for him? I mean, come on, he's the only advertiser in Larry's *White Power Times*."

"I've, uh, never read *White Power Times*."

"Yeah, well, you're pretty much contributing to it."

Why did Donnie have to tell me this shit? I had thus far managed to be willfully ignorant. I thought I was working for an old religious man who had trouble finding help. And maybe he had some peculiar ideas and was a little racist but, I don't know, I didn't think he was hateful in a conscious, organized kind of way. If he happened to not have any minorities working for him, it was probably because there weren't many minorities in Gethsemane. It was impossible to find a job I was morally okay with. I didn't think I'd had that since I worked in a bookstore out of high school. It seemed like everyone else either discriminated against people, destroyed the environment, or were hellbent on keeping their own employees among the poorest part of the population.

I pulled to the curb in front of our last stop for the day, the Carmichaels'.

I checked the bank app on my phone to make sure my paycheck had gone through.

It had.

"It's almost dark, man," I said. "You wanna just blow this one off?"

"I don't give a fuck."

I drove back to the shop and dropped Donnie off. Then I went back to the apartment where I masturbated to a scenario of hate fucking Mrs. Bachman with her bent over a Pilates ball, but thoughts of Dawn kept interfering and I ended up finishing to the thought of eating her out.

I dozed off relatively early and was awakened a few hours later to a loud sound coming from the street. I sat up in the bed and looked out the window.

I first noticed Barcie and grew momentarily excited, thinking Dawn would be with her but I didn't see any sign of her.

The loud sound was the lawnmower running. Barcie stood in the middle of the truck's bed wielding the leaf blower like a supervillain.

I sighed and thought, "I guess I need to deal with this."

But I didn't. Not really. This was Mr. Billups' problem and I was pretty sure I was going to use the money I'd just gotten paid with to fix my truck and tell him he could come and pick up his whenever he wanted because I was done.

Still, I was going to go down and confront Barcie because Barcie was close to Dawn and I had to see Dawn again.

I still wore my work uniform. I changed into jeans and a black t-shirt so I didn't feel like a clown before putting on some shoes and going down to figure out what the hell Barcie was doing.

Once at the sidewalk, I looked around to see if she had attracted anyone else's attention but, of course, there wasn't anyone else around.

"What the hell are you doing?" I asked over the roar of the lawnmower.

Donnie must have been so harried by having to drink his own jizz that he hadn't even removed the keys.

"This stuff yours?" she called.

"Well, it's . . ." I reached up to the lawnmower and turned it off. "It's Mr. Billups'."

I gestured for the leaf blower and she handed it to me so I could turn it off.

"You know how to use all of it?"

"Well, yeah, it's what I do."

"That's what you been up to, huh? Workin?"

"Pretty much."

"You gonna show me how to use it? It'd be a lot of fun. I ain't never done chores before."

"I don't think that'd be a great idea."

"Why not? Fraid of gettin in trouble?"

"Well . . ." I thought about saying not really, that I was done with Billups, but it's what I'd been doing all day and didn't think I wanted to do any more of it.

"Cause Daddy's real tight with old Billups so you wouldn't get in no trouble."

"No . . . it's just . . . I'm tired."

"Come on, take me out and show me how to use it. I'll suck your dick."

She lifted up her shirt to show me her nipples. I liked skinny girls but Barcie was too thin even for me. I really didn't want her anywhere near my cock but, as far as taking Billups' equipment out for a midnight spin, what else was I going to do?

"Fine," I said. "But you don't have to suck my cock."

"I'm totally goin to though." She leapt out of the truck and went to her car, coming back to the truck with a partially depleted case of Bud. She cracked one open and said, "Lawn and garden party!"

She headed for the driver's side of the truck and I cut her off.

"I'll drive." It wasn't that I really cared. I just wanted control of where we were going.

"This is really exciting," she said.

"Yeah. So . . . I haven't heard from Dawn lately."

"I seen her earlier today. She's real busy."

"So . . . what is it she does exactly?"

"I can't really talk about it."

"Why not? It's just us."

She smirked a little. "That's what *you* think. It's never just us.

Somebody's always watchin or listenin. Sides, I signed one of them whaddyacallits."

"A confidentiality agreement?"

"Yeah. That's it."

"Well that pretty much just means you can't talk about it public-ly." I didn't know if this was true or not. "I'm not really asking for specifics just . . . like what's the nature of her business?"

"Makin people happy. That's the nature of Dawn's business. She makes people happy."

I couldn't help but laugh a little. "Really? What about that girl you beat with a chain? What was her name? Taylor something?"

"Taylor Dream. She'll be a lot happier. Sometimes you just gotta wait and see."

"Did Dawn do that to you?" I had thus far not wanted to point out Barcie's obvious wounds or deformities or whatever they were but her reluctance to tell me about Dawn was driving me insane.

"You bet!"

"And that's . . . a good thing?"

"The best. I asked for it. Wanna see what I looked like before?"

"That's okay."

But she already had her phone out, scrolling through photos until she came to one pre-beating.

She held the phone over to me.

"I'm driving right now," I said.

She leaned over farther and held it up a little behind the steering wheel.

It looked like an old school photo and not at all like the girl sitting next to me. The girl in the photo was bright-eyed and innocent looking. Healthy looking. And beautiful. Flawlessly beautiful.

I almost said, "Wow, you were really pretty," just to say something, but stopped myself.

"I was really pretty, huh?"

"Yeah," I said, and added, "You're still pretty."

"Stop tryin to make me feel good. I know I'm not pretty. I don't wanna be pretty. That was sorta the whole point. Bein pretty is confusing for a young girl. Everyone's nice to you. Mostly because they want to fuck you—guys especially—but partly cause it just makes em feel good to have a pretty person pay attention to em. A girl that looks like that doesn't even know what it's like to want somethin. Didn't help that Daddy's so rich and spoiled me rotten with, like, material things? So it's okay if you think I'm a monster cause you know what?"

"What?"

"Even though you think I'm hideous you're still out here spendin time with me but now I know it's cause you like me, not cause you want to fuck me. I mean, you might fuck me if you wanted to fuck somethin bad enough but it's not the first thing on your mind."

I was probably only spending time with her to pick her brain about Dawn but didn't really feel like I needed to tell her that. She probably already knew anyway.

"So," I said, "you figured out what it was you wanted?"

"Mm-hmm."

"And?"

"Dawn. I wanted Dawn the first time I saw her. Same as you."

"Is she your girlfriend?"

"She's my master. You can't really have Dawn. She ain't never gonna be nobody's girlfriend. You can only serve her but, yeah, I guess we do some stuff together."

"Look, I know Dawn's married to Sheriff Bando. He's not her fucking dad."

"You must be like a detective or somethin."

"Well, I mean, that kinda sounds like Bando *has* Dawn, if he's married to her."

"They don't do nothin."

"What, like, they don't sleep together?"

"Dawn's never been with a man."

"Oh, come on."

"I swear. She can't."

"Can't?"

"I ain't too comfortable talkin about Dawn's private matters."

I flashed back to going down on Dawn, combing my memory for any anatomical abnormalities. I'd been up close and personal with a few vaginas in my life and everything seemed normal with hers so I thought maybe when Barcie had said she couldn't be with a man it had to be more of a mental thing.

"Fine," I said.

"Just know this," Barcie said. "Dawn ain't like me or you. She's special. She's gonna to do big things. She's *doin* big things. She's got real callin."

"She seems kind of like a teenage psychopath."

"Well maybe that's exactly what she wants you to think."

I pulled down the gravel access road to the field behind Travis's house.

"Where we at?" Barcie said.

"A friend's house. We're gonna mow this field."

She squealed. "I almost forgot all about our lawn and garden party!"

"It's starting really soon."

Barcie suddenly remembered the beer she'd brought along. She bent down to dig one out of the case, pop the top, and chug it down.

I stopped the truck and we got out. Barcie had opened another beer and lit up a cigarette.

"Want some coke?" She held out a little plastic baggie.

"No thanks."

"Help yourself to the beer."

"Maybe later."

"Don't worry about it. If you get stopped on the way home I'll just give the cop a blowjob."

"You know the world isn't run on blowjobs, right?"

"So says you."

I slid the slats down out of the truck and brought the lawnmower down.

Barcie stood drinking her beer and smoking her cigarette and twitching with her weird energy. It might have just been the coke.

"You gonna show me how to use that?"

"Sure. But I need to ask you about something first."

"I'm finished talkin bout Dawn."

"It's not about Dawn. Follow me."

I walked across the field to Travis's presumably mock grave.

"Oooh, creepy," Barcie said. "Is someone buried there?"

I grabbed my head in frustration and said through clenched teeth. "That's what you're supposed to tell me."

"Why? I don't know nothin bout that."

"I know Dawn is fucking with me. And I'm pretty sure you helped so just . . . tell me what happened to Travis."

"Who?"

I pointed at the crude wooden cross.

"That says Tarvis," she said.

"*Fuck me.*"

"Now?"

"No." I rolled my eyes. "Not ever."

"We'll see."

"If you're not going to tell me that you and Dawn created that grave to fuck with me then you're going to help me dig it up."

"I ain't helpin you dig until you show me how to run that lawnmower."

I could have continued arguing with her but I already felt like it was one of the stupidest arguments I'd ever had.

Resigned, I walked over to the lawnmower and climbed in the seat.

"Come on," I said.

"Let me get another beer."

She got another beer and came over to the lawnmower and sat in my lap.

"This ain't so bad," she said.

I flipped on the headlights. I'd always wondered why riding mowers had headlights since I didn't really know anyone who mowed his grass at night but, then again, here we were doing exactly that.

I fired the engine up, briefly explained the throttle and the clutch, and told her she didn't ever really need to be out of first gear. Then I showed her how to engage the blade and rode with her on a lap around the field.

I stopped it and told her I was getting off the mower.

"Sure you don't wanna mess around for a bit. You're kinda hard. I can feel it."

"I know. I'm sorry. I can't help it. Besides, I've got a body to exhume. Maybe if I knew there wasn't a body in there I'd have time to mess around with you."

"Oh," she said. "Yeah, that was just me and Dawn fucking with you. There's nobody in there."

I again squeezed my head in frustration.

"Ah! Now I don't believe you."

"Does it really matter?" she said.

It probably didn't, but I felt like I needed to know.

She hopped off my lap to go back to the truck and get the rest of the beer and I went to the truck to grab a shovel.

I stuck the shovel in the dirt of the grave and took a picture. I sent it to Dawn and said: "I'm opening Schrodinger's box."

I got to digging. I hoped, if it really was a grave, whoever dug it was as lazy as I was. I was well aware of the 'six feet deep' thing but if I ever had to bury a dead body, there was no way in hell I was going that deep.

I found this small field peaceful when it hummed with the sound of insects. Now, unfortunately, the constant roar of the mower made me feel frenzied and frustrated. I glanced up to see Barcie mowing in no discernible pattern whatsoever. She'd taken her top off and was manipulating the steering wheel with a beer in one hand and a cigarette in the other. She disregarded my advice of keeping it in first gear and raced around with it on its highest possible setting.

I went back to digging.

I stopped to check my phone. Dawn hadn't texted me back.

I dug quickly. I wasn't really trying to exhume the potential body. I just wanted to dig down far enough to see if there was one in there.

Sweat rolled down my face, my scant hair plastered to my scalp, my shirt stuck to my back.

I glanced up and spotted Barcie. She was still on the lawnmower but it had stopped. She'd removed her shorts and had her legs spread on either side of the steering wheel, her phone focused on her crotch.

A couple of seconds later my phone vibrated.

I pulled it out of my pocket and looked at it.

It was a photo of Barcie's vagina. Well, the right half of Barcie's vagina.

The accompanying text said: "My pussy got swetty."

I didn't glance back at her, instead redoubling my efforts on the grave.

After she was finished fucking around on her phone, Barcie shut the lawnmower off and stumbled over to me.

"I'm bored. Can we fuck now?"

"I'm not going to fuck you. Go get a shovel out of the truck."

"I don't want to."

"Help me dig and I'll fuck you."

"Nuh uh. Yer lyin."

"Only one way to find out."

She huffed and turned around, her pale body skeletal in the moonlight. She got a couple of steps away before a car pulled up the access road. I felt a moment of panic and thought about dropping my shovel and darting off into the woods.

It was a cop car.

My moment of panic was replaced with one of hope. Maybe it was Dawn.

The driver's side door opened and Barcie began waving frantically.

I realized it could look like I was possibly digging the grave of a person who'd been missing for the last few days and part of Dawn's fucking with me was really just a moderately elaborate frame job.

I dropped the shovel and approached Barcie from behind as Sheriff Bando approached her from the front.

"Hey, Barse," he said. "Whatcha doin out here?"

"Hi, *Sheriff*," she cooed.

"Why aren't ya wearin any clothes?"

"I got all hot and sweaty doin chores."

"All right. Well, I just came out cause the owners called. This is private property."

"We was doin em a favor. Mowin their grass! Brad here was showin me how."

He pulled out his flashlight and shone it on my face.

"Why don't you come over here, son."

I approached and stood next to Barcie.

He flicked the flashlight over his shoulder toward the truck.

"You work for Billups?"

"Yes, sir."

"He's a good guy. He know you use his truck for extracurriculars?"

"Um . . . probably not."

"Hmm, yeah, maybe he might like to know that. You know this girl here's under twenty-one?"

"I have no idea how old she is, sir."

"She's under twenty-one. She's a good friend of my wife's. And she seems quite drunk." He shone the flashlight around the field. "And I see quite a few beer cans scattered around the field. You know it's illegal to buy beer for underage girls?"

"I didn't buy anything for her."

"Well, a judge might see it differently."

"Other than trespassing, I don't think I've done anything wrong. Besides, I know the people who own this place. I'd be happy to explain—"

"Just shut the fuck up. What were you doin back there?"

"Nothing."

"Want to show me this nothin?"

Again I debated taking off running.

"Okay. This might be of concern to you."

"Just shut the fuck up and show me."

We all walked back to the grave and stood around it.

Bando waved the beam over the grave and the discarded shovel, letting it come to rest on the marker.

"Diggin a little grave, huh?"

"No. I found it. I was trying to see if there's anyone in it."

"Who's Tarvis Stanely?"

"I think it's supposed to say Travis Stanley. He lives here. He's a friend. I haven't heard from him in a few days."

I wanted to tell him to ask his wife who Travis was, since she seemed to have his phone.

"I see."

"You could . . . probably investigate it."

"Or I could just arrest you for trespassing, stealing company equipment, providing alcohol to an underage girl, murder, and probably even rape."

"Rape?"

He shone the flashlight between Barcie's legs.

"You ain't gonna take Brad in, are you?"

"I don't have much to do but I'm not really looking forward to the paperwork. Maybe you wanna come back to the cruiser with me and we can talk about it?"

"Sure." Barcie beamed.

They went off toward his cop car.

I thought about digging but felt like turning up any bones or body parts would only further incriminate me. Besides, I'd dug down about three feet. The soil had even stopped feeling like it had been freshly turned. I was reasonably satisfied there wasn't a body in the grave. I grabbed the shovel and took it back to the truck. I put the lawnmower in the back of the truck and headed back home.

A couple hours later, a pounding on my door awoke me and I was terrified it would be the entirety of the Gethsemane Police Department ready to arrest me for murder and rape.

I opened the door to find Barcie standing there, red blotches and shit stains painting her naked skin. She smelled atrocious.

"What?" she said. "I still got some gag drool on my chin?"

She did, actually.

"I'm stayin here tonight."

"Okay, but you have to take a shower."

"That sucks."

"You're covered in shit."

"So?"

"I'm not letting you in unless you agree to take a shower."

"Fine, but if I take a shower I get to sleep in your bed."

"I don't fucking care."

She came in and I shut the door and locked it behind her. I showed her where the bathroom was and handed her a towel and washcloth.

I got back into bed and pretended to fall asleep. She got in the bed, smelling mostly fresh and clean, excepting the reek of beer and cigarette smoke wafting from her mouth. Sometime during the night she reached down and gave me a handjob.

I pretended to remain asleep, thought about Dawn, and came within a few minutes.

I was pretty sure I heard her licking the come from her hand but didn't want to open my eyes to find out.

I thought I would be too exhausted to dream but when I drifted back off I had a dream about Barcie.

Dawn was in the dream. Living in my apartment.

We both wore Billups' Interior and Exterior shirts and I had the vague sense we worked together although she could have just been borrowing my shirt for some reason. She seemed more like an average young woman, lacking the edge of dark menace.

We sat at the kitchen table watching a young girl in a bathing suit scrub a pale, doughy fat man. He was nude and lying on a plastic tarp over what was presumably a bed. He had an erection that seemed tiny compared to the girth of his body. Dawn sipped her coffee and smiled, carefree.

The apartment was filled with sunlight and it felt like morning.

There was a knock at the door.

"I'll get it," I said.

I crossed my small apartment and opened the door. It didn't have a peephole and I wondered what had happened to it.

Barcie stood in the hallway.

She was naked and covered in neon green pustules. They wriggled as if they had a life of their own. It was alarming but she didn't seem panicked or distressed.

"You . . . have a condition," I said.

"I've been to the beast farm. They were cutting hay. I got a nosebleed and had to leave."

She pointed between her legs. A trickle of blood ran down her inner thigh.

I was confused by what she said.

"Come in," I offered, stepping aside.

Dawn stood near the entrance to the kitchen area.

The two girls moved toward one another.

I had a sense of foreboding for Dawn. I wanted to tell her to be careful, as though she couldn't see the writhing green pustules on Barcie, but I couldn't force myself to talk. I just stood there by the open door as if frozen in place.

"Oh, Barcie," Dawn said. "You look beautiful."

"You know how it goes at the dangle. I've got fun patches."

Dawn moved closer to her. She reached out and began stroking the protuberances.

"They're coming in so nicely," she said.

"It was forty-six degrees and half the universe was in darkness. The headline people were fake."

Dawn leaned forward and took one of the protuberances in her mouth, gently suckling it.

I became both disgusted and aroused.

She sucked on it until it grew so large it made her gag.

Then she moved on to the next one.

I woke up with a painful erection and the fuzzy thought that if

Barcie were still here, I would fuck her. I didn't care.

But she was gone and by the time I shook the dream away my brain felt clearer than it had since meeting Dawn. Probably clearer than it had in a long time. I realized the clarity I thought I'd felt when going down on Dawn was not clarity at all. It was a false clarity. Like your first cigarette or first beer or first joint or first trip. And I wondered if that was *exactly* like what it was and it had taken this long for that hit to wear off.

I pulled back the curtain from the window and looked toward the street.

Billups' truck was still there.

I checked my phone.

No messages.

I went to the kitchen and started some coffee, taking a hot shower while it brewed.

While drinking my coffee, I opened my laptop and did a Google search for 'humiliation' and 'blackmail.'

Thinking that wasn't specific enough, I searched for the terms and added 'gethsemane ohio'.

Then I added the name 'Dawn Bando.'

It turned up a few results but none of them were relevant.

What I had seen Dawn and Barcie do seemed to diminish in my memory.

It didn't really seem that bad and, besides, Dawn hadn't even contacted me in days so maybe I didn't have to worry about her.

But those photos were still out there.

I couldn't shake the feeling of dread. Like either Dawn was going to cajole me into doing something that would land me in jail or she was going to rat me out to White Power Larry and land me in the hospital. Or worse.

I could just go back to work on Monday and keep my head down. Ignore Dawn if she contacted me.

But I knew I couldn't ignore her. The worst thing was that I didn't know why. Or I did know why and the truth was so carnal I didn't want to admit it. Carnal or otherworldly, which just seemed absurd.

And what Donnie said about Mr. Billups really bothered me. I knew I'd worked around racists and probably worse for years but to actually have it framed the way Donnie had framed it shed new light on it. Made me feel more complicit. I knew if I continued working for Billups I would grow to hate it so much I would end up sabotaging myself. Ultimately, I knew it was just an excuse to quit my job. But things were different now that I didn't have my parents as a safety net. Still . . . did I really want to go back to that? Especially if there were an alternative?

Plus White Power Larry was on the route now.

What if I had to start taking care of *his* lawn?

It all felt like some kind of weird trap.

I'd always felt like somewhat of an outsider in Gethsemane but felt that way more than ever now. It felt like everyone was connected. How had I managed to live here my entire life and not feel connected to anything?

I thought back to some of the bizarre things Travis used to talk about when he got really drunk and wished he were around to talk to now. I had just dismissed it as the conspiratorial ramblings of someone who'd basically been drunk or high since he was fifteen or so. It went in one proverbial ear and out the other.

But a lot of it mirrored what Donnie had talked about in the truck yesterday and I'd actually found myself listening to him.

To even begin thinking about it made my head spin.

If there were some kind of conspiracy, who was at the center of it?

Dawn?

Sheriff Bando?

White Power Larry?

Dr. Weishaupt?

Mr. Billups?

The military base?

The Point?

The FDA?

The White House?

How far did it go?

What was the intent?

And why Gethsemane?

This was what crazy people did, right? They lost focus of themselves and drew connections between things that had no relevance to them because it somehow exempted them from any real responsibility. All they were left with was the somewhat exulted abstraction of themselves as some kind of noble truth finder. So it really just seemed like ego. Do you know what you have at the center of every conspiracy? Some egotistical lunatic who thinks he is special because *he's* the only one who knows.

I wasn't going to let this drive me crazy.

As far as I was concerned, my involvement with this began and ended with Dawn.

And I felt like I needed to get as far away from her as possible.

I didn't think it was at all coincidental the longer I went without going down on her the more I thought about leaving. There was something about her that hooked me. Maybe something as physical as it was mental.

I figured I could drive for sixteen hours before becoming dangerously tired.

I opened Google maps.

I could make it as far as Denver if I left now. It might take closer to eighteen hours. Nineteen including stops.

I found the motel with the lowest rate in Denver and booked it online.

I got into Billups' truck, some paranoid part of my brain telling me it wouldn't start, but it did.

I pulled away from the curb, not knowing what the hell I was going to do.

But I knew where I was going and, for now, that was enough.

By the time I got to I-70 West, I felt an amazing sense of freedom.

I felt alive.

I felt like I was finally doing it.

Escaping.

DENVER

I made it to the outskirts of Denver just before dawn on Sunday, my body vibrating with fatigue, caffeine overload, and the collective grit of I-70. My body still felt like it was moving. I slung my backpack over my shoulder and went into the lobby of the Super 8. Hollow-eyed and shaky, I gave the male clerk my driver's license and credit card, wondering if he thought I was strung out on something. But he was probably beyond wondering. I was probably in good shape compared to a lot of their other clientele. He asked if I'd be checking out at noon or if I wanted to go ahead and book that night too. It was a good question. How far did I want to go? I didn't know. I'd had the past eighteen hours or so to think about this question, but I hadn't. It was like my critical thinking had completely abandoned me on the drive here. I'd had my phone plugged into the truck's surprisingly decent stereo and had tranced out on my music. It wasn't even interrupted by the GPS app for anything other than "Continue along I-70." I didn't think about stealing the truck from Billups, or Dawn, Barcie, White Power Larry, the possibly insidious conspiracy affecting Gethsemane. None of it. If I checked out at noon, that would give me about five hours of sleep then I could get something to eat and try to figure things out. If I paid for another night then it would have almost been cheaper to get a one-way plane ticket somewhere. Why hadn't I done that? Then I wouldn't have had to steal Billups' truck. Or, at least I could have left it abandoned at the airport. But, fuck, now I'd crossed state lines with it. That probably made it some kind of federal offense. Nothing that had happened in my life gave me any reason to believe I could possibly get away with this. Oh man, I was completely fucked. If I left at noon tomorrow then I could be back in Gethsemane around the time Billups opened on Monday morning. Shit. Was I really going to do that?

"Sir?"

"Uh . . . I'll be out at noon."

He typed some things into the computer, slid the key card across the counter, and directed me to my room, told me where I could park.

"Can I leave my truck where it is?" I didn't want to get back in it just yet.

"If you're checking out at noon, that's fine. I don't think there's going to be a rush at this hour." He laughed and I thought about how lonely his job must be. I could have probably stood there and talked to him for an hour.

"Thanks, man." I left the lobby and walked to my room.

I dumped my bag on a chair and wished I had a cigarette or a beer. Anything. I turned the TV on instead. Local news. The top story was about a man who drove his family off a mountain road. They said they didn't know if it was murder-suicide or not, but of course it was. It seemed unfathomable to the reporters. They probably wouldn't ever be able to understand the pressures some people live under. They couldn't understand how that warps and twists a person, turns him into something he isn't. Or brings out the thing he always was. I turned it to the Weather Channel. Sure there might be tragedy there. But it would be mindless, unavoidable tragedy brought on by nature and to me that seemed a lot less sad.

The phone rang and I jumped. I couldn't remember the last time I'd heard a real phone ring.

I picked it up and said, "Hello?"

There was garbled static and then an unrecognizable voice, sounding very far away, said, "Come home. To the stars."

At least, that's how I heard it.

"Who is this?" I said, but the line had already gone dead.

I placed the phone back in its cradle and took a deep breath in an attempt to calm myself.

I turned the TV down to a reasonable volume and lay back on the surprisingly comfortable bed. I set the alarm on my phone for 11:30 a.m.

I had a dream I was at a massive outdoor rally. I was pretty sure it was at Barcie's place but, for some reason, it was actually Dawn's. White Power Larry and Billups stood on a stage in front of a massive flag that looked like a weird hybrid of a Nazi swastika and the Confederate flag. I felt a mix of shame and horror. I was talking to someone standing next to me, possibly Donnie, and trying to think of a racist joke but it wasn't coming to me. I scanned the sizeable crowd. It seemed like nearly every resident of Gethsemane must be here. But these weren't the people I knew. Some of them looked vaguely familiar but they were all glowing a neon shade of green. I felt like that color had some significance but I couldn't think of what that was. I began walking through the crowd but it felt like I was underwater. White Power Larry or possibly even Billups was making some kind of speech but the words seemed like gibberish. I was looking for someone but I didn't know if it was Dawn or Barcie. I found myself in the fluorescent-lit kitchen of my childhood home. My dead parents were at the kitchen table, arm wrestling.

"You guys are dead," I said.

"They found a way to bring us back," my dad said. "Now we're stronger than ever."

"Just have to find out which one's strongest," my mom said.

They didn't look strong. They looked weak and emaciated.

I wandered out of the house and into a field. Maybe it was the one behind Travis's house. It was either dawn or twilight and I could hear the chanting of the rally from somewhere in the distance.

It was warm and humid and I thought I woke up for a second but when I closed my eyes I was immediately back in the dream, looking for Dawn. I was in the torture shed out behind Barcie's house. Taylor Dream lay naked on the concrete floor, surrounded by the familiar houseplants I took care of every day. I moved closer to her. I crouched down next to her and touched one of her arms.

It felt cool and then turned to rust. I stood up. Her whole beautiful body had turned to rust except for where I'd touched her. There was a neon green dot, maybe even a fingerprint.

I left the storage shed and saw a line of girls. The line went into a building that looked like a smaller version of The Point Medical and Research Facility. I moved up the line and into the building. Inside it was just one massive room that reminded me of a Catholic church. I continued moving to the front of the line. I felt like Dawn was there.

I continued moving forward.

I awoke to the sound of my phone's alarm.

I had a lingering image of a girl at the front of the line lying on her stomach and lapping at Dawn's vagina but knew I hadn't actually seen that.

Then I had to ask myself if we ever really saw anything in dreams.

I was covered in sweat and shaky. My heart hammered. Nausea clenched my stomach. I raced to the bathroom and vomited a gallon of black coffee into the toilet.

I lay on the bathroom floor until the snooze went off on my phone.

I stood up and went to turn it off.

I glanced at the TV. It wasn't on the Weather Channel anymore. It looked like a talk show. The banner across the bottom said: FORMER CULT MEMBERS SPEAK OUT.

I turned it off and put the phone back in my pocket.

I was going back to Gethsemane.

Just the thought of going back calmed me. The nausea was already subsiding. Despite the bile at the back of my mouth, I could taste Dawn on my tongue.

EMBRACING CHANGE

As June slowly turned into July, I stayed in the apartment, checking my email every half hour or so, eating whatever shit I had lying around, and half-reading a Murakami book but mostly starting up at my ceiling and wondering what the hell I was going to do.

It felt like my back had to be firmly planted against the wall before I could make any decision whatsoever. Or maybe I just wanted to put myself in such a position I couldn't say no to Dawn if she came around again.

I got back to Gethsemane around nine a.m. and drove the truck directly to the shop.

Billups and Donnie were there. Donnie was in the lobby eating a massive beef stick and drinking Mountain Dew. It looked like his eye was working again but there was a massive green pustule at the corner. I tried not to stare.

Billups was in his office, bent over some paperwork.

I walked in and dropped the keys on his desk.

"Finally get your truck fixed?"

"No. I'm quitting."

He stopped what he was doing and leaned back in his chair.

"You can't quit."

"I'm quitting."

He narrowed his eyes and stared at me, as if seeing me for the very first time. He crossed his arms over his chest.

"You need some time off, take some time off. I guess me and Donnie can handle it."

I immediately regretted what I had done and now felt like crying, telling him I was sorry, of course I'd stay. But I couldn't do that. I had to stand my ground.

"I don't think I'm coming back."

"What're you gonna do?"

"I don't know yet."

"This is a good job, ain't it? Why're you quittin?"

I briefly thought about trying to explain it to him but my head felt like such a jumbled mess I was pretty sure I would just ramble incoherently for a few minutes before ultimately throwing up or weeping.

"It's just . . . something I have to do."

"Okay." He uncrossed his arms and leaned forward in his chair. "But you're really leavin us in the lurch here. This is our busiest time and we're down to just the two of us. If you're quittin, that's it, don't think about comin back."

"I understand."

"You're sure about this?"

"Absolutely," I said, but that wasn't true at all. "Do you, um, think you could give me a ride back to my place?"

"Sorry," he said. "We're too busy for that."

I turned and walked through the office.

Donnie was outside loading up one of the trucks.

"Hey, man," I said. "Think you can drop me off at my place?"

"Sure," he said. "You off today?"

"No. I quit."

"Really?"

"Yep."

"Good for you."

We both got in the truck and Donnie drove me back to the apartment in a truly harrowing fashion, not stopping for a single red light or stop sign. Fortunately there weren't many cars on the road. I wanted to ask him about his eye but didn't want to distract him any more than he apparently was.

That evening, Dawn finally contacted me via text.

It read: "Barcie's dead. I'm coming over."

She texted me when she got there.

I went down to meet her.

Another girl sat in the passenger seat. Her head was wrapped in black gauze, except for her eyes, and she wore a blond wig.

I sat in the back.

"You remember Taylor," Dawn said.

I did but didn't think that went far in explaining why she was here in the car with Dawn. I wouldn't have thought she wanted anything to do with her. But all I had to do was think about Barcie and her allegiance to Dawn and it made some sort of sense. Dawn instilled envy and fear in her acolytes.

She pulled onto the road.

"So what happened?" I asked.

"Barcie died," Dawn said.

"I know. How did she die?"

"I don't want to talk about it."

I leaned forward from the backseat. They both wore all black. Taylor wore a black bodysuit with a wide red stripe running down her torso. With the gauze wrapped around her head, I thought she looked like she was in a science fiction movie. Dawn wore a simple black dress, so short it rode up nearly to her crotch.

"Are we going to the funeral?" I would be really underdressed if we were.

"That's where we came from. We're going to Barcie's. There's something I have to do."

Dawn turned into the sand and gravel company, driving past the unreal blue gravel pit and up to Barcie's house.

She stopped the car and we all got out. She had a camera with her and I wondered if I was going to have to do something terrible.

She handed the camera to me.

She pressed a button and said, "It's recording. Just keep the camera on us. Make it look good. This is what she would have wanted."

I fell back a couple of steps and filmed them from behind. The bodysuit accented Taylor's nearly flawless body and I made sure to hold her rounded ass in frame for a couple of seconds before flipping over to Dawn. Her dress barely covered her ass so I let the camera take in her tan, fit legs, waiting for the skirt to flip up just enough to catch a glimpse of her underwear. It didn't happen.

We entered the house.

No one else was there.

We walked through the house, up the stairs, and down the hall to Barcie's room.

Dawn swung the door open.

She reached up and slid her black underwear down her legs.

"Okay," she said to Taylor. "Let's put our pussies on everything."

I didn't think I'd heard her correctly.

She turned Taylor around and slowly unzipped the bodysuit to the waist. Taylor peeled it the rest of the way off and stood completely naked except for the mask and the wig. I circled around her, getting her all in camera. My cock was uncomfortably hard.

For the next several minutes I filmed the girls walking around the room and laughing as they rubbed their vaginas on everything they could find.

Dawn pulled an 8x10 photo of Barcie from the wall. It looked like it could have been her senior photo. She removed it from the frame and rubbed her crotch on the back of it and then stuck it to the front of Taylor's gauze wrapping.

Dawn approached me, looking into the camera before reaching out and taking it. She was so close to me I could hear her breathing and wanted her to touch me.

"Barcie really wanted you to fuck her," Dawn said. "I think, in the end, it was really all she wanted."

Taylor now stood in front of me, her hands reaching down to unbutton and unzip my pants.

I looked at her perfectly firm tits, trim stomach, and bare cunt.

I tried not to look at the photo of Barcie stuck to her face.

"So fuck her," Dawn said. "Fuck her really hard. Just like she would have wanted."

I didn't protest.

I don't know if it was submission or some kind of genuine desire for Taylor. Maybe some desire to perform in front of Dawn.

I turned her around and pushed her over the edge of the bed, guiding myself into her wet cunt. I grabbed her around the upper arms, bending them back while I rammed into her.

Maybe having the camera on me was making me nervous but I lasted a lot longer than I thought I would. I kept fucking her as hard as I could, ramming the bed against the wall, smacking her ass until it was red. I felt out of my head.

I pulled out and rolled her over, yanking her legs apart and reentering her, trying not to catch even a glimpse of the photo.

"She wants you to finish in her ass," Dawn said. "That's the way Barcie liked it."

I continued fucking her hard before pulling out. I ran some of her juices around her asshole, spit into my hand and rubbed that over my cock. Taylor pulled her legs back, reaching down and spreading herself for me. I pressed my cock against her tight asshole, thinking it probably wasn't going to work.

"Don't be gentle," Dawn said. "Fuck that little asshole. Some girls like to hurt."

I wasn't gentle.

I ignored Taylor's twisting and whimpering and came inside of her a couple of minutes later.

After getting dressed and heading back to the car, I felt awkward and weird. The girls, on the other hand, seemed ebullient and chatty.

We went back to Dawn's house.

Outside the car, she said, "Follow me."

I followed her through the house and down a short, carpeted staircase into a fully finished basement. On the far side, she opened a heavy wooden door and I followed her through it. I half-expected some kind of torture dungeon or something with a sinister aura, but it was a completely normal looking home office. I felt like it was probably Sheriff Bando's but didn't really know.

Dawn sat behind a heavy wooden desk.

"Sit," she said.

I sat in one of the two chairs facing the desk.

"Am I in trouble?" I said, feeling like I'd been called into the principal's office.

"Cute."

"Thanks."

"But, actually, you are in trouble. Quite a bit."

I didn't say anything. I just kept looking at her face and trying not to fidget. I felt like anything I said would be incriminating. I glanced into her eyes but it was tough to keep eye contact. There was something empty and soulless there. At first I'd mistaken it for some kind of sadness.

"I guess you liked what happened back at Barcie's? You didn't resist at all. Came *a lot* too."

"Resisting hasn't really helped a lot."

"I thought it was because you had some chemistry."

I shrugged. I didn't really know what she meant.

She tapped something into her phone.

A few seconds later there was a gentle knock on the door.

"It's open," Dawn said.

Taylor stood in the doorway.

"Sit," Dawn said.

Taylor sat in the chair next to me.

"Go ahead," Dawn said, tapping her phone and training it on Taylor.

Taylor reached back and unclipped the gauze wrapping her head. She slowly removed it. My heartbeat increased. She turned her head away from me as she removed the last of the gauze.

Something wasn't right.

I knew there had to be some horrible reason for what had just happened. Making fuck videos might have been part of what Dawn did, but not when it came to me.

Taylor's hair had been long and blond.

This girl's hair was short and black.

I recognized the hair.

How had I not recognized the body?

My heart pounded faster and faster.

She finally brought her head back up and turned to face me, a malicious smile spread across her face.

Stasia Warner. White Power Larry's wife.

Fuck me.

She put her hand on my knee. "That was *so much* better than the last time. I guess all it took was thinking I was somebody else."

My mouth was dry and I couldn't speak.

My mind raced.

The first time we'd done anything I was pretty drunk and it had happened in the relative darkness of my bedroom. I distinctly remembered the swastika tramp stamp and thought there'd been more tattoos. The girl I'd fucked a little while ago definitely didn't have any. Was it possible I had just fucked Stasia again or had they swapped her out while I was in the office with Dawn? Why would they even do something like that? Maybe Stasia had covered the tattoos or maybe they weren't even real in the first place.

"I know," Dawn said. "It's a lot to take in."

"Why?" I managed to croak out. "Why are you fucking with me?"

"It's what we do. It's just business."

"It's fucked up."

"Not really. It's pretty practical if you think about it. Beats the hell out of college."

"I'm gonna go find something to eat," Stasia said. She stood up. "Bye, lover."

"Before you go," Dawn said. "I have a question for Brad. Brad, who was the last person you jerked off to?"

"You," I said. "It's been you ever since we met."

"That's it," Dawn said to Stasia. "You can go now."

I watched Stasia walk to the door, still trying to figure out if this was the same girl I'd followed into Barcie's house.

"What was the point of that?"

"What? It was just a question."

"Were you trying to make her feel bad?"

"Bad? Stasia never feels bad. I guess I was just curious."

"You could have just asked me. She didn't really need to hear that."

"Oh, I think she did. I'm pretty sure her answer would have been the same."

"I quit my job today."

"I know. How was Denver?"

Her question momentarily took the wind out of me. How did she know I'd gone to Denver? Of course she knew. I was beginning to think Dawn knew just about everything about me.

I swallowed and coughed, my throat dry. "I missed you," I said. "So I came back."

Dawn stood up.

"I want you to lick my pussy again."

She pulled her underwear down and sat on the edge of the desk, spreading her legs.

I pushed the chair back, got down on my knees, and went to work on the sheriff's wife.

This was all I'd wanted, all I'd been able to think about since the last time I'd done this, and greedily lapped up every bit of her I could. Everything else melted away.

I was hard the entire time.

She seemed mostly unresponsive.

I again went to that same heightened place I had the first time I'd done it. If I had any regrets about coming back to Gethsemane, they were all erased.

Later we went to a party in a house in the middle of nowhere. Most of the people there were much younger than me. The main purpose of the party seemed to be to destroy the house. I drank way too much. By the time we left just after midnight, the house was nearly demolished. We had to leave because someone started a fire. I had no idea what the point of it was but I had a lot of fun. It seemed relatively non-threatening compared to a number of the things I'd seen Dawn do up to that point.

Stasia drove. Dawn sat in the passenger seat and I sat in the back.

Dawn pulled up an image on her phone and held it up to me.

"Do you think she's pretty?" she asked.

This always seemed like a loaded question coming from another girl. Then again, I supposed there really wasn't anything happening between Dawn and me, other than the occasional vagina licking, and she had recently coerced me into fucking her very attractive friend only a few hours ago so I thought I could be honest.

"Sure," I said. "But I've had quite a bit to drink." I decided to qualify the statement because Dawn still terrified me a little.

"Good," she said. "We're meeting her in a few minutes."

"I don't think I'm up for much," I said.

"You don't have to be *up* for anything. This isn't about you."

She opened the glove compartment and I heard the rattle of the chain.

"I definitely don't think I can take any more of that," I said.

"Any more of what?"

I pointed to the chain. "That."

Dawn quickly turned around and brought the chain down across my thighs. In my attempt to not howl out in pain I let out a defenseless whimper that sounded even more pitiful and embarrassing.

"This chain is transformative," she said with probably more passion than I'd heard her say anything. "Do you want to get out of the car?"

"No." I kept my head down and gently rubbed my burning thighs.

Stasia pulled the car into a Krispy Kreme parking lot somewhere outside of Dayton. I was pretty sure it was Kettering again.

A couple parking spaces over, a slender attractive girl—the one from the picture—sat leaning against a Volkswagen convertible eating a donut that looked huge in her small hand.

Dawn got out of the car and approached the girl. I rolled my window down and asked Stasia if she had a cigarette. She handed me one and I lit it and it wrapped me in a layer of comfort as I inhaled all the sense memories that came with it.

"Are you Kat?" Dawn asked.

"Yeah."

"I'm Dawn."

"*Wooow.*" The girl drew out the word like meeting Dawn was

some kind of honor. "I didn't think you'd come."

"Come on. Let's get in the car."

"Okay," the girl said. "Lemme get my purse." She turned and flung the donut out into the parking lot before staggering and nearly falling down. "Aw, fuck it."

Dawn placed a hand on her back and guided her toward the car. She opened the door opposite mine and the girl collapsed onto the seat. I was fairly drunk and the alcohol fumes wafting off this girl still seemed overpowering.

She didn't acknowledge Stasia or me at all. She sat at a slight angle, her glassy eyes fixed on Dawn.

I rolled my window up a little and continued smoking. I didn't really know what was going on. I figured this girl—Kat—was another one of Dawn's actresses and we'd be taking her to a motel or something, maybe back to the storage sheds behind Barcie's house. Or maybe not, since Barcie was dead.

"I hate to be a buzzkill," Stasia said, "but if I'm not home by three I'm going to catch hell."

"It shouldn't take long," Dawn said. "You need me to talk to him?"

By 'him,' I assumed she meant White Power Larry. The thought of tiny little Dawn somehow rationalizing to a six-and-a-half foot Aryan lumberjack seemed hilarious but, well, maybe Dawn had some control over him too. She was married to the sheriff, after all.

"Should be okay," Stasia said. "As long as I'm not too late."

Stasia continued to drive toward Dayton. We ended up back in East Dayton in the well-lit but abandoned and overgrown parking lot of a closed up warehouse.

Dawn and Stasia got out of the car. I got out too, a little wobbly on my feet. Dawn went around to the trunk and opened it up. When I glanced back into the car, Kat was sitting up straight, breathing deeply with her eyes closed.

Dawn pulled out the camera and tripod and set it up a few feet from the car.

"Go," Dawn said.

Stasia opened Kat's door and brutally pulled her out. Kat went down on the grass-veined asphalt. Stasia crouched down and fumbled with the button of Kat's tiny shorts. She yanked them down, revealing light blue underwear with a yellow flower in the crotch. Stasia smirked and ripped those off too.

Kat didn't struggle. She lay on her back, staring at Dawn who swung the chain slowly in her hand.

Dawn pointed at Kat's cunt, looked at me, and said, "Get down there."

"I didn't think I was going to have to do anything," I protested.

Dawn lashed out with the chain, striking me hard across the lower back.

I stumbled toward Kat and got down on my stomach between her legs.

Stasia grabbed her wrists, pulled them well above her head and then stepped on each hand with a heavy black boot.

I began licking the girl's pussy, parting her lips surrounded by blondish peach fuzz. She tasted like strawberries with just the faintest hint of urine and chemicals and I wondered if she had prepared for this or if she always preferred a strawberry-scented crotch.

The chain whistled through the air and across Kat's face.

Kat screamed and twitched, her bladder letting go.

I pulled my head away from her and looked up at her face in time to see the chain come down again. The tip of the chain licked the asphalt and created a spark. I couldn't look at Kat's face. I looked at her lower stomach as it clenched and unclenched and went back to work on her pussy because I knew that was what I was supposed to do and didn't want to get hit with the chain again.

After Dawn hit her several more times, Kat released some sort of mighty, final spasm before lying still.

I stood up, careful not to look down at her.

Stasia stepped off Kat's hands, bent down, and yanked the girl's shirt and bra off. Then she spit on her and headed back to the car.

Dawn quickly dismantled the camera and tripod and did the same. I followed.

Once we were back in the car I said, "Do you think she's going to be okay?"

Dawn and Stasia laughed.

They laughed most of the way back to my apartment.

PUSSYLICKER

I felt lost and restless in my apartment. I had begun to not only expect but to look forward to my adventures with Dawn.

What else did I have?

After beating the girl in the warehouse lot, Stasia had dropped me off in front of the apartment and Dawn had said, "I'll call you when I need you. Keep your phone on you."

And I had.

And I'd found myself doing almost nothing but waiting for her to call or text.

I didn't just sit around. I was way too anxious for that. I read some of the Murakami book I'd been working on for the past month but had a hard time getting into it and couldn't seem to focus on more than a couple sentences at a time. An hour would pass and I wouldn't remember a single thing I'd just read. It was the same thing with the films I tried to watch. I cooked little meals and cleaned the apartment. I kept music playing in the background constantly because I didn't think I could take the silence but I couldn't tell you what song was playing at any given time.

I began monitoring the crime section of the Dayton *Daily News* website to see if there was any mention of the girl, Kat. I didn't see anything. Maybe she'd been okay after all. Maybe they just hadn't found the body.

I got another idea and searched Gethsemane obituaries for Barcie's death. I didn't see it listed and thought that was a little curious but supposed some families may not want to list that kind of thing. Maybe they were embarrassed of her. Maybe she wasn't dead at all.

I grabbed my phone and texted the number I had for her.

"How's the grave? Comfortable?"

I began scanning Google for images of mass graves and ended up jerking off to brutal rape porn.

When I picked up my phone again, I saw Barcie had texted me back.

It said, "I'm so cold."

I was too freaked out to respond.

I went back to the internet and scanned through the past few weeks of the Gethsemane paper's very modest crime section, looking for something about Travis. Surely, if he were dead or missing, there would be something about it in there. Hell, that would probably be big news in Gethsemane.

I didn't see anything.

My thoughts drifted to Dawn again.

What did I want from her?

What did she want from me?

What was she doing when she wasn't around me?

Did she ever act in her own videos?

Did she spend the days her husband was away getting fucked senseless by guys she met on the internet? She'd said she didn't like cock but how much of what she said could really be believed? I mean, she was married, after all. Did that doughy old cop get to come home and fuck Dawn every day? I couldn't really imagine it but didn't see how it could really be any other way.

Was Dawn just fucking with me or did she have bigger plans for me?

I didn't want to run around the greater Dayton area assaulting young girls with chains but . . . maybe I would?

I wanted to say I wouldn't but I was starting to think that almost anything would be better than sitting around this apartment, broke, unemployed, and bored out of my fucking skull. It felt like what I'd been doing since graduating high school, for the most part.

I walked to the convenience store a block away.

Stepping into the Snack Barn, it was like the harsh fluorescent glow threw a bright light on my internal fear. Stasia and White Power Larry stood at the counter. Neither one of them acknowledged me and my heart slowed a little. I glanced at them on my way back to the beer cooler. Stasia looked good, all pale skin contrasting with her black clothes. White Power Larry looked menacing. Huge and bald, his physique hinting he'd been athletic at one time. A giant swastika screamed from the back of his skull. Maybe he was stocking up on energy drinks for the next rally.

I crouched down, out of sight, pretending to scan the beer. When I popped back up they were gone.

I still wanted to make sure they were completely off the premises before leaving the store so I grabbed a twelve-pack of beer and wandered around grabbing things like Doritos and Funyons and beef sticks and a couple of frozen breakfast burritos for in the morning. I took my haul up to the register and asked for two packs of cigarettes, figuring I might as well go all in.

My eyes went to a pamphlet on the counter. It was a cheap Xeroxed thing, the front covered with swastikas and the American flag. The title or headline or whatever read: PREPARE FOR THE COMING MIDDLE EASTERN BLACK PLAGUE.

The clerk, a teenager with a mop of black hair and stoned red eyes, saw that I was looking at it and said, "Dude told me to give it to the owner. I'm gonna read it for shits."

"I'm sure it's Pulitzer material."

"Scary dude."

"Mind if I borrow it?"

It took him a couple seconds to digest what I'd asked him. He rubbed his fingertips across the top of the pamphlet. I glanced at his nametag: Kren.

"I guess. Bring it back?"

"Sure." I grabbed the pamphlet and shoved it into my bag.

I paid for my stuff, went back to my apartment, drank and smoked until I vomited, and went to bed.

I woke up in my bed but it may as well have been a bar floor. The stench of smoke, along with the nearly floral odor of slightly stale beer, hung in the apartment. I'd drunk the twelve-pack of beer and smoked most of the two packs of cigarettes. I didn't feel as bad as I thought I should.

I got out of bed, opened the two windows the apartment had, dumped the overflowing ashtray into the overflowing trashcan and ran it down the hall to the garbage chute. I took a shower and made coffee and one of the breakfast burritos and sat at my tiny kitchen table.

White Power Larry's pamphlet sat next to my laptop. I'd forgotten all about it. I leafed through it as I drank the coffee and ate the burrito. It made me feel slightly ridiculous I was afraid of this guy. There were very few words in the pamphlet. It was mostly pictures of him in various poses. He had his shirt off in most of them, his massive torso and arms decorated with swastikas and 'SS'es and wolves and skulls and iron crosses. In most of the photos he held some kind of weapon—a battle axe, a sword, several different kinds of guns. I wondered if he'd ever killed anyone. He was probably a lot more harmless than Dawn. If he were truly dangerous, there wouldn't be a need for the clown costume and all the theater.

What did someone like Stasia see in someone like this? I couldn't figure it out. She was attractive and reasonably intelligent. I was sure she had a host of mental disorders and probably wasn't every guy's type, but it still seemed like she could do a lot better than some narcissistic douchebag who ran on hate. Maybe hate was what they had in common, although in the one conversation we'd had over the course of our drunken evening together, the hate she exhibited didn't seem to be particularly racist. Maybe he made her feel protected. That was the only thing that made any sense to me.

I had so much fun looking at his pamphlet I felt like his MyFace page would have to be like the 3D version or something. Maybe he didn't have one. Or if he did maybe it was set to private. But that wasn't possible. With as narcissistic as this guy was, he definitely had a public profile. He wanted to be seen. Besides, wasn't the goal of any good racist to recruit and train more racists? So you felt better about something you knew was socially abhorrent?

I flipped my laptop open and tried to bring up the browser.

NO INTERNET CONNECTION

Fuck.

When was the last time I'd paid the bill?

It was at least a month ago.

I could have paid it on my phone but I didn't really have the money to pay it with. What little money I had in my account I needed for beer and cigarettes. Maybe I could get Dawn to pay it. She probably wouldn't though. It was a lot better for her if I just remained ignorant and couldn't do any research. Not that my research had turned up anything too significant.

With my phone's screen being fucked up, I couldn't really do anything on it other than listen to music and text. I could have made calls but I didn't have anybody to call.

What had happened to everybody? I'd had friends in high school. Most of them had moved away. A couple of them had died. Travis had disappeared. I wasn't on speaking terms with any of my failed long-term relationships. It seemed like a person should acquire more friends as they grew older, that their lives should become fuller and fuller, not emptier and emptier. Everyone was connected via the internet and social networking yet loneliness seemed to be a modern plague. It almost made sense a group like Larry's could exist. Almost made sense that girls would seek Dawn out to come and beat them with a chain. It made them part of something, at least.

After breakfast, I took my coffee over to the bed, lit a cigarette, and tried to read more of the Murakami.

Once I'd finished the coffee, I decided to take a nap, even though I'd been up less than an hour.

I didn't sleep long but I had a dream. I was at the end of a long hall. There was an endless row of women sitting on the floor with their backs against the wall. They wore thin hospital gown type things and they all had their legs parted. I had an overwhelming feeling of fatigue, vague nausea, and a sense of duty. I got down on the floor and slithered toward the first woman's vagina. It was pink and perfect and shaved. I began licking her. She was not demonstrative although she did get wet. She had the familiar taste of pussy with that now almost equally familiar chemical tang underlying it. She tasted just like Dawn. I pulled away from her and noticed, rather than a trickle of pearly girl come, a tiny rivulet of some neon green fluid. The dream had the feel of a video game and this meant I'd advanced to the next level.

I rolled over to the next girl.

The dream seemed to last forever and I was extremely hard when I woke up. My tongue felt super dry, probably from sleeping with my mouth open, something I tended to do more when I was smoking. I tried to generate some moisture in my mouth and glanced at the time on my phone. I'd been asleep less than an hour.

I got up and staggered to the bathroom. Once I managed to collect enough saliva I took down my pants and spit into my hand. I slowly masturbated while imagining Dawn giving me head. It took a while for me to come and by the time I did, I was imagining fucking her in the ass while she lay on her stomach on my bed.

I wiped myself off, zipped up, and washed my hands.

I checked my phone again. It was seven o'clock. Plenty late enough to go back to the Snack Barn. I told myself it was to return the pamphlet to Kren but I really just wanted more beer and cigarettes. I grabbed the pamphlet and headed out into the humid, fragrant evening.

Gethsemane was a quiet town and tonight was no exception. I didn't pass a single pedestrian. I didn't see any cars on the street. It was like the whole town was in a coma.

When I reached the convenience store, I was glad to see Kren behind the counter. He stood behind the register staring intently down at his phone, which seemed to be roughly twice the size of mine. He didn't look up or acknowledge me. I was the only person in the store.

I went back to the beer cooler, grabbed another twelve-pack, convincing myself I was being responsible by not getting the case, and took it up to the register.

It took him a couple seconds to tear his gaze away from the phone and glance at me with eyes as stoned red as yesterday.

"Oh, hey, man," he said. "Sorry. I'm, like, really high right now."

"I'm not in a hurry. Can I get two packs of Camel Blues too?"

He reached over his head and grabbed the cigarettes, dropping them on the counter. He tried to ring me up but had a hard time.

"I can't do it," he said.

"That's all right."

"I guess you can just have it." He seemed frustrated.

"I'd give you something but I don't have any cash."

He waved the notion away. "I *know* I can't work the credit card machine."

"I brought this back for you."

I placed the pamphlet on the counter.

"Aw, man, I'm . . . not really interested."

"No, I'm not a racist. That guy with the swastika tattoo left it here yesterday. You let me borrow it. You asked me to bring it back. Remember?"

"Not really. I guess I could review security footage later."

"It's probably not that important."

"You wanna go out back and get high?"

I wanted to remind him he was already too high to run the cash register but I think I also wanted someone to hang out with who wasn't me.

"Sure," I said.

"Maybe then I'll be able to figure out this thing." He motioned to the register. "Follow me."

He stepped out from behind the counter with a bobbing, loping gait and I followed him toward the restrooms. We went down a short, dim hallway and he opened a door with an EXIT sign glowing above it. The door shut behind us and he sparked up the joint.

I pulled a can of beer out of the pack and handed him one.

"Oh, thanks," he said around his exhale.

He handed the joint to me and I took a satisfying drag, feeling instantly relaxed and looking forward to being back in my room, sitting on my bed and thinking fuzzy thoughts while sipping beer, smoking cigarettes, and listening to music without words.

"I'm Brad," I said after exhaling.

"Right on, man. I'm Kren. It's like Ken with an 'R'."

"Yeah. The nametag."

"Oh, yeah, right," he laughed.

We finished the joint and continued sipping our beer in the short lifeless alley.

"Man, I think I'm gay," Kren said out of nowhere.

"That's okay. No judgments here."

"I don't know many other gay people around here."

"Yeah, there probably aren't many. Just go to Dayton."

"That's too hard."

"It's like fifteen miles away."

"I think I'm too stupid. You want a handjob?"

"No thanks, man. I just jerked off like an hour or so ago. I don't think I'd do anything."

"That sucks, dude. Did you come a lot?"

"Not really. I've been jerking off quite a bit lately. Might have something to do with it. Low reserves."

"You want to give *me* a tug job? I haven't done that yet today."

"I don't have anything against it but it's not my thing. My heart wouldn't really be in it. I mean, I have a girlfriend."

"Yeah, I hear you. Fuck! I'm gonna go take a come as soon as I'm done with this beer. Sometimes it burns though. Is it supposed to burn?"

"I don't think so. You maybe should have that checked out. It'll probably pass."

I lit a cigarette and smoked that while I finished my beer. I offered Kren one but he didn't smoke cigarettes.

When I was finished, I said, "Well, I'll let you get back to work."

"Right on. It was cool hanging with you."

"You too."

I turned to walk toward the opening of the alley. Kren tugged on the door we'd come out through.

"Fuck, man. I'm locked out!"

I stopped and turned back to him. "You could probably, um, just go in through the front?"

He hit his forehead with the heel of his hand.

"Right! Duh. See, I'd never be able to make it to Dayton."

Dawn called a few days later, disrupting what had become an established routine. My phone ringing always slammed me with a sense of panic and I tried to remember when the last time I'd heard it ring was.

The night Travis had called.

The panic seemed warranted.

I tapped the answer icon and said, "Dawn."

"Did you watch the video of you and Stasia? I emailed it to you."

Her voice was breathy. You never really know how a person

sounds until you experience their voice isolated from everything about them. Not even a voice can be heard objectively.

"No," I said. "I lost my internet. Which video? The one in Barcie's room or . . ."

"That one. I'm thinking of sending that and the photos to White Power Larry. I'm getting bored."

"Please don't do that."

"Maybe I won't." She took a deep breath. My hand went to my stiffening cock. Part of the routine she'd interrupted had been an at least once daily masturbation session. Always while imagining her. I wondered if I could keep her on the phone long enough to jerk off.

"Why do you keep threatening me with that." My voice had already thickened and grown a little shaky.

I unbuttoned and unzipped my pants, sliding them and my underwear down a little as I stood and made my way over to my bed.

She took another deep breath.

"I'm helping you," she said. "It's a motivational tool. I need someone who's going to do what I ask him to do. I mean, you would tell me I don't really need to hold this stuff over your head, but how can I really trust you? I'll keep threatening you with the photos and you'll keep helping me do what I do."

"But what if what you're doing is illegal?"

"I don't do anything illegal. I give people what they want. No one does anything against their will. That's the beauty of it. It's like fitting puzzle pieces together."

"Through blackmail."

"You want the photos destroyed. I want you to do some things for me. It's not blackmail if I'm not asking for money."

"Regardless. It's unnecessary. That's what I'm saying."

"I'll decide what's unnecessary." She paused before saying, "Are you jerking off right now? You sound weird."

I thought about lying and wondered what the point would be.

"Yeah." I made an attempt to sound normal.

"Do I turn you on?"

"You know you do."

"It's never gonna happen," she said. "Besides, I told you, I don't like cock."

"Then why are you married to a dude?"

She didn't say anything.

"I know you're not Sheriff Bando's daughter."

I stroked myself harder and faster.

"I know you know. Barcie told me. Way to do your research.

"When I was fifteen I fell into a bad place. I had always been a good kid and I had good parents, if a little overbearing. They both had degrees and made good money and I was their only child. They wanted me to be just like them. But I knew from a very early age I didn't want to be just like them. I wanted more. I wanted every-thing. I'm not talking about material things. I'm talking about expe-rience. I wanted to experience everything. They had all the material things you could ever want but they had a deep emptiness inside of them. Do you know how hard it is to get away from that yawning emptiness? It's like a black hole, a huge cosmic vacuum trying to suck everything around it into it. So I got out. I met a guy who lived in Cincinnati. He wasn't a nice guy. But after being around him for a few days, I didn't want to be anywhere else. He had it. He had that secret knowledge. He had that endless thirst for experience and we did everything together. The summer I was with him, I spent every day in my upstairs bedroom, drunk or doped to the gills, whatever I wanted. I never wore clothes. I would just lie on the bed and watch daytime TV as an endless stream of guys came to meet me. I didn't have to do anything. They didn't want me to do anything. I would just lie there and spread my legs and smoke cigarettes and watch TV. And they would fuck my little pussy. Some of them were rough, some of them were gentle, and I never came. Sometimes I'd see ten or twenty guys a day. They'd fuck me and throw their condoms in a trashcan beside the bed and leave. Most of them came back. It was exactly what they wanted until they decided they wanted someone else. And I was okay with that because there were always hundreds of men to take their place, but no one could take my boyfriend's place. At the end of the day I'd take a shower and put on something nice and meet him in his room. We did everything to each other. I let him go where the other men never went. He had the biggest cock and I let him slide it halfway down my throat. I let him fuck me in the ass even though it felt like he was ripping me in two. I wanted to be covered in his come, inside and out. I let him tie me up. I let him hit me until my skin was red and bruised. I liked it when he bit me."

I turned and came onto the bed, trying not to call out or grunt or anything.

Dawn continued.

"I asked him if it ever bothered him that I was with so many other guys and he said he liked it. He said it was his way of absorbing them. Anyway there was some trouble and he had to disappear. He said he had to go back to the stars for a while and my life got a little darker until I was returned home and Sheriff Bando was assigned to keep tabs on me. He was an all right guy but my homelife felt like a prison. I told him I would give him anything if he got me out of there. My parents went missing when I turned seventeen. The courts decided I was old enough to live on my own. When I turned eighteen, Bando asked me to marry him, and I said yes. That was all he wanted. The young trophy wife. Between my parents and then him, no one knew about my past and they probably never will. And that's all I give him. Poor guy. I know he probably wants more but he's too much of a sweetheart to ask and I'm not sure if I'd give it to him anyway.

"So, see, I trust you with that story. Have you come yet?"

"Um . . . yeah."

"Which part?"

"When you were, uh, talking about your boyfriend fucking you."

"I'll pick you up in half an hour. There's something I need you to do for me."

In my post-orgasm stupor I thought about the wild story she'd given me. It had to be a story. Dawn was tough and manipulative, sure, but she still didn't seem to me like someone who'd led a particularly rough life. She seemed pretty driven, so I supposed she could have put a lot of work into being the type of girl she wanted people to perceive her as.

I watched the street from my apartment window. I thought I saw Kren walk by on the sidewalk, but couldn't be completely sure. Maybe he was on his way to work. I hoped whatever Dawn had planned included beer and cigarettes. She texted me almost exactly thirty minutes after she'd hung up with me.

I went down to meet her. A morbidly obese girl sat in the passenger seat. She looked about Dawn's age. I got in the back.

"This is Plopsy," Dawn said, motioning to the girl.

"Hi, Plopsy," I said.

She didn't say anything, just stared glassily out the front window.

"Plopsy's not real talkative. She'll be taking Barcie's place."

"Sure," I said. "Barcie. Who died."

"Yep."

"She did die, right?"

"Pretty sure. I went to the funeral. For all intents and purposes, she's dead to me."

"So she's not dead?"

"She is until she's reborn, I guess."

"Schrodinger's cat again?"

"No. Not really. That's about something simultaneously existing in two states. Not one state. A person who's dead doesn't really have anything to do with Schrodinger's cat. They're just dead. We've been over this."

"So . . . never mind." I shook whatever I was going to say away. "What are we doing?"

"Going to a party."

Dawn and Plopsy were both dressed really well and wore a lot of make-up.

"I look like trash," I said. "I haven't even showered today."

"That's fine. Besides, don't you always look like trash?"

"I guess. I never really have a need to wear decent clothes."

"I know. I'm surprised you haven't graduated to sweatsuits yet."

"I guess that leaves me room to grow anyway. So what's the party?"

"It's a Republican fundraiser outside of Columbus. I don't really know the specifics. It's not like I organized it or anything. I'm just there to help get donations."

I could have asked her more about it but didn't really care. Politics bored the piss out of me. I was just relieved we weren't picking some young woman up to whisk her away to a gangbang before beating her in the face with the chain.

I leaned back, lit a cigarette, and cracked the window.

"Throw it out," Dawn said.

"What?"

"Don't smoke in here."

"Are you serious?"

"Plopsy and I don't want to smell like white trash. Throw it out."

I took a deep drag and tossed the cigarette out the window before putting it back up.

Dawn cracked the window again from the front.

"Gotta give it a chance to air out," she said.

I settled back in the seat and closed my eyes. Columbus was a little over an hour away so I'd be able to get a decent nap in. If the night was going to be as uncomfortable as I thought it would be then I was going to want my rest.

It was pretty easy to doze off. There was no music playing and Dawn and Plopsy didn't say a single word to each other.

When I opened my eyes a little later, Dawn was looking at me in the rearview mirror.

"Did ums get his sweep out?"

I didn't respond to her. I kept to myself until we reached a line of cars, most of them Mercedes and Cadillacs and BMWs, pulling into the circular driveway of a palatial mansion, complete with massive white columns and twinkling golden lights. It was the kind of place I'd driven by and wondered who lived there. Apparently it was the type of person who threw fundraisers for the Republican Party.

"Who lives here?" I asked.

"Dunno," Dawn said. "All I know is that I got paid to do a job and I'm doing it."

"And the job is . . .?"

"To enhance the evening."

"And that means . . .?"

"You don't know what 'enhance' means?"

"I do, but . . . How are you going to do that?"

"Don't worry about it. You don't have to. Why would you want to concern yourself with something that isn't your responsibility? Just relax and have fun. You're learning how to do that, right?"

"Not really."

"Not really?"

"Everything still seems kind of . . . I don't know, tinged with dread or something."

"And maybe some day you'll come to appreciate that too."

"Half the time I don't know what the fuck you're talking about."

"And maybe you'll grow to appreciate that too. Mystery."

We pulled up to a young valet wearing a black vest and the competitive cold blue stare of a Nazi. We all got out of the car and Dawn handed him the keys. For the first time, I noticed it was a black Mercedes and I felt really oblivious I hadn't noticed it the entire ride up here.

"Is that Barcie's car?" I asked.

"It was always my car. I decided to take it back after she, you know, died."

We walked toward the house behind a small flock of well-dressed, well-preserved elderly people, the cloud of perfume and cologne nearly choking me.

Dawn handed a cream-colored card to Plopsy and me. I assumed it was an invitation and didn't open it.

An elderly man in a tuxedo stood behind a podium or maître d' stand or something. He smiled at the group in front of us and they passed into the house. Maybe it was a well-known politician and his family or something. I wouldn't have known.

The old man gave us a summoning look.

Dawn approached first and she handed him her invitation. He looked down at it, smiled, nodded, and said, "Have a lovely evening, Mrs. Bando."

He did the same with Plopsy and said, "Have a wonderful evening, Ms. Plopsy."

Plopsy Plopsy? I thought.

I approached and handed him my invitation. He started to say something—possibly about how I was dressed—before looking down at the invitation. He applied more scrutiny to mine than he had the girls' before saying, "Please go in, sir."

I joined Dawn and Plopsy just inside the door. They each held drinks in their hands. The man carrying the tray had turned away from them. I quickly reached around him and plucked a drink off the tray. White wine. Not my favorite but it would have to do.

I looked at Dawn. "What now?"

"We've got work to do," she said. "I'm sure there's a place to smoke out back or something."

I guessed that was her way of telling me to get lost.

I wandered through the room. I didn't know what to call it. A reception area, maybe. I lived in a place without a bedroom or separate kitchen. This house made me extremely uncomfortable. I could see tall French doors leading out to a veranda and I made my retreat toward it. I would attempt to not step foot back in the house for the rest of the night. I kept my head down and tried not to look at anyone.

Outside, two long tables draped in white tablecloths were arranged in an open 'V' pattern. I walked well past those toward a couple of old men standing around a gray pole. As I got closer, I could see it was one of those cigarette disposal things that look like an upside down lollipop.

I stopped and fished my cigarettes out of my pocket.

The other two men standing around the stand chuckled.

I lit my cigarette.

One of the men, the color of leather, said, "Are you sure you're in the right place?"

"Pretty sure. This is the smoking area, right?"

"Aren't you with the staff?"

"I don't think so. I had an invitation."

"Oh." He smirked. "I'm Bob Sanders." He held out his hand.

"Brad Renfield." I shook his hand.

"Poke Roberts," the other man said, coming forward. His skin was the color of old paper and he reminded me of a lizard.

"And what do you do, Brad? Are you in tech?" Sanders asked.

"Um, no," I said. "I don't really do much of anything."

"Must be nice," he said. "You'll have to give me the name of your consultant."

At first I didn't know what he meant and then I laughed a little and said, "Oh, I haven't retired from anything. I'm just unemployed."

He gave me another glance up and down, the look on his face completely changing. I'd gone from a tech wizard who was too autistic to dress himself for a formal gathering to what I really was—a trashy, unemployed deadbeat. The two men quickly crushed out their cigarettes and went back up toward the house.

When I finished that one, I lit another one and looked at the continually shifting mass of people. For the first time, probably because I'd tried to keep my head down, I noticed a number of girls milling around. Dawn hadn't said anything about it but it looked like what I assumed a coming out ball would look like. Most of the men were very old. Some of the women I assumed were their wives were also quite old, but on the whole the women looked considerably younger than the men. And then there were the much younger girls. All of them wore a slightly similar white shift kind of thing, their hair either straight or done up in braids. They could have been the daughters but I didn't see any young men of around the same age.

About halfway through my second cigarette, one of the girls approached me.

She didn't say anything. She just looked at me with huge green eyes, unblinking. It made me nervous.

"Want a cigarette?" I said.

She nodded her head. I didn't really know if she was of smoking age or not. I just felt like I had to say something.

I handed the cigarette to her and lit it for her.

"Having fun?" I asked.

She didn't say anything. She just puffed her cigarette lightly, like she didn't quite know how to do it, and stared toward the house.

"So . . . are you here with your parents?"

No response.

Dawn emerged from the crowd and made a beeline toward us.

"Serena?" she said when she spotted the girl. "What the fuck are you doing?"

Dawn grabbed the cigarette and handed it to me.

She grabbed the girl around her thin arm and dragged her back toward the house.

"You need to get back to work!" Dawn shot a murderous gaze over her shoulder at me. I wasn't sure if she'd been talking to the girl or me.

I held up both my cigarettes and nodded at her. I took a drag from the one the girl had been smoking but it didn't taste right so I crushed it out and put it in the disposal. I polished off the wine in my glass and went in search of more.

As I waited in line at the outdoor bar, Dawn approached me.

"You're not to talk to any of the girls," she said.

"Jealous?"

"Hardly. I don't want you distracting them."

"I didn't. I thought they were people's daughters."

She laughed a little. "Well, we let them pretend they're whatever they want them to be but I think most of them would be a little disappointed to have daughters like this."

She didn't really need to say anymore. I got it. The girls were whores. I was hoping they were at least eighteen. I wasn't going to ask. I started to wonder what it would be like to be with one of them and quickly tried to put the thought out of my head.

"Just get your drink and go back over to the little smoking stand. Don't sit at the table during dinner."

My face flushed a little when she said this.

"So I *am* the help?"

"What do you mean?"

"Some guy asked if I was the help or something earlier."

"You're more like the entertainment."

"What am I supposed to do?"

"Just be yourself."

Then she took off.

I asked the bartender if she had any beer. She gave me the same type of scrutiny the doorman had given me and pulled a bottle of Stella Artois—the beer for rich people with no taste—from a cooler of ice, wiped it off, and pulled the top. I tucked a dollar into the tip jar and made my way back to the butt stand.

I saw Dawn talking to a tall, white-haired man. She held her phone in her hand and looked at him with a very serious expression. He smiled briefly, as though humoring her, and directed his attention toward the phone. The smile dropped away and one of his hands shot to his forehead.

I moved a little closer, careful to remain behind Dawn, so I could hear what she was saying.

". . . and that's why the campaign would really appreciate whatever contribution you could make."

"My wife, Marilyn, has the checkbook and obviously . . ." He waved a thin, bony hand at the phone.

"Right. You wouldn't want her to see this. Fortunately we also take credit cards or I could even write you a receipt for good old American cash."

The man reached into his blazer and produced a wallet. He quickly looked around, probably to make sure his wife wasn't nearby, and handed a black card to Dawn, who swiped it on some sort of gadget she had on her phone. Was that called a dongle? I didn't know. Probably. Leave it to America to come up with names for things that were even more ridiculous than what the names represented.

I couldn't risk getting any closer without being noticed, especially with how I was dressed, so I continued walking back to the smoking area.

What was on Dawn's phone?

Was it more blackmail?

Or was it some kind of emotional reel of something like abused dogs or starving children in Africa or amputee veterans of war? I could certainly understand the man saying he didn't want his wife to see any of that, but I didn't think Republicans cared about those things. Maybe it was an emotional reel of people enjoying free education or free healthcare or walking down a street where no one was carrying concealed firearms. That might get a Republican's blood boiling.

As I got closer to the smoking area, I pulled my cigarettes from my pocket and heard a disturbance near a row of shrubs toward the back of the property. I wandered back a little farther, just in time to see Plopsy punch one of the younger girls in the face.

"Mr. Cuatro likes bruises," she hissed.

She mechanically punched the girl two more times in the face. I thought about asking her to stop but then thought about the chain. I'd already gotten the chain a couple of times and didn't want it any more, especially in the face. I entertained the thought of saving this beautiful young girl from Plopsy's fists and escaping into the night and her ultimately begging me to fuck her. But I felt like in the end she would be vapid and boring and right now just kind of wanted to move out of view of Plopsy so I wasn't somehow enlisted to help beat the poor girl.

Bob Sanders stood by the butt stand. It was just my luck the one guy here who enjoyed smoking as much as me was also the biggest douche.

"Hello, Brad," he said.

"Bob. How's your evening?"

"Quite splendid so far."

I pulled a cigarette out and lit it.

"I forgot to ask earlier," Bob said. "You said you didn't work. Are you living off some kind of trust fund?"

This was a really invasive question and I felt like he must know the answer or he wouldn't be asking.

"No," I said. "I'm just poor."

He smirked. "That's what I thought."

The next couple of minutes were awkward and silent.

Then Bob said, "You know, I'm glad you're here. You remind me of why I've worked so hard to achieve what I have. I'm living a dream, boy. Living a fucking dream. I've done things and will do things you've never even thought about. Don't let people tell you money can't buy happiness. The only people who ever say that are poor people."

"I've never said that," I said absently.

"Good! Maybe there's hope for you yet. I'm about ready to enjoy a fine dinner and then a couple of hours in the company of a fine young woman." He picked out one of the milling girls in white and said, "I swear, it's like they create these girls in a lab somewhere."

I didn't know if he was looking for a pat on the back or waiting for me to match his exchange of lechery but I didn't really have anything to say.

"Of course," he said, "sometimes concessions have to be made. Which brings me to something of a proposition."

I tried to think of what this old man could possibly ask from me and couldn't really think of anything.

"My wife has certain . . . fantasies."

I didn't like where this was going. I brought my free hand up to my forehead and massaged my temples.

"I don't really do that," I said.

"Really?" he said. "The pretty young woman with the phone said you would be more than happy to cooperate. She also said for me to tell you, 'Jingle jangle.'"

The chain, I thought.

I knew where he was going with his request and could only manage to think about the female equivalent of this man, some overly coiffed emaciated grandma.

"I'll cut through all the nonsense and get right to the point. My wife fantasizes about being raped. Although, I've tried to argue with her on this point. I don't feel it's really rape if I'm buying the rapist. I think it's a pampered rich girl fantasy. If she really wanted to be raped, she would just go wander around Niggertown on a Saturday night. *That*, I think, would be rape. Although I guess it would still be debatable if that were what she was actually looking to have happen to her. Plus she'd probably get AIDS."

He took one last drag of his cigarette and popped it into the disposal.

"Her name's Fiona. She'll be sitting to my left at dinner. She will get up under the auspices of using the restroom before the food is even served. My Fiona doesn't really eat, especially not in public. Then, you know, make a game of it. I'll certainly be having my own fun after dinner. Don't let me down, Brad."

He turned to walk away and doubled back.

"Oh, I almost forgot. Your young lady friend said to give you these." He reached into his pocket and produced two blue pills. "I'm sure you're plenty virile but, well, sometimes nerves can get the best of you."

I held out my hand and he dropped the pills into my palm before turning and drifting back up toward the house.

Jingle jangle.

A shudder ran through me.

I continued smoking until I saw people making their way to the large tables.

In the interim, I was approached by a number of people, most of them older, all of them well dressed, about only half of whom were smokers, and they asked me questions like:

"Do you buy your clothes at the thrift store?"

"Do you have indoor plumbing?"

"Do you use public transportation?"

"What's it like to rent?"

"How many illegitimate children do you have?"

"What's it like not to have insurance?"

"Do you wish you'd gone to college?"

I got it. I was the token poor person. Some kind of ridiculous clown these people would have never approached outside the safety of their confines. Was this the main reason for Dawn bringing me here or had all those questions arisen from that initial conversation with Bob Sanders. I could ask Dawn about it later, but knew I wouldn't get a straight answer.

Once everyone had gathered around the tables I drifted up toward them. The setting sun hit the backyard in such a way that everything seemed to glow—the white of the contributors' hair and the dresses of the girls, the freshly watered lawn, the white tablecloths, the crystal blue of the pool. I got just close enough to hear the hushed conversations, the comforting clack of silverware, and the sloshing of water and coffee and wine being poured.

I spotted Bob Sanders, his wife sitting next to him. What had he said her name was? Sophia? Fiona. I was pretty sure that's what he'd said. She wasn't as old or hideous as I thought she'd be. From this distance, she looked like she was probably even around my age, possibly a little older. Her blond hair was swept up and she wore some kind of black spaghetti strap top. Since she was sitting down I couldn't really tell what else she wore or get a good idea of her figure. She was probably thin. I thought most rich people—women, at least—were obsessed with being thin.

My phone vibrated.

It was a text from Dawn.

It said: "U should probably take those pills."

I reached into my pocket and grabbed the pills Bob Sanders had given me. I still had a little beer left so I popped the pills and washed them down with that. I'd never taken anything like that and had no idea how long it would take them to kick in. Or if I'd even need them. I'd never had any problems in that department before but, then again, I'd never attempted to rape anyone, either.

A team of waiters emerged from the back of the house carrying many shiny silver trays heaped with bowls of salad. It took a few minutes before they finally got to the Sanders. Once the bowl of salad was placed in front of Fiona, she excused herself and stood up, smoothing the front of her cocktail dress down over her thin thighs. She casually looked around and headed toward the house.

I had a moment of fear and paralysis. I didn't know if I'd be able to do this or not. I should have drunk a lot more. My mouth went dry. I didn't feel aroused at all. What if Bob Sanders was just setting me up? What if he hated poor people so much this was all worth it just to see me go to jail for attempted rape? Wasn't jail where most rich white Republicans felt like poor people should be anyway?

I forced myself to move because if I didn't I thought my fear would eventually force me to take root where I stood.

I walked quickly in an attempt to close the distance.

By the time she reached the back doors I was only about fifteen feet behind her.

I dumped my beer bottle in a trashcan and entered the house.

Fiona walked through some kind of very formal dining room. Most of the guests were out at the tables and the servants were apparently taking this opportunity to clean up after them.

I tried to come up with some sort of game plan but it almost seemed too ridiculous. I wasn't a violent person. I felt like, if Bob wanted me to do this, he should have given me something like PCP or bath salts. Something that would turn me into a raging lunatic.

Fiona cast a lingering gaze over her shoulder.

Somehow, I told myself this made what I was about to do okay.

She'd spotted me. It felt like she was aware of it. We were the only two people in the room who were not staff or young prostitutes. This was her last chance to back out. She'd seen me. She knew I was the guy. If I was too repulsive or she didn't want it to happen, she would have shifted course.

Before reaching the grand reception room, she turned to her right and started down a dimly lit hallway. I assumed the areas with the lights turned off were the places guests weren't supposed to go.

Toward the end of the hallway she made another right and disappeared through what I assumed was a doorway.

My heart pounded and I tried to regulate my breathing so it didn't run away with me.

I turned into the open doorway and went down a few steps.

I stood in some kind of finished basement. The lights were turned low but it looked like it was used as some kind of recreation room. I spotted two pool tables, a ping pong table, a wall of dartboards, and a wet bar. Toward the back of the room, fluorescent light spilled from another opening.

I paused and took a series of deep breaths. Tried to slow my heart. The Viagra probably wasn't helping. What if I had a heart attack during my first attempted rape? I was middle-aged and hadn't really taken care of myself at all. I tried not to think about it. It was just something else to worry about.

Maybe as a stalling technique, maybe in an attempt to make it a more genuinely authentic experience, I went over to the bar and rummaged around until I came up with a corkscrew. It was the most threatening thing I could find.

I held it in my hand so it was plainly visible and walked toward the bright light.

I walked into the laundry room filled with white tile and stainless steel machines.

Fiona stood toward the back of the room.

She turned to me, laughed a little, and said, "I think I got turned around."

I grabbed the heavy wooden door and shut it, turning the lock.

"You don't want to do this," she said. "Just let me go back to the party."

I began walking toward her.

She ran toward me on the opposite side of a bank of folding tables. She reached the door quickly, cranking the handle with one hand and pounding on the door with the other. She made no attempt to actually unlock it.

"Help!" she yelled. "Rape!"

I didn't know if anyone could hear her or not but felt completely terrified. The Viagra was kicking in, however, and my cock felt like it was about to shoot off into space. Maybe the sudden rush of blood to that area removed the last bit of judgment I had in my brain.

I grabbed her arm and yanked her away from the door, throwing her to the floor.

She sat up and looked up at me, an expression of maybe genuine terror on her face. She was quite beautiful. Almost like an older version of the young girls wandering the property.

Her legs were parted slightly and I could see the crotch of her black underwear.

"Help me!" she shouted. "Somebody help!"

I pointed the corkscrew at her and said, "Shut the fuck up." I hoped my voice didn't quaver too much.

She kept screaming.

I grabbed a washcloth from one of the laundry bins. It was folded so I imagined it was clean.

Fiona scooted away from me on her ass.

She stood up quickly and came at me with her nails. She gouged and slapped my face. She was only a few inches shorter than me but probably only weighed a hundred pounds at most.

I held the corkscrew in front of my face with my right hand and grabbed her around the throat with my left. Her neck was so thin my hand nearly encircled it. I pushed her back against a bank of dryers and squeezed her throat until she stopped screaming. Her eyes grew watery and a vein in her forehead bulged. She opened her mouth, trying to get air, and I shoved the washcloth in with the hand holding the corkscrew. I turned her around, dropped the corkscrew, and mashed her face against the glass of one of the dryers. She now furiously breathed through her nose. Her eyes were watering and a trail of clear snot leaked from her nostrils. She couldn't really get at me with her arms. All her attempts to kick me in that backward fashion just meant there was more pressure on her face against the dryer. Keeping my left hand on the back of her head, I unfastened myself with my free hand, tugging my underwear over an erection that seemed painful and nearly foreign to me.

I plunged my hand between her legs and put all of my weight against her. I massaged her pussy roughly through the thin fabric of her underwear. I listened to her gagging and attempting to scream against the washcloth. I pushed her dress up and hooked my hands into the band of her underwear, yanking them down. She renewed her efforts, slamming her hands against the dryers and trying to push back against me. Now that both of my hands were free I wrapped them around her upper arms and took her down to the floor. I pulled her thin arms behind her and clasped one of my hands around her wrists, pressing them against her lower back. I rested my weight on the backs of her legs and pushed her dress back up with my free hand. Her ass was pale and round and small and amazingly firm. I split her cunt with my hand, sticking two and then three fingers into her. I grabbed my cock and pushed myself into her. She was tight and wet and I took my time. She struggled against me as I thrust against her. I thought I would come right away but I didn't. I went slow and then hard and fast until I got tired. Time seemed to expand and stretch out. There was no music or sound of any kind, other than the faint buzz of the lights and my ragged breathing and her muffled grunts. The wet sound of our flesh smacking together. I took myself just to the brink of coming and slid out of her and stood up. I quickly took off my shirt and grabbed the corkscrew. I looked down at her, limp and sobbing on the floor. I noticed some clothesline draped over a portable clothes rack.

I pointed the corkscrew at her and said, "I want you to stand up and face me. If you take the rag out of your mouth, I'm going to kill you and finish up with your dead body."

She slowly and shakily stood, her skirt falling back down into place.

She turned and looked at me.

I pulled off my shirt and shook the corkscrew at her.

"Take off your dress."

She reached down and pulled it over her head. She wore a black strapless pushup bra. Bruises were beginning to form at the bottom of her ribcage and her hipbones.

"Take off the bra."

She took it off.

"I'm going to tie you up now. If you try anything . . ." I again shook the corkscrew.

I grabbed the clothesline and approached her.

"Turn around," I said.

She turned around.

"Put your hands behind your back."

She did that and I sloppily tied her wrists.

"Now put your ankles together."

I bound her ankles.

I put the corkscrew down and picked Fiona up and took her over to one of the folding tables. Now that we were both completely naked, more of our skin was touching and I became even more aroused. I bent her over the table and again entered her cunt, massaging her asshole with my thumb as I did so. Once my cock was wet with her juices, I pulled out and pressed it against her asshole. I used one hand to spread her ass cheeks and the other to press the tip of my cock against her tight sphincter. Once I broke the seal I slowly slid in to the hilt. I fucked her slowly, sliding the entire length in and out until moving faster and faster. She stopped struggling after a few minutes. I fucked her harder and harder, banging her thighs against the table. I looked down at her reddened little ass and noticed her hands were balled into fists. She opened and closed her hands and I felt her asshole spasm around my cock. I had to stop or I was going to come. I stayed in her until her asshole stopped constricting. I pulled out. Her legs were shaking.

"Now I want you to get on your knees."

She dropped to her knees.

I bent down and spit into her face. She looked surprised. My spit blended with the snot and tears already there.

"I'm going to pull the washcloth out now. Don't scream."

I pulled the washcloth out.

I was still really hard.

"Open your mouth."

She looked at my cock. She didn't open her mouth. I grabbed the corkscrew off the table and pressed it against the side of her head. I looked down at her pussy and noticed a string of girl come extending to the floor.

"Open it."

She opened her mouth.

I pressed the corkscrew against her temple, braced the back of her head with my free hand, and filled her mouth with my cock. I was so close to coming I felt out of my head. I started fucking her mouth harder, feeling the tip of my cock press against her esophagus and disregarding her choking and gagging. When I was finally ready to explode, I held the back of her head hard and pressed myself as far as I could into her as my penis swelled and constricted, releasing burst after burst of come into her throat.

I pulled out and she slumped over, sobbing and gagging.

Now we'd reached the awkward stage.

I wanted to say something to her. To make sure that was really what she wanted or whatever but figured it was probably a little too late for that anyway. I quickly put my clothes on and got the hell out of the laundry room.

I thought I should probably get the hell away from the house but as I was in one of the bathrooms washing the blood off my face, my phone vibrated with a text from Dawn.

It said: "Get back to your post, Marlboro Man."

I felt weird. Not good at all. I didn't know if it was a fear thing or an ethical thing or just the fact it felt like I'd been wrestling with someone for the last hour and that was more exercise than I'd gotten in a long time. And the scratches on my face hurt pretty badly. Before leaving the bathroom I disappeared into a stall and had a small breakdown.

I became extremely paranoid I had actually just raped that woman. She had certainly acted like how I thought someone being raped might act. But maybe that was part of it. Part of the thrill. She'd yelled a lot and no one had made any attempt to intervene. Maybe the house was that soundproof. Maybe everyone felt so secure that, even if they'd thought they heard something, they'd told themselves there was no way that could happen here.

There wasn't really anything I could do now. If there were going to be consequences, I'd just have to deal with them.

I left the house and went back to my spot near the butt stand.

There were more people around it now, probably because the drinks had been flowing for a while and people's resolves had lessened. Or maybe it was because everyone had sneaked off to the nearly infinite areas of the house to have their little flings they'd most probably paid for and this was their afterglow smoke.

My cock was still hard and this made me a little self-conscious.

Bob Sanders drifted over. He seemed drunk and exhausted. Why did he keep talking to me if he hated me so much?

"Looks like you got a little roughed up." He moved his hand in a circular fashion a couple inches from his face.

I didn't say anything.

"Fiona said she had a wonderful time, although it was maybe not as much as she'd wanted." He exhaled a plume of smoke in my face. "The next time somebody asks you to do something like this, don't be such a fucking pussy."

I wanted to hit him but just lit the cigarette I'd been cradling in my hand instead.

He went over to a group of men who were more like him and they all stood around smoking and looking at each other's phones and laughing. They all had erections tenting their slacks.

I continued smoking and drinking, going back and forth between the butt stand and the bar.

Later into the evening I noticed almost everyone was carrying a gun. Some of them were lethal semi-automatic looking things.

Others had futuristic looking pistols. Some had large rifles and shotguns that seemed almost quaint. Even the women carried guns.

I didn't see any sign of Dawn or Plopsy. I caught a glimpse of Fiona, sharing a drink with her friends, laughing and looking radiant.

The dining tables had been removed and replaced by something large, draped in a white cloth. I noticed music was playing. Light classical music. I hadn't noticed it before.

Eventually an air horn sounded and everyone gathered around the draped structure. The cloth was removed and shouts of anger and laughter erupted from the crowd.

A massive piñata wearing a turban and a beard hung over the crowd of people.

They all raised their firearms and began firing at the piñata. I wondered what it contained but it didn't take long for bullets to begin shredding it. Blood began pouring out of it. Or something used to simulate blood. I expected the guests to move away from it, but they didn't. They moved toward it, letting the blood rain down on them, smearing it all over themselves.

"You smell like pussy." Dawn stood to my left. "I mean, like, you smell really bad. Ready to go?"

I looked at the horror in front of me and said, "Please."

PINING

I didn't hear from Dawn for three days. I spent most of my time in a semi-depressed state of near paralysis. If you ever ask yourself how poor people can take the jobs they do—things like factory work or a call center or construction or data entry or landscaping or fast food or retail—it's because whatever that job is is probably an alternative to this nothing. I was never a person with big ideas or an imagination or drive or initiative of any kind really. The modern world is rigged so it costs money just to leave the house. I'd had hobbies at some point in my life but somewhere along the way they'd been ironed out or expunged through lack of money and free time. The hobbies I'd been left with were really more like addictions—drinking, smoking, sex when I could get it. Maybe the internet.

Mostly I lay in my bed, tried to conserve cigarettes, and thought about Dawn. I began to place things in two contexts: with Dawn and without Dawn. With Dawn was the preferred context. It was dark and kind of scary, sure, but it was exciting. I never seemed to be crushed by boredom and a sense of meaninglessness when around her. It seemed like there was the possibility of something. With her I'd already done and seen things I wouldn't have imagined. And there was always the possibility of more. If I still hadn't figured out what I wanted to do with my life it seemed like she had and there was a part of me that wanted to see her achieve her goals. Sure, there may be consequences for some actions—like the chain or the looming thought of blackmail—but it seemed kind of pure. Quick and painful. Black and white.

Time spent without Dawn was very familiar territory. What if it lasted forever? What if I never saw her again? I almost texted her the day after the fundraiser but didn't want to seem too desperate. I wasn't exactly sure what I was to her. Maybe texting her would show her how much I desired her, but I was afraid it would make me seem too needy. Everything had happened without me doing much of anything so far so I imagined she would eventually get in touch with me. Still, the longer she went without contacting me, the more I'd have to think about going back to my old world. Finding some kind of dead end, practically temporary job so I could make just enough money for gas and cigarettes and cheap food that came from a can or the freezer section. No bonuses. No highlights. No vacations. Beer would be a fucking luxury. Just mindless drudgery until whatever undiagnosed illness the lack of good insurance allowed to fester in my body overtook me, hopefully swiftly. Thinking about a world without Dawn seemed completely hopeless.

Still, I was cautious. Aside from the perceived neediness, this was the other main reason for not reaching out to her. It had always seemed like the more I wanted something—the harder I reached out for it—the further away it got.

When I was younger I thought I would live life to its fullest. I never wanted to be able to say I hadn't tried. Now that I was forty, I wished I hadn't wasted so much time trying. Trying had become synonymous with failing.

Not to sound too clichéd, but Dawn had become something of a drug and I needed a fix. Not a big one even. Just a little hit would do. I imagined myself going down on her again, running my tongue along the lips of her pussy, pulling her clit into my mouth. And I thought about doing a lot more and wondered why I hadn't tried it yet. Maybe it was because, until a few days ago, I'd actually thought of myself as a good person. I didn't really think that anymore. And I didn't really care.

Surprisingly, I refrained from masturbating. I didn't need an erection to go down on Dawn but I felt like if she was going to have any 'assignments' for me, like my encounter with Fiona Sanders, I should be able to perform. Apparently I still had that robotic worker drone mentality.

When my phone vibrated, I became unrealistically excited. It had to be from Dawn.

It was.

"I'm dropping off a present for you."

Dawn's interpretation of a present could be a little ambiguous so I wasn't as excited as if someone else had said they were dropping off a present to me but by that point I didn't really care. At least it was something. Dawn hadn't forgotten about me.

I sat up and swung my legs over the edge of the bed, the lack of food and sudden rush of blood making me a little dizzy. I went into the kitchen, opened a can of ravioli, and ate most of it cold.

There was a soft knock on the door.

I tossed the can into the trash, wiped my mouth off with a paper towel, and went to answer the door.

It was one of the prostitutes from the party.

My stomach did an odd flopping. I hoped she was here for the reason I thought and that made me excited but standing there looking at her made me uneasy.

Maybe she was legal.

I told myself she was legal.

But deep down I just didn't see how it was possible.

The only thing I was certain of was that it wasn't Dawn.

I thought about what Bob Sanders had said: "It's like they grow them in a lab somewhere."

Was that how they managed to take advantage of these girls and not feel bad about it? Convince themselves they weren't even real?

The girl wasn't wearing a dress like they all had been the other night. She was dressed like any other teenage girl on a hot summer night. Red tank top hugging small firm breasts. Tiny denim shorts barely covering her. Untied high tops.

She was nearly a foot shorter than me and stared up at me.

"Come in," I said.

She came in from the hallway and I shut the door after scanning to make sure none of my neighbors had seen her.

"Do you have a name?" I asked.

She moved to the edge of my bed, facing me, staring at me. She briefly glanced up at the ceiling and took a couple of steps to her left. I looked in the direction she had and noticed the tiny little camera for the first time.

How could I have been so stupid?

How many more of them were scattered around the apartment?

How many times had Dawn and Barcie or Plopsy or, fuck, Officer Bando or whoever shared a laugh over something ridiculous I'd done while I thought I was alone?

No.

I couldn't let myself think about any of that right now.

Dawn had given me a present.

I was looking forward to unwrapping it.

The girl, not taking her eyes from me, kicked off her shoes and peeled down her shorts and underwear. She sat down on the edge of the bed and pointed to her cunt.

I walked over to her, got on my knees, and went to work.

The taste was familiar. If given a blind taste test, I couldn't have distinguished between her and Dawn. This girl was actually responsive, though. She twisted her hand in my hair and moved her hips and moaned. I felt a little of what I felt when going down on Dawn. It was like a diluted version of Dawn.

When I decided I was finished I stood and removed my clothes. Took off her top. She had a jewel stud in her bellybutton. Looking more closely, I wasn't even sure she had a bellybutton. I tried not to let it distract me.

I thought about being gentle but kept flashing back onto my sexual encounter with Fiona Sanders. Thought about Dawn saying, "Some girls like to hurt."

By the time I was finished, I was completely exhausted.

The girl grabbed her clothes and went into the bathroom.

It looked like she'd cleaned off all the blood when she came back out.

She headed for the door.

I was physically tired but the encounter had renewed some sort of life within me.

The girl shut the door and I quickly put on my clothes and went after her.

The hot day had suddenly turned cooler with nightfall. Mist swirled around the blue streetlamps and I thought I'd already lost the girl.

I caught the outline of her to my left and went in that direction. Because I was following her, I had it in my head I should keep some type of discreet distance but she was so acquiescent and passive I couldn't imagine her stopping if she heard me, let alone telling me to get away and leave her alone. For all I knew, I could follow her to wherever she was going, break in and do the same thing I'd just done to her and it would not be met with any aggression or hostility.

A couple blocks away she turned to the left.

I thought the municipal building was in that direction, housing the police and fire department and public works utilities. There was also Veterans' Park.

The fog gave everything a hushed dreamlike quality. I liked it.

She reached the sidewalk across from the municipal building and turned right.

The houses around us were silent and dark. Even the midsummer insect sounds were faint. The fragrance of some night blooming flower hung in the fog and had a nearly narcotic effect. I passed a house with a car idling in the driveway, its lights off, no one in it.

The girl continued to move robotically through the fog.

I don't know what I was expecting.

I wouldn't have been surprised if she turned and walked up to one of the houses. I could just as easily imagine her going down to the darkened basement and powering down as I could imagine her sneaking past her parents and going up to her high school girl's room.

A black car waited at a stop sign at the end of the street.

The front doors opened and two men wearing black suits got out. I thought back to my night in the motel.

I stopped short, took a few sliding steps back. I wondered if I should be recording this.

"Please come with us," one of the men said.

The girl didn't say anything.

"Get in the car."

I would like to say I detected a humiliated slump to the girl's shoulders, anything denoting some semblance of humanity or resistance, but I didn't. She simply bent and slid into the car with that same borderline lifeless demeanor. What were they going to do with her? She was filled with my come and I didn't know why that made me uneasy.

The car turned to the left and came toward me. I took a step back, trying to find the foggy shadows, but the guy driving the car, maybe a federal agent, maybe not, must have spotted me because he shouted, "Go home, retard!" without slowing down.

I instinctively turned to do just that but after getting to the end of the block, I no longer wanted to go back to my sad, monitored apartment. I patted my pockets out of habit and had a brief flash of panic when I realized I'd forgotten my phone.

The panic quickly transitioned into relief.

I felt free.

The phone was like the final tether. I could feel myself surrendering to Dawn more and more and decided to utilize what remained of this one evening. I didn't know how many more there would be.

I continued walking through the neighborhood, careful to avoid the main road in case the men in the car were still out.

I began walking up a hill toward one of the small suburbs populated with little brick ranch houses on the outskirts of Gethsemane. While I felt freer than in the presence of Dawn or in my apartment waiting for my phone to vibrate with a message from her, I flashed back to our first encounter and again had the realization that I wouldn't feel completely divorced from this unless I was somewhere very far away. After all, hadn't she originally snatched me by finding me wandering along a road late at night?

Snatched?

That seemed like a funny way of looking at it but it felt true, in a sense.

How could things have really happened any other way?

I looked up toward the neighborhood at the top of the hill and noticed the large ghostly white water tower looming over it. They'd had to rebuild it nearly a decade ago after the bizarre storm had rolled through the area. A number of people had died and they'd built a memorial in front of the water tower with all the names of the dead. Seemed as good a place as any. It was surrounded by a park I hadn't been to since I was a kid.

I briefly thought about going to the carryout to see if Kren was around but decided I would rather be alone and take advantage of my lack of communication.

This was nice. I didn't know why I had never really done it before. I thought it would be especially nice at dawn.

Dawn.

There was that name again.

The name of a person. The name of a thing. Maybe I was trying to make too much out of it.

What was dawn?

The end of the night? Or the beginning of a new day?

Both?

What was Dawn?

Some kind of savior sent to liberate me from my boring life? Or some kind of witch, out to control and ultimately destroy me?

That seemed like a perversely egotistical thought. Who was I to be sought out for control and destruction? I was nobody. If I was anything to Dawn, it was simply for use as a cog in the larger machine of whatever she was running. But who knew? Maybe I fit some type she was looking for. Almost every employer typecasts. During my first long term relationship right out of high school, I'd spent a few years going to college and working in a bookstore. Eventually, I'd decided poverty was the most obviously overt strain on our relationship and decided to seek out a higher paying job. I began applying to a number of factories. I filled out the applications neatly and accurately, listing my job history that only consisted of the bookstore and my couple years of college. I showed up well dressed and well spoken at the interviews. I never even got called back. I even got rejected from the factory my dad had retired from. Finally I filled out an application very sloppily, misspelled things, didn't list any previous employment or college. I showed up at the interview wearing a stained t-shirt and jeans. I didn't talk a lot. I wanted to seem quiet and desperate. I got called back and hired two days later.

They were looking for a type. They wanted someone they could mold into their way of thinking.

I worked there one day and never went back.

Turned out they were right.

The days past threatened to break into this thick night and poison it with some kind of overly sunny nostalgia.

I quit thinking about the past.

I thought about the impending dawn.

Dawn.

The future.

Dark and beautiful and cruel and so close I could taste her on my tongue.

I took a deep breath of the damp night air and looked up at the looming water tower.

I looked around the park. Some swing sets, a merry-go-round, a baseball backstop, a slide and a wooden jungle gym, the whole park rimmed with tall pine trees.

A bench sat across from the water tower. I thought it was an odd place for a bench. Who wants to sit in the park and stare at a somewhat ugly, slightly rusty water tower? For that matter, why was the water tower in the middle of the park at all? Maybe this was the highest point in Gethsemane. I didn't know if that mattered or not. Then I remembered the memorial and figured that was probably why the bench was there. The sculpture was of a tornado, the names of the dead engraved into it. I thought it seemed a little weird, but then Christians saw the cross as some kind of memorial so maybe it made sense to a certain type of person.

And why was there a man sitting on the bench?

I went over to the bench and sat down next to the man.

He stared glassy eyed at the tower, looked haunted, and smelled strongly of whiskey.

"Would it bother you if I sat here?" I asked.

He jumped a little, as though this were the first time he'd even noticed me.

"No," he said. "I . . . sometimes I do this." He stood up. "You can have it. It's all yours now."

Then he made his way through the fog swept park and disappeared out of sight.

I sat and listened to the very distant sound of traffic and the faint jingling of a flagpole but mostly there was silence. And a hum. Coming from the water tower. Some kind of low hum I felt as much as heard. Probably some sort of engine running within it. After a while, I closed my eyes and had a sense the water tower was pulling me into it, swallowing me.

I must have fallen asleep because I had a seemingly endless dream of walking through a massive junkyard and beating on the trunks of cars and yelling for Travis and woke up to a crazy old man with a trenchcoat and wild hair beating me with a newspaper.

I mumbled, "Popular spot," and wandered back to the apartment amidst the explosion of sunlight and birds.

Dawn had arrived.

A couple days later, back in the apartment, I again felt like I was going out of my head. I was one of those people who prided themselves on being able to cope with boredom. Now I saw that in a somewhat sad light. It wasn't that I really never got bored before, it was just that I'd never really had anything else to do and had become adept at entertaining myself. I had probably been bored my entire life and just too blind to notice.

I convinced myself Dawn had grown tired of me. She had probably found some other poor schmuck who entertained her more. I resolved to try to be more entertaining but didn't really know what that would entail. Being more ridiculous than I already had been, maybe. I was a novelty to Dawn. Novelty always wore off, nearly by definition.

If she had grown tired of me, I feared it was only a matter of time before she forwarded the images on to White Power Larry and then I'd be fucked. I again came up with plans of leaving but hit the inevitable roadblock.

Funds.

Maybe I could rob Kren.

But how much would that really yield?

Given my last attempt at escape, I couldn't even say funds were the only problem. I didn't know if I'd physically be able to stay away. I could quit thinking about leaving. Gethsemane was where I belonged. It was where I needed to be.

I couldn't remember the last time I'd masturbated. I'd come a couple of times when Dawn had sent the girl over but hadn't touched myself except to go take a piss since then. That was exceptionally hard being as bored as I was. Especially when the focus of my thoughts was Dawn, a girl who I very much wanted to fuck. I almost thought about employing a technique I'd used in the past when obsessed with certain girls who were unobtainable. That technique would have been to masturbate to them as much as possible. That way I was almost bored with them before anything even had the chance of happening. Ultimately though, it was probably just because my obsession shifted to someone else. In order for that to happen, I'd have to leave the apartment.

Dawn's unobtainable quality was what made her worthy of obsession. After all, my focus hadn't shifted to Stasia or Fiona Sanders or the girl. And that was probably because I'd had them in one way or another.

Therein was a possible difference between men and women. I couldn't imagine a woman being obsessed with a guy—no matter how good looking—who just wanted his cock sucked and nothing more. Because, really, that's all I'd done with Dawn, and still wanted her more than ever.

Maybe the next time she asked me to do that, I'd try to do more.

Or would I?

Even if I got away with it, if it were something she didn't want, she had a way of making my life hell.

My phone vibrated with a text from Dawn.

"Meet me out front."

I practically ran to the door.

She was in the refurbished cop car. Sitting in the back. She pointed to the back passenger side door. I opened it and got in.

She swiveled around, slid down so she rested against the door, and spread her legs.

She wasn't wearing any underwear.

I was hard but knew what I was supposed to do.

"Close the door," she said.

I closed the door and put the seat in front of me up as far as possible. I bent down and greedily went to work on her pussy. The present she'd sent over had provided a sip, but this was the gulp I needed. It wasn't even dark out. There wasn't a lot of foot traffic in downtown Gethsemane but there also wasn't a lot going on, not a lot of distractions, and I felt something like this would surely be noticed. That's what made it so exciting.

I reached between Dawn's legs, pressing my middle finger

against her.

"Just your mouth," she said.

I heard the chain before I felt it.

It only came down once, hard, connecting with the back of my neck and shoulders.

"That girl you were with the other night, did you like that?" she asked as casually as if I didn't have my mouth on her pussy.

I pulled my mouth away, looked her in the eyes, and said, "Yeah, but she wasn't you."

"Keep working. You don't have to answer my question. Besides, we both know this is as much of me as you're getting."

I took her clit into my mouth and began suckling it, running my tongue down to taste more of her juices.

"Anyway, she's dead. The cops found her this morning. She had semen in her vagina and ass. They're still waiting on the contents of her stomach but they'll probably find some there too. They found her in Veterans' Park. Probably looks bad for you.

"Your friend, Travis, Barcie, that girl. I'm starting to think a few photos of you banging the local racist's girl are the least of your worries."

I should have felt anxious or panicked but I really didn't. The difference between those photos and the deaths was that I was guilty of the photos.

"So you should probably be careful about what you do, especially in regards to me. I haven't asked you to do anything too bad. Just provide some content, that's all. Provide the entertainment at a party. Nothing major. But eventually I'm going to need you to do something bigger."

I was barely listening to her and it didn't really make a lot of sense anyway.

"So I've got something very special I need you to do."

I sucked and licked her harder, snaked my tongue as far as I could within her, pretending she was enjoying this, like she was capable of getting pleasure out of anything that didn't involve sadism.

"I have a client who has some special interests that don't involve pussies."

I froze. I guess I was wondering how long it would take to get to this. I wasn't attracted to other guys. I had nothing against people who were, it had just never been my thing, despite having more opportunities with men than women. I probably could have even done it if I had more or less a passive role. But knowing the crowd Dawn seemed to hang with, I didn't think I'd want to subject myself to the degradation it would most definitely contain.

I took my mouth off her and said, "Let me fuck you and I'll do it."

She pushed down her skirt, smiled sarcastically, and said, "Wow. That's pretty pathetic. And no. Besides, you're not who I had in mind although it's nice to know you're still so egotistical that was your first thought. You're too old."

I motioned toward her lap, "I wasn't finished."

"No. You were."

I shrugged.

"Okay. Well, he wants the meeting set up at his house in two days. I've already agreed to it so my back's kind of against the wall. But I've been busy so I need you to find someone. I guess you know what happens if you don't. And I had so many plans for you."

I adjusted my cock and tried my best to think of some way out of this.

"I don't really know anyone."

She licked her lips and stared out the front of the car. She tilted her head to one side and her lips pulled back in a slight smirk.

"I'm going to give you the time and the address. As long as there's a dude there who isn't a hideous monster, he won't really care. But here's what you have to do: watch it. Just so you know what you're selling someone else into."

"I'll do that," I said, wondering if I should have hesitated.

"So I'll pick you up around then and we'll watch together. I'll make popcorn and invite friends. I'll text the details to you. Now get the fuck out of the car."

RECRUITMENT

Kren stood with his hands on the countertop, a joint tucked behind his ear. A video played on his phone in front of him but he wasn't watching it, just staring vacantly into some middle distance.

"Hey, man," I said, "want to go out back and get high?"

He snapped to the closest thing he came to attention and said, "Right on. This place is fucking dead."

We went out the same way we had before. This time he took off one of his shoes and used it to keep the door from shutting all the way. He reached into the pocket of his company issued smock and brought out a lighter and baggie of pot.

I reached out and plucked the joint from behind his ear. He didn't even flinch.

I held it up in front of him and said, "Magic!"

"Awesome!" He smiled ear to ear. "Customers never get *me* high!"

"I got it . . . Never mind."

"Spark it up!"

It always amazed me how chronic pot smokers could be so animatedly excited about getting high time after time. I had been a cigarette smoker for many years, and while it was an admittedly much lower grade buzz, I rarely if ever expressed excitement about smoking a cigarette, even though I pretty much lived for it.

I lit it and inhaled deeply before passing it to him.

"Do you remember what you told me the other night?" I asked.

"Aw, man, I don't even know who you are."

"My name's Brad. We got high together out here a few nights ago. You locked yourself out and I helped you get back in. I borrowed that racist pamphlet from you."

"Oh, right! That was pretty great shit! Being white is great! Everyone else is horrible!"

I had come here with a mission and didn't want the conversation to take too many weird turns. I had to focus. Although if I'd provoked Kren into some kind of racist diatribe, it might have eased my conscience.

"Well," I said. "I . . . don't think you really have to worry about them around here."

"Prolly cause of the guy who wrote that book. He's like a fucking superhero!"

"Anyway, you mentioned to me that you were pretty sure you were gay."

"Yeah, man, did we suck each other's bathroom parts? I don't remember."

"No. My herpes was flared up pretty bad. But you said you had a hard time finding anyone around here."

"It's pretty dry, man. I used to get beat up just for asking dudes so I decided to stop. Somebody told me I should move to Dayton but I don't know."

"You don't need to move to Dayton. Besides, there are too many black people there."

"*Fuck!*"

"Don't worry. I think I've found someone who's interested."

"Really? Did you pimp me out?"

"It came up. I told him where you worked. Described you. He knew who you were. He's interested. Want to meet him?"

"I guess. Is he cool?"

"He's . . . older but, sure, he seemed all right. Into some kind of weird shit."

"I'm down."

"He wants to get together tomorrow night."

"I work tomorrow, man. This sucks."

"We'll just take the money out of the register so no one can steal it. Leave the doors open. People'll leave money if they take any-thing, right? Most people are pretty decent. It'll probably only be for a couple of hours anyway."

"Prolly wouldn't be a problem."

"So I can come over around seven and we can ride over there."

"Well, I only have a moped, so you'd need to drive."

"I think I can get us a ride."

"Awesome!" He took another massive hit of the joint. He'd nev-er handed it back to me. I was okay with that. I lit a cigarette.

Were it not for the fact that I was probably selling Kren into white slavery, I would have felt pretty good about arranging tomorrow evening. Like a matchmaker. As it was, I didn't really feel good. Unless relieved counts as good. It was something, at least.

I finished my cigarette and we went back into the store. I grabbed a case of beer and two packs of cigarettes from behind the counter. I anticipated a long night spent alone in my apartment wrestling with dread and felt like the beer would make it a little more bearable.

As I got close to my building, I thought I saw Barcie walk into it.

I thought about calling out to her but didn't. I just walked a little faster, thinking maybe I could catch her in the hall.

Once in the building I didn't see any sign of her.

I texted Dawn.

"Could've sworn I just saw Barcie."

She didn't respond.

A few hours later she sent a text that said, "UR high."

I didn't think I was anymore. But I *was* drunk. Very.

Dawn picked me up in the Mercedes. She drove me to the carryout. Kren was there. There was a customer at the register when I entered.

"You ready?" I asked.

Kren had dressed for the occasion. He wore a sleeveless black mesh shirt and skintight black skinny jeans. His hair had an abundance of some product holding it in place about six inches over his actual head.

"Yeah, man," he said. "A little nervous."

"Don't worry about it. Let's empty out that register."

Kren popped the register open.

"I can't put anything in my pockets, man. Pants are too tight."

"I'll hold on to it for you."

He handed me a few stacks of bills and I put them in my pockets.

"What about the change?" he asked.

"I'll hold on to that too."

He handed me handfuls of change and a couple rolls of quarters.

I went over to the drink station and grabbed a huge sixty-four-ounce cup.

"You have a marker or something?" I asked.

He rummaged around under the counter until he came up with a black Sharpie. He handed it to me and I scrawled 'HONESTY JAR' on the cup and, under that, 'Be back in a few.' That way anybody doing anything wrong would feel like they were always in danger of getting caught.

Kren wadded up his smock and shoved it under the counter. We headed for the front door, the cloud of Kren's cologne hanging around us.

I got in the back and let Kren have the passenger seat.

"Hey, Dawn," he said.

"Hi, Kren! Brad didn't tell me it was you we were picking up."

"Who's Brad?"

She hooked a thumb over her shoulder at me.

"Oh, right," Kren said. "So are you guys, like, going out?"

Dawn laughed.

"Yeah, he's kind of old," Kren said. "But, wait, didn't you marry Bando?"

"That's why I'm driving a Mercedes and you ride a moped. Call it a big head start."

Dawn and Kren had a light and mostly evasive conversation about what they'd been doing since high school. It was a pretty short conversation since the place we were going was less than a mile away and in the couple of months they'd been out of high school Kren had only gotten high and worked at the store and most of what Dawn had done was so hideous she couldn't really talk about it. It hadn't occurred to me we might actually be watching this in person. It had been my idea to escort Kren there because I couldn't really see him making it any other way, even though it was so close.

We pulled up to a gated driveway. The gate swung open and Dawn pulled around to the lush backyard of a Victorian mansion.

"Aw, man, this is Dr. Weishaupt's house! You didn't say anything about Dr. Weishaupt. He's *super* old and gross!"

"You don't have to do anything," Dawn said. "Brad can take your place. But, you know, older guy with a lot of money and experience . . . You could learn a lot from somebody like that. I mean, you could probably find yourself doing things like this all the time instead of working in that shitty carryout. How great would that be, huh? Your whole life could be like one big party. I guess I can drive you back to the store if you want me to."

He didn't take too long to think about it.

"I'll check it out," he said.

"You'll have a really amazing time," she said.

Kren got out of the car and adjusted his tight clothing. I was relieved Dawn didn't get out after him.

"We should hurry back so we can watch this," she said. "You want to get up front so I don't feel like a fucking chauffeur?"

I almost opened the back door to move up front that way but an overwhelming feeling stopped me. I didn't want to step on the ground surrounding this house. I felt immediately relieved I was not the one going in there. I didn't know if it was the house itself or the guy who lived here, but I felt a sense of evil.

So I crawled into the front seat.

"That's one way of doing it, I guess," Dawn said.

As she pulled away I looked toward the house to see Kren standing in front of the back door. I had the thought I might never see him again.

Dawn drove us back to her place. There were a number of cars in the driveway.

"The Sheriff here?" I asked.

"He's in Columbus for something called sensitivity training."

We walked into her house. Voices came from the kitchen. Stasia came out to greet us.

"Plopsy's already downstairs with the girls. I made popcorn. A lot of it. I didn't know if you were serious or not."

"I'd love some," I said. I was starving and a little nervous. Eating sounded like a good idea.

"Follow me," she said.

"I'm gonna go on down," Dawn said. "It's probably going to be starting soon. Don't you lovebirds get into any more trouble."

I followed Stasia into the kitchen and loaded up a bowl of popcorn from the nearly industrial-sized drum she'd filled.

"There's beer in the cooler there."

I grabbed a couple of those too.

"Hey," I said. I was going to apologize for spreading the photos of us fucking but stopped myself. I figured she knew I took them but we were both pretty drunk so maybe she didn't. It was possible she didn't know I'd sent them to anyone, even though her supposed friend was the one lording them over my head.

"Yeah?" she said.

"Never mind."

"Don't worry," she said. "Larry's not here."

"It wasn't that."

"Okay. You seem nervous. I thought maybe that was why. I guess we should probably get down there."

"Are you—"

"Not now." Her eyes flicked up toward a camera and I got what she meant.

I wasn't even sure what I was going to ask her:

"Are you Dawn's new girlfriend?"

"Are you being blackmailed too?"

"Are you a human or a monster?"

"Are you really a Nazi?"

I followed Stasia down to the lower level and crossed the rec room. She pulled open a heavy door and held it for me, since my hands were full. My pants were so loaded with money and change it felt like they were about to fall down. I entered some kind of mini-theater, about the size of the few art houses I'd been in. There were maybe twenty-five seats, larger and more comfortable looking than in most theaters. The huge screen flickered on the wall. Right now the only thing on the screen was a well-lit room, which seemed to be some kind of sex dungeon. There were maybe about ten people in the theater. Plopsy sat in the front row like a soft boulder. Most of the others were the young prostitutes. Dawn sat in the middle of the back row. I sat next to her. Stasia sat to my left.

Eventually Kren entered the well-lit room, followed by Dr. Weishaupt. He was a thin, wraithlike old man. Kren seemed drugged, wandering around the room and looking at the cuffs and chains hanging from the ceiling, running his hand along something that looked like a stainless steel autopsy table.

"Wow," he marveled.

Dr. Weishaupt slowly removed his clothes, methodically folding them and placing them off screen.

"You're really into all this stuff, huh?" Kren asked.

"I think I'm going to have to put something in that mouth of yours to keep those words from coming out."

Kren turned away from the cross with shackles he was examining to look at Weishaupt, who stood with his hands on his hips sporting an impossibly huge erection.

"Get on your knees, boy."

Kren obediently dropped to his knees.

I don't know how long it all went on. Two to three hours, at least. I dozed off at one point and woke to Dawn jostling me awake. It was still going on. I drank my beer and ate popcorn. The people around me, all women, laughed and responded as though they were watching any feature film at a theater.

The good news was that Weishaupt didn't seem to kill Kren. His acts became increasingly degrading and sadistic as the scene ground on. By the time it ended, Kren was shackled to the table, a ball gag in his mouth, completely naked, bleeding and covered with shit (Weishaupt's) and piss (also Weishaupt's) and vomit (his own).

I felt nearly comatose. I stood up and stretched, wondering why my pants felt so heavy, until remembering the pockets were filled with bills and change from the carryout. I still didn't know if I was going to give it back or not. Probably not unless Kren asked for it.

"You did pretty good," Dawn said. "Maybe I should turn you into a recruiter."

I wasn't sure Dawn had ever given me a compliment before.

"Thanks," I said.

"Don't get cocky," she said.

"What now?"

"I've got some things to do. There are drinks and shit upstairs."

Another beer sounded great. And I really needed a cigarette.

I grabbed a beer from the kitchen and went out to the front porch and smoked a cigarette. The one girl who'd approached me for a cigarette at the party the one night came out and I gave her another one. This time I didn't even attempt to engage her in conversation. She stood next to me, smoking, and I thought I could smell the machine oil coming from her. Maybe it was just the cigarette smoke. Maybe it was my imagination.

About halfway through the cigarette, Plopsy trundled out, holding her sizeable stomach. I thought about taking Barcie to the hospital only days before she'd apparently died. I wondered if Plopsy enjoyed having random dead animals shoved up inside of her as well.

Plopsy seemed like an odd successor to Barcie. Opposite in almost every way. And she didn't seem oversexualized like the rest of Dawn's gang.

She continued to wander around in the turnaround of the driveway, holding her stomach and moaning. I thought about asking her if she was okay but I didn't really care. Plopsy seemed mean.

I tossed my cigarette out into the yard. The girl had already disappeared back into the house. I wondered if she had a bellybutton. If she didn't, what did that mean? I took a sip of my cold beer and contemplated smoking another cigarette but Plopsy's distressed presence made me uncomfortable. Besides, it didn't seem like there was really a lot going on and I didn't really think I'd been around Dawn when there wasn't much going on or I wasn't incredibly fucked up. I imagined she had somehow engineered it that way.

It looked like most of the girls were in the living room, dancing oddly to infuriatingly minimal electronic music, their limbs liquid, their eyes vacant.

I went into the kitchen to grab another beer, the very first fingers of intoxication beginning to knead my head.

One of the girls was in the kitchen amidst a loud noise. I couldn't figure out where the noise was coming from until I noticed the girl pulling stuff from the refrigerator and jamming it into the sink. The garbage disposal was what was making the noise. I walked over to the sink and turned the garbage disposal off. The girl froze and straightened up. It looked like she had been in the process of feeding a can of biscuits to the disposal.

She didn't look at me. Just continued staring at the half-devoured can of biscuits with what I projected as a longing look. The air from the can made a weird wheezing sound.

"Have you seen Dawn?" I asked.

The girl still didn't look at me or answer me.

I poked her in the arm. Maybe she only responded to commands, not questions.

"Suck my cock," I said.

She immediately turned toward me and dropped to her knees. I had to stop her before she actually started.

"Never mind. Stand up."

She stood up but continued looking at me.

"Tell me where Dawn is."

The girl pointed up.

"Thanks." I turned the garbage disposal back on and she went back to feeding the can of biscuits to it.

I went up a small flight of stairs. Dawn's house was many floors connected by a series of half-flights of stairs. There was probably a name for that kind of house.

I hadn't been this far into it before. This was probably the floor with the bedrooms on it. The thought of being near Dawn's bedroom excited me a little even though this was probably where she had sex with Sheriff Bando, even though she said she didn't.

Slapping and moaning came from farther down the hall. A door was open, bright light spilling from it. I moved to the doorway and looked in.

The room was bedecked with swastika banners and a large poster of Hitler at a Nazi rally. Dawn stood near the doorway with her camera trained toward the center of the room. Stasia was on her knees. Her top was pulled down over her breasts and her jeans were unbuttoned and unzipped. Three well-muscled and naked black men surrounded her. She had one of their cocks in her mouth while a second man pushed her head from behind and the third stood beside her and stroked himself.

Dawn, spotting me skulking at the door, set the tripod down and came over.

"What are you doing up here?" she said.

"I don't know. Just wanted to see what you were doing."

"I'm busy. Obviously. Go back downstairs. You can mess around with the girls if you want. Keep your phone on you."

I took one last look in the room to see the man whose cock Stasia had been sucking slap her in the face several times with it. Then she spit on him and he crammed his cock back into her mouth. I headed back down the hall.

In the living room the girls were still dancing. A few of them had removed most of their clothes. There were two couples making out—one couple standing up, the other couple on the couch. The erection that had begun with seeing Stasia on her knees was now fully formed.

I wandered around the room, inconspicuously bending and checking the naked ones' bellybuttons. The light was low so I couldn't be entirely sure, but I didn't think any of them had navels. They all had piercings—large green jewels, for the most part—to possibly distract the eye from noticing their lack of bellybuttons. Maybe I should have been repulsed but I wasn't. I was out of my head with lust, like they exuded some kind of aphrodisiac.

I stripped off my clothes, thankful for the dimness of the room. Still, if this were a room of normal girls, I never would have done that for fear of embarrassment.

I went over to the couple on the couch. The girl on top was busy sliding the girl on the bottom's shorts down her hips. I watched her do this while guiding my cock toward the girl on the bottom's mouth. She quickly and expertly took me in. The top girl finished removing the bottom's shorts and underwear and began licking her pussy.

Much like the other night with the other girl, there was a part of me that couldn't believe this was happening. I thought of the old clichéd adage, "If it's too good to be true then it probably is," and added to that my favorite adage of all time: "Fuck it." I was just drunk enough to not really care too much and what this girl was doing to me felt amazing. I fucked the slight suction of her mouth with the length of my cock, watching as her stomach muscles tensed, watching the back of the other girl's head as she worked on her cunt. It wasn't long before I felt like I was going to come so I pulled my cock out of her mouth.

I went around to the back of the girl on top. I watched her ass as she continued working on the bottom girl. The bottom girl moaned and lifted up her shirt to play with her nipples. I reached around and unfastened the other girl's shorts, sliding them over her ass. She wore a pair of white underwear. I pulled those down to the base of her ass and ran a couple fingers along her labia, sticking my middle finger into her tight cunt. I clutched myself with my right hand and pressed into her.

A few girls stood around the couch watching us.

I fucked her harder and harder until I was nearly ready to explode.

I pulled out of her and turned to the girls who were watching.

The girl who'd been in the kitchen feeding things into the garbage disposal was on the far left.

"I want you to suck me off," I said.

She obediently approached me and dropped to her knees. She took me into her mouth and I wrapped my hands around the back of her head and pressed my cock in until she gagged.

On the verge of coming, I heard an angry Dawn say, "Goddammit! I thought I told you to keep your phone on you! I've texted you like ten times."

She approached the girl attached to my shriveling dick and shoved her away by the forehead. She fell to the floor and the two girls who'd been on the couch swarmed her and began removing her clothes.

"Follow me," Dawn said. She held a camera in one hand and a chain in the other.

I went over to my clothes and Dawn said, "There's no time for that."

I followed her through the kitchen and outside.

Plopsy was still out there. She was on her hands and knees on the manicured grass at the center of the turnaround. Her dress was hiked up around her waist. Dawn moved over top of her and turned the light on the camera on. It lit up Plopsy's ass in a harsh bright light. There was some kind of bright green discharge oozing from Plopsy's vagina. That killed what remained of my erection.

"You gotta push, Plopsy! Push!"

"It fuckin hurts!" Plopsy said. "Fuckin hurts like fuck!" Now her cheek was against the grass, her huge rump stuck up in the air.

"I told you it wouldn't be easy."

Dawn brought the chain down hard across Plopsy's upper back.

"Oh, God, please make it stop!" Plopsy cried out again.

"Push, dammit!" Dawn barked and hit her with the chain again.

Plopsy made a strained grunting noise and I saw something press from the inside of her dilated vagina.

Dawn hit her with the chain again. Plopsy held two fistfuls of grass. Blubbering and drooling, she again heaved and I saw whatever was in her break the surface of her vagina.

Dawn looked at me and said, "Get over here."

I was too dazed to move. I barely registered her speaking to me.

"Now!"

I slowly approached whatever abomination was happening in front of me.

"You've got to grab it," Dawn said.

"Grab what!" I was on the verge of hysteria. I wondered if Dawn was trying to permanently ruin sex for me and then felt ridiculous for even thinking that.

"The head! Wrap your hands around it and pull. You won't hurt it."

This was the first time it had occurred to me that Plopsy was giving birth. I didn't even think of an actual baby because as I bent down to take hold of the head, it was so much larger than what I imagined a baby's head would be.

Suddenly glad I wasn't wearing any clothes, I slid my hands in between Plopsy's dilated labia and the head. It was warm and slimy.

Dawn hit Plopsy with the chain again.

"You have to pull when she pushes," Dawn said.

I got as much of a grip on the head as I could. Dawn brought the chain down again and I leaned back.

I pulled about two feet of whatever was in Plopsy out before my hands slid off and I went staggering back, landing on my ass.

Whatever was in her was . . . not normal. I didn't even think it was human. It was glowing green and hairless, and the parts of it that were outside of Plopsy were bone thin.

I continued sitting on my ass and watching as it began digging its sharp elbows into the grass, pulling itself out of Plopsy. I feared it was coming toward me but I was too paralyzed to move.

Finally, with a sickening popping sound, perhaps imagined, it pulled itself from Plopsy and continued crawling toward me.

Dawn now straddled the thing, bringing her chain down on its head until it was a quivering heap in the grass, an acrid vapor rising from its body.

I leaned over and vomited up all the beer I had drank that night.

I stood up on shaky legs and watched as Dawn scanned the whole incident with her camera.

"What is it?" I said.

"Dead, hopefully. A parasite. But it could have been a beautiful girl."

I thought about what I'd been doing to the girls in the house only a few minutes before and shuddered.

"I'm gonna need you to run Plopsy to the hospital. They'll know how to take care of her."

I was going to say no way but I wasn't wearing any clothes and Dawn was holding the chain.

I headed back toward the house.

"Where are you going?" Dawn asked.

"To get my clothes."

"Afraid not."

She tossed her keys to me.

I wasn't planning on driving Plopsy to the hospital but I didn't think I'd get too far in the car with no clothes, money, wallet, or phone.

I felt drained and exhausted.

Plopsy was collapsed on the grass.

I nudged her with my foot. "Can you walk to the car?"

"Help her up, for fuck's sake. She's not a monster just because she's fat."

I thought of her as a monster for reasons other than that, not the least of which was what I'd just seen her do.

I bent down over her, grasped her under the arms and did my best to heave her up.

She got up to her knees before collapsing back onto the grass.

I went over to the car, started it, and pulled up right next to her. I got out and again tried to help her up. This time I managed to get her to the car and she collapsed into it.

I was too mad to even look at Dawn. I got in the car and furiously sped down the driveway.

I began driving toward Dayton but felt exhausted. I turned down a wooded side road. I pulled the car onto the shoulder. After making sure I didn't see any lights coming from either direction, I got out of the car and went to the passenger side. I opened the door and Plopsy practically tumbled out.

Easy enough, I thought.

I dragged her into a ditch at the side of the road. I patted down her dress and found her phone. I activated the screen and pressed the emergency icon. Then I dropped the phone into the ditch with her, got back in the car, and drove back to my apartment.

I freaked out when I realized I didn't have my keys. I wasn't going back to Dawn's. I wanted to but felt like she would know what I did to Plopsy and there would be some form of punishment involved. I got out of the car and glanced up and down the street to make sure there were no cars or pedestrians. It was late enough this wasn't a problem. There weren't even many lights on. I went to the front of the apartment and started hitting buzzers. While standing there, a teenage boy came running down the street. He wore regular clothes and breathed heavily. No one was chasing him and he didn't notice me.

"Yeah?" a voice came through the speaker.

"Sorry to bother you. It's Brad Renfield from 2B. I seem to have locked myself out."

There was no other response other than the clicking of the door unlocking.

I got to my apartment and forced the door open. Luckily, everything used to construct this building was so cheap I was able to do it with minimal commotion.

I felt like I'd be able to sleep for a week.

SHERIFF BANDO

I felt isolated with no phone, wallet, money, or internet. I found a certain amount of comfort in this isolation.

I thought Dawn would probably get in touch with me right away, if only to exact some form of punishment or the other but I hadn't heard from her. Of course, there was really no way for me to hear from her unless she showed up. I did check out front to see if the car was still there, but it was gone.

I couldn't even think about what I had seen happen with Plopsy. There would have been a time when I would have obsessed upon it and let it terrify me. I was surprised at how easily I was able to put it out of my head. I thought, not for the first time, that Dawn was training me for something. Like everything I'd seen and done had prepared me to not really be shocked by much. My conscience, dubious to begin with, was being drained away.

I cleaned the apartment really well.

I listened to the music I had on vinyl since I didn't have any way of streaming anything.

I finished the Murakami book and debated finding another book to read but decided not to. I had read the few books I had in my apartment. I only kept the ones I'd really liked and was always leery about re-reading anything because I was afraid I wouldn't like it as much the second time around. There was something depressing about art losing its magic.

I masturbated once but couldn't think about anything except Dawn and her creepy girl army and, after I came, I still found myself thinking about them. It was like you couldn't get enough and would always want more. I decided not to jerk off again. Besides, it kind of burned.

I had smoked through all the butts I had left in the ashtray and managed to last about twenty-four hours before I wanted another one so much I was willing to leave my apartment. My only option was if Kren was working, since he'd have to basically just give me a pack.

I'd pick up some beer if he were there too.

Once I mustered up the energy, I left the apartment.

The afternoon air was stifling. By the time I reached the carryout, I was sweaty and my clothes were sticking to me.

Kren was not behind the counter. Instead there was a balding, middle-aged woman who only had one arm. Although the air conditioning in the store felt great, I didn't waste any time looking around and pretending I had the money to buy anything.

I walked to the counter.

"Is Kren working tonight?"

"Nope. He don't work here no more."

"Really?" I don't know why this alarmed me so much. I guess I saw Kren becoming a high profile male prostitute while holding down his position at the carryout to stay in touch with his roots. Of course, he could also be dead.

"He ain't showed up the past two days."

"Okay. Thanks."

I turned to leave.

"Wanna touch my stump?"

I turned back to the woman, thinking I couldn't have possibly heard her correctly. "Sorry?"

"I ast if you wanted to touch my stump." She held her stump arm toward me to make her point. "I'd let you rub it real good."

My first instinct was to get the fuck out of there as quickly as possible but, dammit, I'd come for a pack of cigarettes.

"Will you give me a pack of cigarettes if I do?" I felt like the absolute cheapest, lowest form of whore at that point.

"Ain't none of this stuff mine. I'll let you take whatever you want."

With employees like Kren and this woman, how did this place even continue to exist? It was like whoever owned the store hired the worst person he or she could find for the job.

"Where do you want me to do it?" I walked back toward the counter.

"Better go back to the break room."

She reached below the counter to grab something and came up with the honesty cup. It was flattering to see it become a fixture.

She came out from behind the counter and I followed her back to the break room. She was about twice as wide as me.

She pulled a molded plastic chair out into the middle of the brightly lit room. I noted the absence of vending machines, coffee makers, or microwaves before realizing they didn't need them. A carryout was pretty much a public break room. They already had all that stuff.

She sat down heavily in the chair and waggled her stump at me.

"All right," she said. "Here ya go."

I moved closer to her. She smelled like a bar. An overpowering smell of smoke clinging to her hair and clothes with hints of booze and sweat and a faint back note of something that reminded me of urinal cakes.

I'd never felt a stump before and found myself genuinely curious. I reached out and touched it with my fingertips.

"Get in there good," she said. "No need to be gentle."

She unbuttoned her pants and slid her one hand into them, an even more vile smell rising from her.

I palmed her stump and began squeezing it. I made a mental grocery list. Might as well grab some food while I was here.

"Wanna know how I lost it?"

"What?" I was thinking about bread.

"Want to know how I lost my arm?"

Not really, I thought. *I want to keep all the stuff I'm going to rob from you locked in my head so I don't forget anything.*

"Sure," I said.

"I went to my doctor up at The Point a few years ago cause I thought I was gettin that corporate funnel syndrome. He tells me he thinks it's a lot more severe than that n wants me to get x-rays of it. So I do that thinkin they just want some way to make a little more money off me and he comes back and tells me there's some kind of *worm* livin in my arm!" She rubbed herself quickly, almost angrily. I lit into the stump with the same passion. "So he tells me they need to operate right away or it's gonna come out through my pussy and I might die and I go in the next morning and they put me under n when I wake up I only got one arm!"

She shuddered with a rapid climax and I felt a sticky substance against the palm of my hand. I quickly pulled it away and watched an anemic waterfall of sickening greenish brown liquid ooze from her stump.

I searched the break room for a paper towel or napkin while she sat in the chair with a far away look in her eyes.

"I hope I lose the other arm one day," she said softly.

I wiped my hand off and got out of the break room before I threw up. I marched up to the counter and grabbed a couple of bags and a carton of cigarettes and quickly filled the bags as full as possible. I went back to the coolers and grabbed a case of Bud and got out of the carryout as fast as I could. She hadn't come back up front the rest of the time I was there. That made things a lot less awkward.

When I got back to the apartment, there was a sky blue Xeroxed flyer taped to the door of the building.

It said:

ARE PLAGUED BY **DEMONS** OR **WITCHES**???
BLACK MAGIC RUINING YOUR LIFE???

CONTACT **DR. BLAST** TODAY AND

LIFT

THE

CURSE!!!

Below the text was a black and blue photo of an affable looking bearded man wearing a turban and at the bottom were a number of tabs with a phone number on them.

I ripped the whole sheet down and stuffed it into one of my bags.

Maybe I was cursed.

If so, I had no way of contacting this Dr. Blast character to lift the curse. Even if I could contact him, I had no way of getting to him or paying him so I guessed I'd just have to remain cursed.

Back in the apartment, I dived into my bags of junk food and the beer, taking breaks to smoke, lifting the curse the only way I knew how.

A couple days later I had a dream I was at the dentist's office. I had some kind of apparatus on my head holding my mouth open and the doctor was in the process of shoving a severed hand down my throat. I wanted to tell him I couldn't breathe but couldn't make any coherent sounds come out.

I woke up to the crushing weight of Plopsy on my chest, her meaty hands wrapped around my throat.

Once she noticed I was awake, she took her hands away but didn't get off.

"Dawn told me to come and get you," she said.

I was slightly hungover and sick with junk food. I couldn't remember the last time I'd had a shower.

"Okay." My voice felt hoarse and weak. "What time is it?"

"Late. Almost dark."

"Do you mind getting off me? I think I'm going to be sick."

She hoisted herself off me and fell to the floor. She struggled to stand up and I felt really embarrassed for her. She was remarkably thinner than she had been, but still pretty large.

"I'm gonna have to take a shower," I said.

"No rush," she said.

I went into the bathroom to vomit and brush my teeth and take a quick shower.

I expected to find Plopsy powered down and standing in the middle of my apartment staring into space in a slightly unfocused manner.

Instead she had her dress hiked up and was rubbing her vagina against a Chet Atkins record.

"I got bored," she said. "So I was puttin my pussy on stuff."

"Yeah. That's fine."

I held out my hand and she gave me the record. I walked into the kitchen area and threw it in the trash.

I followed Plopsy out to the former police car. I sat in the passenger seat, not feeling all that great. Plopsy drove to a McDonald's on the outskirts of Gethsemane and ordered an abundance of food. She didn't offer me any of it. I was okay with that. I'd eaten so much shit since rubbing that woman's stump the idea of eating any more bad food made me queasy.

By the time we got to Dawn's house I was really excited to see her.

Plopsy didn't knock or anything, managing to get the door open with her two bags of food and massive soda.

Dawn was waiting for us.

She looked really good in a tiny pair of denim shorts and white t-shirt so tight I could make out her darker colored bra beneath it.

"Hey," I said, trying not to sound too needy.

"Follow me," she said.

She wasn't wearing any shoes. I didn't have a foot fetish and I'd had my mouth on her pussy but, still, the sight of her naked feet excited me.

Christ, I needed to start jerking off more.

Plopsy didn't follow us. I imagined she was going to go dig in to all that food.

I followed Dawn downstairs and through the rec room and into a small bathroom next to the office she'd taken me into the one day.

"I know you want me," she said.

It was true. I didn't say anything.

"So I want to play a game. The winner gets me."

I wasn't a competitive person and had no idea what game she wanted to play.

"What's the game?" I asked.

"I'm going to get into the bathtub. Someone else is going to come in. The first one of you who pisses on me gets to fuck me."

I was a bit lost for words. I felt relieved it didn't involve killing animals or beating people in the face with a chain but knew I could never win. I could barely piss at a public urinal if there was anybody else in the bathroom. I didn't see how I could possibly stand next to another man and piss on a girl I was more or less obsessed with. That was a lot of pressure. There was also the thought of someone else having sex with her if I lost. That lit a sort of jealous rage in me and maybe that was her whole point. I knew the jealousy was unreasonable. Dawn had never expressed the least sexual interest in anything other than my tongue, I knew she was married, and she'd also repeatedly told me she wasn't into any guys. Well, I guess she'd admitted being into one guy, her pimp or whatever from her delinquent days, but I'd assumed that story was mostly bullshit.

"If that's what you want," I said.

"And the loser has to watch the winner fuck me."

She probably meant this to be a huge deterrent to losing but the thought of seeing her actually get fucked by anyone, seeing her with more than just her pants off, seeing her penetrated, excited me quite a bit. Men are animals.

"Okay," I said. "We doing this now?"

She nodded, looking deep into my eyes.

"You can come in now," she called outside the bathroom.

Suddenly White Power Larry was filling the doorway and my little pussy heart was suddenly hammering. I wondered what Stasia thought about this and remembered the last time I'd seen her she was getting fucked by three large black guys.

Dawn got into the bathtub and lay down.

"Why don't you take off yer clothes, honey," White Power Larry said.

"Come on now," she said in an almost purring sexual voice I'd never heard her use before. "I don't want to ruin the surprise."

Larry moved up to the side of the tub and began unfastening his black cargo pants. I moved to his right and began unfastening mine with shaky hands.

I didn't even have to piss. I'd peed before leaving the apartment and hadn't even drunk anything since.

Larry was probably full of Jagermeister and hate. He probably pissed on people all the time. I'd never pissed on anyone. Maybe as a kid. Not with anything sexual in mind. Not that this felt very sexual.

I flopped my sad dick out and tried my best not to look over at Larry's. Not only did I imagine he was much larger than me, I was pretty sure he would lynch me for even glancing.

"May the best man win," she said.

"Win what?" a voice said from the doorway of the bathroom.

Larry and I both turned toward it.

I wondered if Larry was as panicked as I was.

Sheriff Bando stood in the doorway.

"Larry?" Bando said. "Dawn? What the fuck is going on?"

He moved into the bathroom and realization broke across his face.

"This is *sick*," he said.

Maybe him saying that meant he was into it. I remembered the night Barcie and I had run into Bando in the field. I remembered her coming back bruised and covered in shit.

Larry had already hoisted up his pants and quickly shoved past Bando.

Did that mean I won by default?

Looking at Bando's angry red face, I should have been worrying about a lot more.

"What's wrong, baby," Dawn said in the same voice she'd used with Larry earlier.

The thought of watching Dawn and her old husband have some kind of marital tiff was almost as menacing as getting murdered by Sheriff Bando. I knew it would probably get me the chain, but I bolted for the door anyway.

And was blocked by the solid flesh wall of Bando.

He grabbed me around the arm and drove me to the floor. He dropped on top of me, yanked my arms behind my back, and quickly fastened handcuffs around my wrists. This was something he'd probably never had to do before and, fresh from sensitivity training, he seemed extremely brutal.

Dawn now stood above us.

"You gonna hurt him, baby? He was tryin to pee on me. I don't even know who he is. He just showed up with Larry."

"None of that is true," I think I said. I tried to say, anyway. I was nervous and panicked and it was hard to breathe.

"Shut the fuck up," Bando said. "I know who this piece of shit is. I should have arrested him when I caught him gettin Barcie wasted that one night."

"I'm so sorry, baby. Did I do somethin wrong?"

Bando dragged me out of the bathroom, lifted me up, and forced me into a chair.

He pulled his gun out, making the situation a thousand times tenser.

"Now don't do nothin stupid," Dawn said.

"I think the stupidest thing I did was marrying you."

Dawn was still in the bathroom and I couldn't see her. Bando aimed the gun into the bathroom and fired three times.

Holy fuck.

The sound was deafening. I'd heard gunshots before, but never up this close. The smell of burning machine oil filled the room. Maybe this was what I'd always heard described as 'cordite' in crime novels. I was doomed.

I thought about bolting but Bando now stood only a couple of feet in front of me.

"Don't move," he said. "I just want to talk."

My whole body was vibrating. I might have been crying. This was not how I expected the night to go.

"How long have you been fucking her?" he said.

"I . . . I haven't."

"Don't lie."

"I'm not. I swear."

"Larry's probably been fucking her for a while. He's my best friend. Or, at least, I thought he was. Were you guy's gonna fuck her together?"

"No. I . . . didn't know that was going to happen."

I thought I could tell him the truth—that she occasionally had me go down on her—but didn't see how that would help things.

"I've never fucked her. Maybe I should do it now but . . . I'm too sad. I should have known something was wrong. She said she had a condition. Didn't like to be touched. I married her anyway. She said she loved me. Said she'd love me forever. And we were good to each other. She was nice to me. I thought she'd cave in eventually but the most she'd ever do was watch me jerk off. I was forced to lower myself and bed the dirtiest of whores. I confessed every time. I couldn't keep anything from her. She never judged me. You know, people think she married me for the money but she has a lot more money than me. I don't know where it comes from. I probably should have looked into that too."

Bando was now crying and that further complicated my assessment of the situation.

"I thought she'd be with me when I retired," he blubbered. "Thought we'd travel together. Now I have nothing. Nothing. Oh God, what have I done?"

"I . . . I'm really sorry," I said.

There were too many things to process. Bando had distracted me with his talking and I could barely think about Dawn being dead.

What was I going to do?

"She was everything to me. And now she's ruined my life. Made me into a murderer. I think she needs to give me something. She owes me." His blubbering turned into a steely resolve.

He came toward me and I thought it was going to be all over. Instead he put the gun on my lap. I stared down at it, completely aware of its deadly weight.

He disappeared into the bathroom and came back out carrying Dawn. He laid her down on the floor.

There were three large bloodstains on her chest. Blood soaked into the carpet.

He got down on his knees, still weeping, and unbuttoned and unzipped her shorts, tugging them down her legs. Her underwear came down partway with them. He hooked his fingers into the waistband of those and pulled them down. He wiped his tears away, the look of miserable sadness suddenly replaced with one of excited frenzy.

He straightened up and began fumbling with his belt.

I glanced at Dawn's face.

Her eyes were open.

And moving.

She was alive.

Once Bando's pants were undone he looked at Dawn.

She had raised herself up onto her elbows.

Bando began trembling.

He stood up and fastened his pants.

"What the hell are you?" he said.

Dawn didn't say anything.

Bando took a couple steps toward me and grabbed the gun from my lap. I expected him to shoot Dawn again, but he plugged the gun into his mouth and blew his brains out.

I turned and vomited and sat in the chair shaking, my nerves completely shredded.

Dawn stood and approached Bando's body.

She nudged him with her foot.

"I think he's gone," she said. "Oh, before I forget . . ." She grabbed her shorts from the floor and grabbed my phone and keys from one of the pockets. She tossed them to me but since I didn't have my hands free, they hit me on the shoulder and fell to the floor.

"I had some money in those pants too."

"You did." She still stared down at Bando's lifeless body. "You don't anymore."

"Do you think you could undo my cuffs?"

"I'm going to have to call the cops. I think I should leave you like that. I don't want to tamper with anything."

"I'd like to leave before they get here."

"I can't let you do that. It's better to have a witness."

"What do you want me to tell them?"

"Tell them whatever you want."

"Should I tell them about why I'm here?"

"What? To piss on me?"

"Yeah."

"That's not really why you're here. *This* is why you're here." She again nudged Bando's body.

She grabbed her own phone from the pocket of her shorts and came over to me. She put one foot on the back of the chair and moved her vagina in front of my face. Just the familiar scent of her made me crazy. I eagerly began lapping at her, instantly hard. I forgot about what I'd just seen. Her juices were like a balm, quieting my nerves.

She called either the local police station or 911. I guess there wasn't really a need to call 911, since the emergency was over. Something about this was exciting her, although not outwardly or anything. She didn't even move her hips. But her juices mixed with my saliva and made a trail from her to my lap. I couldn't get enough.

"I need to report a suicide," she said. She did her best to sound sad and slightly panicked. She rattled off her address.

I continued to lick her until we heard sirens and then she stopped and said, "I need to change shirts."

Dawn dropped me off after midnight. I had to write a statement that was mostly true. I hadn't mentioned why I was there. I had put in the part about Bando shooting at Dawn but didn't offer any real speculation. The whole thing was a lot more cut and dried than I thought it would be. The major surprise following Bando's suicide was Plopsy's death. Maybe suicide. Maybe not. They actually found her body first, sitting on the couch in front of the TV, a sack of McDonald's congealing on her lap, and a look of utter terror twisting her dead face. One of the EMTs speculated that her heart had probably just given out. With her size, nobody bothered arguing with him.

Dawn got a lot of sympathetic hands to the upper arm. One of the cops gave her a hug I found mildly lecherous. I went to bed with her taste in my mouth, her smell on my lips, her juices dried to my chin. I masturbated and fell asleep.

TRAVIS

I woke up the next afternoon and discovered a red spot on my penis while taking a piss.

Great, I thought. *One of Dawn's girls has given me herpes.*

After taking a shower I decided I was coming down with the flu or something. My skin felt sensitive and my bones were achy.

It hurt to put on clothes so I didn't. For, like, three days.

I mostly just lay in bed and shivered with the fear.

It felt like something was coming to a head but I had no idea what it was. I found it impossible to think coherently about anything. I knew what I had seen. I had seen Dawn recover from three gunshot wounds as though they'd never happened. But the more I tried to think about it—the more I tried to think about what that could possibly mean—the foggier the memory became until I began questioning if it had happened at all.

Maybe I was just losing my fucking mind.

I thought jerking off might help me focus but every time I even contemplated it I saw that red bump and lost all desire.

I was pretty sure the bump was getting bigger.

Dawn didn't contact me. I felt cheated. I would have rather she picked me up every day and had me do terrible things rather than sitting around and wondering what she was doing.

I thought about putting on clothes and stealing a paper to see when Sheriff Bando's funeral was. I contemplated going if I hadn't already missed it. To help reaffirm its reality, if for no other reason.

By the time I was able to take a shower and put on clothes, I was so stir crazy I had to leave the apartment. Also, I discovered I didn't have any electricity that morning. It was probably time to go rub the stump again.

I walked to the Snack Barn. It was oppressively hot. Gethsemane was a ghost town.

At the carryout, there was no one behind the counter at all. Just the honesty cup. I almost felt bad about not honoring the honesty cup, since it was my idea, but I needed things like beer and cigarettes and food that didn't need cooking. I contemplated getting ice to keep the beer on but decided I was too weak to transport it back to the apartment.

When I was behind the counter getting my cigarettes, I saw an envelope on the counter. It was addressed to 'Kren Doll.' I figured it was probably a paycheck. Kren Doll. That couldn't be his real name.

I popped open the register and stuffed all the paper money in my pockets. Then I pocketed Kren's paycheck. I recognized the address. It was another small apartment building a couple blocks from mine.

I took my haul back to the apartment, quickly ate a Snickers bar and a Slim Jim, wondered how anyone was still alive if this was what they ate, and set out for Kren's.

On the way to Kren's I saw an elderly woman with her dress hiked up around her hips either pissing or shitting in her flowerbed. I wasn't close enough to tell. People weren't right anymore. Maybe we were living too long or something.

I entered Kren's building and walked up to his second floor apartment. I knocked on the door and waited for a while but there wasn't an answer. I thought about sliding the paycheck under the door but doubted Kren ever locked it, if he even knew how. I didn't even see how he was living on his own, but I was also living on my own and hadn't had a mature thought in over a decade.

His door was unlocked. I opened it and went in. It was a studio apartment similar to mine. Kren had a twin bed shoved against the far wall and there was no furniture anywhere. Just piles of things. A massive bong seemed to be the centerpiece for the apartment. A large TV had a scene frozen from a video game bouncing around on it. There was a large swastika flag hanging on a wall near the kitchen area. There was also a large poster of Hitler and what looked like pages ripped from White Power Larry's pamphlet taped around the swastika flag. I walked over to the bed and tossed the envelope onto it. Their was a spiral bound notebook on the floor, opened to a page that just said 'Kren Loves Weishaupt' over and over in what was a surprisingly girlish and legible script. Just being in Kren's apartment felt like it was enough to provoke some sort of identity crisis.

I noticed a laptop sitting on the floor. I felt like there were things I wanted to look up or research but by the time I actually sat on the floor and opened the laptop my mind had gone blank so I spent nearly two hours watching hidden cam public pool videos and people eating until throwing up. Then I Googled 'how to be a terrorist' a hundred times and closed the laptop. I spent a few minutes quickly ransacking the apartment for money but didn't turn up anything. I had to piss before I left and relieved myself on Kren's bed. The spot on my cock reminded me that I wanted to look up images of herpes but then I decided I didn't really want to know.

Also, I couldn't be sure, but it looked like it had changed colors.

On my way home, a car full of teenagers passed a seven-year-old girl playing in her yard and shouted, "Show us your tits!" but they didn't stop the car and the girl probably didn't have tits anyway. Or maybe she did, what with all the hormones in milk nowadays.

I got back to my apartment and hit the beer pretty hard.

It felt like my bladder was going to explode. I had my underwear down before even lifting the seat of the toilet. The piss came shooting out the tip of my cock like water from a showerhead, in all different directions instead of a single, concentrated stream.

My cock . . . What was happening to it?

I held myself with one hand while keeping myself upright by placing the other hand on the vanity, studying my cock while dealing with the burning pain.

The red spot had grown considerably and I was pretty sure the whole thing was swollen. The head of my cock seemed to be about twice as large as it had been and there was an irregular-shaped bulge midway down the shaft. By the time I was finished, I was just glad I hadn't pissed a gallon of blood.

I was pretty sure the red spot now had a greenish hue.

I took off my shirt and studied my torso in the mirror. I turned around. I had two more green spots on my upper back, roughly where the lingering scars from the chain were.

I went into the kitchen, ate half a bag of Doritos and drank some tap water. Coffee would have been great but I didn't have any way of making it. I felt shaky and weak. The flyer for Dr. Blast still lay on the counter. I considered the fact that Dawn was quite possibly a witch and I quite possibly had some sort of demon in me. Or maybe even that she had infected me with something. I'm not sure why I was drawn to the flyer. I wasn't really a believer in those types of things. At that exact moment, though, what I really focused on was the title 'doctor.' Was this guy actually a doctor? Did it really matter? I felt like I would need someone to look at my cock eventually. Not to mention those things on my back. I didn't think it would be possible to make an appointment with any of the doctors in Gethsemane without insurance. Other than my pediatrician, I wasn't even sure there were any doctors besides Weishaupt in Gethsemane. And the way I'd felt when we'd dropped Kren off at his house prevented me from even considering him. I knew I could go to The Point in Dayton and probably have it looked at, but I'd walk away with a bill so large I'd never be able to pay it off. Or I'd end up becoming some test subject or research experiment. Fuck. Maybe I already was.

I tore one of the phone number tabs off the flyer and took it to bed with me. I'm not sure why I didn't just take the whole thing with me. I collapsed back into my bed, checking my phone for any messages. Of course there weren't any.

I sent a text to Dawn.

"What the hell did you do to me?"

She didn't respond.

I lay there in my semi-darkened apartment, clutching the phone to my chest, obsessing about my cock even more than I normally obsessed about it, pretty sure I could feel the spots on my back growing and moving, until I dozed off.

I had to piss again when I woke up. That basic bodily function now filled me with dread.

This time the situation in the bathroom was even worse.

My entire cock was now swollen to nearly double its size, covered in large knots and bumps. Still no blood, thankfully, but the pain of the experience filled me with nausea.

I was thirsty and hungry but I didn't want to drink or eat anything because that would just make me have to pee again.

Dawn still hadn't responded to my text.

I texted her again.

"I think I need to go to the doctor."

I dozed off again, conscious of the throbbing, burning sensation in my cock.

I woke up to a darkened room.

I checked my phone for messages.

Still nothing.

My door was open. I thought about getting up to close it but felt frozen in place.

I went back to sleep and dreamt that everyone in the building took turns standing in my doorway staring at me. Then they went back to their apartments, opened their laptops, and continued watching me.

When I woke up around noon the next day my door was closed. Since I wasn't wearing any clothes, I was immediately aware of the horror show between my legs. My cock hadn't improved. I went to piss and painfully squeezed out a few bright yellow drops that seemed barely liquid.

The original red spot was now definitely green.

Red means stop. Green means go.

I went into the kitchen and had more Doritos and water. I decided to put on clothes. My cock had changed so much my pants fit differently.

Out of boredom and possibly some misguided sense of self-preservation I decided to call Dr. Blast.

"Hello. Thank you for calling the office of the Righteous and Honorable Dr. Blast. How may I help you?"

The voice was weird. It sounded like a man impersonating a woman and I wondered if this wasn't Dr. Blast himself.

"Um, yeah." I cleared my throat. I didn't know how long it had been since I'd said anything out loud. "I'd like to make an appointment."

"There's no need. Come by whenever it suits you."

"Um . . ."

"What's the worst that could happen? Maybe you have to wait for a few minutes. We all have time to wait, don't we?"

I definitely did have time to wait but wondered how many other people felt like they did.

"I don't suppose you make house calls, do you?"

"I'm sorry. We don't. The good doctor has a touch of agoraphobia. Also, much of his diagnosis is based on geographically specific data."

Geographically specific data? What the fuck did that mean?

"Okay. And what are his rates?"

"That's negotiable."

"I don't have a lot of money."

"We can discuss it at your appointment."

I got the address and hung up. I was hoping it would be within walking distance but was expecting it to be in some place like Twin Springs or one of the more posh suburbs of Dayton. But it wasn't in either of those places. It was in a suburb of East Dayton. I didn't think it was a particularly nice one.

I made it a goal to get there. What else did I have to do besides waiting around for my dick to mutate further?

I didn't feel like I had a lot left in me. The only thing I could really think about was Dawn and I wasn't sure if I was getting anywhere with her. I wasn't sure how it was going to end. Maybe that was what made it exciting.

I grabbed my keys to the truck and went down to the street.

There were a number of fluorescent pink and yellow stickers stuck to the windows. I was pretty sure they could tow something if it hadn't moved in a few days and felt like maybe the only reason my truck hadn't been towed was because of Dawn's connections. I felt like it would be a good sign if it started.

It didn't.

I didn't bother taking the key back out of the ignition.

Maybe Kren could give me a ride.

I lit a cigarette and began walking to his building. The air was a little cooler than it had been. I didn't see a single person outside. I imagined everyone was either at work or inside a semi-darkened house, whacked on prescription meds and hunched over some screen or the other, indulging whatever was still able to ignite some sense of pleasure in them.

I got to Kren's building and went in. I knocked on his door. I was somewhat surprised when he answered it. He'd shaved his head.

"Hey, Kren," I said. "It's Brad. Remember me?"

"Yeah, man. Are you here to take me back to Weishaupt's place?"

"No. I didn't really have much to do with that. I need to borrow the moped."

"Aw, man, I totaled it."

"So . . . it doesn't even run?"

"No, man. I threw it in a dumpster. It was trashed. Where do you need to go?"

"I have a doctor's appointment in Dayton."

"Oh, but I have a car now. Weishaupt bought it for me."

I again thought of the weird evil feeling I'd gotten from Weishaupt and wasn't sure I wanted anything to do with anything he had a hand in. But I was desperate.

"That's great," I said. "Do you mind if I borrow it for a couple of hours?"

"You said you're going to Dayton?"

"Yeah."

"Maybe I could come along with you. You could show me how to get there?"

The thought of being in the car with Kren seemed mildly unendurable but he was doing me a favor so I acquiesced.

Kren went back into the apartment to put on a shirt and I followed him down to the parking lot.

When we got to his car, I said, "Dude, this is a Bentley."

"Yeah. I guess it's pretty nice. Better than the moped."

"It's a really expensive car. You could probably quit your job if you sold it."

"I already quit."

"Oh, yeah, I forgot."

"And I don't need it. Weishaupt gives me whatever I need. He says I never have to get a job if I don't want to."

"Maybe be careful around that guy."

"He's pretty fucking twisted!" Kren laughed. "But I like it. He's cool."

We got in the car and I put the address into the GPS app on my phone.

Fortunately Kren didn't talk a lot. We listened to some driving industrial sounding music with white power lyrics.

My phone's battery died and I panicked.

"Just put it in the car's GPS," Kren said. "I don't know how to use it, but I'm sure it has one."

"Right," I said.

It was really simple to use. Of course it was. This was a rich person's car and nothing was supposed to be difficult for the rich.

It was late afternoon by the time we took the Smithville Road exit off Route 35. We passed a Kroger that had ten police cars and three ambulances in the parking lot. Everyone walking around looked like they'd either just gotten out of prison or were about to do something that would send them to prison. Three hoodlums were playing leapfrog by a bus stop. We turned down a narrow street. There were a lot of obese people on their porches or in their yards.

"Jiggle Avenue," Kren said, looking at one morbidly obese teenager wearing skintight clothes and pushing a stroller. "You really have a doctor's appointment or are you just here to buy drugs?"

"This is the address they gave me."

We took what Kren had dubbed Jiggle Avenue until it ended. Then we turned right and went to the last house on the left. It was a tiny cape cod with a wooded backyard. It seemed oddly anomalous.

"This it?" Kren said.

"Yeah. I think."

"Okay. I'm probably gonna take off. Just text me when you need me to pick you up."

"All right."

I opened the door and started to step out.

I stopped.

"Somethin wrong?" Kren said.

"I can't do it."

"Why not?"

"I don't know."

Kren squinted toward the house.

"Well," he said, "he's probably not a real doctor anyway."

"Probably not."

"I guess we can go back if you want."

"Yeah. Sorry to make you drive me all the way out here."

"Now I know how to get to Dayton, at least."

I wanted to point out that he had a really nice car with a GPS in it and could probably go wherever he wanted to at just about any time but what was the point?

"Nobody needs to come to Dayton," I said. "Ever."

He backed out of the driveway and we started back to Gethsemane.

Once we were back in Gethsemane, I thought I saw Travis walking down Main Street.

"Hey, can you just let me off here?" I said.

Kren slowed the car and I thanked him for the ride and hopped out.

I started following who I thought was Travis. As I drew closer to him, I became even surer, although it looked like he'd shaved his head.

"Travis!" I called.

He stopped and turned.

"Oh, hey, man," he said. It was like nothing had happened.

"Where you been?"

"Oh, you know, around."

"Where you going?"

"Just home. I got a new place. Wanna see it?"

"Sure." What else did I have to do?

I walked alongside him.

"I thought something had happened to you."

"Nah, man, I just lost my phone."

"I think I know who has it."

"Me too."

We turned down a side street.

We'd both spent a lot of time on this street with the landscaping company. It was a well-maintained street with a number of one-story cottage-type houses. They weren't the nicest houses in Gethsemane but I felt like they were still well outside of Travis's price range.

He turned up a brick walkway. I followed him.

"This is nice," I said. "You renting?"

"Nah, man. It's mine."

"You bought it?" It wasn't completely unreasonable. Travis had worked the same job as me for a lot longer. And he'd lived with his parents for the majority of that time.

"Sure," he said.

We walked into the house. It was decorated nicely but I didn't think it was to Travis's tastes at all. Of course, since he'd never really had a place of his own and his bedroom at his parents' house hadn't changed since high school, I had no idea what his tastes actually were.

"Can I get you a drink or something?" he said.

"Water's fine."

"Sure, man. Take a seat."

He disappeared into the kitchen. I sensed movement coming from somewhere farther back in the house. One of Dawn's blond girls came into the living room and sat down on a chair positioned catty-corner to the couch.

I looked at her.

She stared at me with large unblinking eyes.

"Let me guess," I said. "You don't talk."

She didn't say anything.

Travis came back into the living room with a bottle of water.

He handed it to me and said, "This is Courtney. She doesn't say much."

"It's . . . very nice to meet you."

"Courtney, this is Brad, my oldest friend." He sat down on the couch, leaning slightly against the arm so he was facing me. "So what's been up with you? I heard you quit Billups'."

"Yeah. Did you know he was a racist?"

Travis smirked a little. "Dude, this is Gethsemane. Everyone's a racist."

"I guess it just didn't bother me until lately. I don't even think I gave it much thought."

"That's just your excuse. You left because it was time for you to move on. You were ready."

"What are you talking about?"

"You're ready to join the community."

"I've lived in the community for years. Still not sure what you're talking about."

"Dawn's community. She's here to do amazing things. She's going to change shit. *Is* changing shit. You do know Dawn, right?"

I felt winded. I took a shaky sip of my water.

"Yeah," I rasped.

"It's nothing to be ashamed of. I'm a member of it too. Almost everyone in town is. It's like Gethsemane created her. She comes to you when you're ready. It's like she just knows. And then, all of a sudden . . . she's just there, man."

"Wait . . . I don't . . ."

"That night I called you. That was my breaking point. The night of my rebirth. You were my recruit." He gestured at Courtney. "She was my reward. Well . . . and the house. And, okay, sometimes I have to do some stuff I don't want to do but I'm able to forget it about it pretty easily. It's not even that I don't *want* to do it . . . it just makes me feel bad sometimes. Well, it used to. I think I've gotten over it. She can set you up with Weishaupt and he'll fix you the perfect cocktail. Every morning's like a brand new day. I finally feel like a grownup, man. I was tired of feeling like poor white trash. Dawn knows how to get ahead. She knows what this town needs."

So many feelings surged through me—anger, fear, confusion, betrayal—that I struggled just to latch onto one of them.

"Why?" was all I managed to say.

"Why what? Why you?"

"Yeah," I said, but what I meant was "Why any of it?"

"I guess because I was desperate. You could be mad. Hell, I know you pretty good so I know you probably are mad, but you shouldn't be. Paradise is just around the corner. You just gotta learn how to let go. In the end, I think you'll see that I did you a really big favor."

"What happened to you?"

He smiled and I realized for the first time this was not the Travis I had known. I mean, physically he was still the same, but the Travis I had known had not displayed a smile that carefree in years. I would be hard pressed to even think of a time he'd smiled when he hadn't been drunk.

"I found happiness," he said.

"You mean you've given up," I blurted.

"Given *in*. I never understood that the tools for my happiness have been around me my entire life. I've done nothing but sabotage myself because I didn't think I deserved to be happy. I closed myself off to the town. I fought against it. Closed myself to all the wonderful people surrounding me. And things just got worse and worse. You should be happy for me. Instead you just sound jealous."

"It's just . . . really hard for me to understand."

"You're not letting yourself understand. It's like . . . remember all that conspiracy stuff I used to talk to you about? You always said something like 'It's not a conspiracy if you're being openly manipulated.' Maybe that's why you were so resistant to it for so long. It didn't have any mystery to it. Imagine it though, man . . . It was like all that conspiracy shit was my religion so finding out that it's all true is like someone proving that God exists. Not to mention that the truth is stranger and more beautiful than I could have ever dreamed of."

"I just . . . I feel like I've been sold out."

"It's easy to feel that way. It's much harder to be happy. Look, you didn't feel sold out when I got you the job at Billups', did you? Trust me, this is something much better."

I glanced at Travis. He had a be-one-of-us gleam in his eyes. I didn't like it but still found myself slightly envious.

"Do you really want to spend the rest of your life fighting? Aren't you exhausted? Do you even know what you're fighting against anymore? Rebellion is a young man's game. Submission to the will of Dawn, to the will of this town, is like opening the door to a dream."

"This all sounds like a sales pitch."

"Except you can't buy it with money. The only thing you lose is your misery."

"I think I need to go," I said.

"Are you sure? I could answer some questions."

I had a lot of questions but felt like Travis would only put some kind of positive spin on the answers, confusing me even further.

I stood up.

"Well," I said, "it was good seeing you again, man."

"Stop by any time."

He asked if I wanted his new phone number and I told him my phone was dead so he wrote it down.

I walked through the humid evening to my apartment, which wasn't very far away. I kept thinking about what Travis said: "The only thing you lose is your misery." But I thought there was a greater price. It was hard to even put it into words, but it seemed like there was some great psychic toll for being a member of the community. It was like some part of their brain had been eaten away and something else had moved in. It was like they were all being drained. But ... then again, wasn't that what I'd felt was happening to me since graduating high school and joining the workforce?

Still, I came back to the only solution—leaving. But the last time I'd tried to do that it had nearly killed me.

On my way back to the apartment, I saw the two men in black leaving my building. I assumed it was the same two men I'd seen on the other occasions. They were so nondescript it was impossible to tell. I froze where I was and they went in the opposite direction.

What business did they have in my building?

Was it paranoia to think they were there for me?

I went back up to my apartment and lay in my bed.

Seeing Travis had been a big surprise. If I'd been telling myself I had become involved with Dawn to find out what had happened to him then I no longer really had any reason to be involved with Dawn, did I?

Of course, I had no reason *not* to be involved with Dawn, either.

My apartment was stifling. I opened the window beside the bed and tried to summon a breeze.

I pulled my useless phone from my pocket. I could take it to the library and charge it but I didn't really have the energy to move. I knew I'd have to leave the apartment at some time since there was absolutely nothing in it for me.

I lay there thinking about Travis and his nice house and his beautiful girlfriend . . . or whatever she was.

It didn't seem too bad.

Who could blame me for giving up and joining the community?

Maybe I was already a part of it.

After all, I'd never really been a joiner and what had it gotten me so far?

Absolutely nothing.

No one was paying attention.

Who was I trying to impress?

I fell asleep and dreamed of Travis. He and his girlfriend were in what I assumed was his new backyard. He had his shirt off. A number of neon green nubs protruded from his chest and back. His girlfriend had a pair of pruning shears and was mechanically cutting the protuberances off. They hit the soil and wriggled into it. I kept thinking I should tell them to stop but I felt like I was hiding and didn't want to reveal myself.

When I woke up, it was dark outside and Dawn stood beside my bed, watching me, and I had a lingering thought that I should have asked Travis about the things growing on my back and my cock.

The room smelled heavily of gasoline.

"I think it's time you come with me," Dawn said.

I was still groggy, possibly from sleep, possibly from the fumes, possibly just from Dawn's presence.

I wanted to resist her, felt like I *should* resist her, but I couldn't.

I sat up. Maybe the fumes had gone to my head. My vision swam in and out and, for a horrifying moment, I was convinced Dawn was going to set me on fire.

"Come on," she said. "These fumes are making me sick."

I pivoted off the bed and stood on watery legs.

"Where . . ." was all I could manage to say.

"Back to my place. You're one of us now."

"No," I slurred.

"Yes," she said. "*Yes.*" And she reached out and put a hand on my shoulder. And for as much as I knew her to be a sadistic psycho, that touch sent a feeling of calm spreading throughout my body. It felt comforting.

I made my way to the door, already open. I stood in the hallway and watched as Dawn turned, flicked a match, and tossed it into the room.

She stood in a state of thrall until the entire apartment was alight.

"Now you have nothing to come back to," she said.

I should have felt a sense of loss, but I didn't.

A NEW REALITY

I felt a little better by the time we got back to her house, which was surprisingly empty and eerily quiet. Most of the rooms were darkened. I followed her through the house and up a flight of stairs. She led me to her bedroom. My cock stiffened. The nubs on my back stiffened also, the sensation oddly pleasurable.

Dawn turned and unbuttoned her shorts, sliding them and her underwear down.

She sat on the edge of the bed and spread her legs.

I knew what I was supposed to do.

And I wanted to.

The first flash of lightning from an incoming storm turned the window a bright blue for a second.

I got down on my knees and leaned into the familiar scent. My body shook with the need and anticipation.

I ran my tongue up and down her labia, pressed the tip of it against her clit. She reached down and wrapped her hands around the back of my head. This was the first time she'd ever done this. I sucked her clit into my mouth and pressed a finger against her opening, expecting her to tell me to stop.

"Just your mouth," she said. "Please."

I felt a momentary sense of frustration, but the more I drank of her, the frustration quickly dissipated.

Thunder rumbled in the distance.

I continued suckling her clit. I tried to get a pleasurable response from her but nothing was happening. I didn't care. I could have kept doing it for hours. To taste her was to understand her. Embrace the nebulous gray shape of her mystery, some essential part of her that had been here forever, in this place, in Gethsemane, and I wondered if every town and city had a guardian like her.

She moved her hands around to the sides of my head, pulled me from her, and said, "It's time."

I quit suckling her, stood up, and stripped off my shirt.

"Kiss me," she said.

I leaned over, shaking with anticipation. Our lips met just as another bright flash of lightning lit up the room and I thought it was like she was controlling the heavens. Our tongues entered each other's mouths, probing and snaking around each other. While locked together, I could feel her taking something from me. It wasn't stealing, as I gave it to her willingly. And I excused her and forgave her, thinking it was possible she was so sadistic because she did this, absorbed other people's pain, drank it up. And I again caught a glimpse of that ancient shadowy being somewhere in her core and knew this girl in my hands was only one version of Dawn. I was guessing her physical appearance changed every year. She may have even looked different to everyone who knew her. I saw what I wanted to see. I felt like she was always female, always eighteen. In appearance only. I wondered when this Dawn became who she was, when she had changed, what would happen to her body when that thing inside of her moved onto someone else.

Dawn wrapped her arms around my torso and raised her fingers to the protuberances on my back. Her touch stiffened my cock even further. I felt the protuberances tauten my skin, tingling with a million nerve endings.

I slid my fingers under the hem of her shirt, again expecting a protest.

I slowly lifted her shirt. I couldn't believe this was happening.

For the first time, I looked down at a fully naked Dawn.

Maybe there would have been a time when I would have been repulsed. Instead the sight of her naked body sent my cock and the nubs on my back throbbing.

Her nipples were not nipples. They were neon green protuberances.

She looked down at her chest and said, "We need to make more."

She slid off the bed and came to rest on her knees in front of me. At first I thought she was going to take me in her mouth but she didn't. She angled my cock down so the protuberance touched one of the growths on her breast. My green nub reached out to touch her green nub. They slid and rubbed together as our tongues had only moments before. It felt amazing. I lost myself to it. Every part of my body felt alive and trembling.

We eventually moved up onto the bed. I lay on my stomach while she straddled my lower back and leaned her breasts into the nubs below my shoulders. I felt them writhing together, faster and faster. I slowly ground myself against the bed, Dawn's satisfying weight pressing down on me. The feeling grew so intense I felt I was going to scream and then my cock and the other protuberances stiffened and quivered in spasm.

With my orgasm came a burst of clarity.

Clarity always came too late.

Everything I'd experienced since meeting Dawn had been scripted, and it all led to this exact moment.

I had dreamed of fucking Dawn and, in a sense, that's what we had just done. But I was now just her incubator. My biology had begun changing from the first time I'd gone down on her but I'd been . . . distracted.

Was that what all the filming and adventures were about? Diversion?

I had gone into some kind of fog since meeting Dawn and now felt that fog lifting, replaced with a sense of wide-awake terror. Or awareness. Maybe those things were not mutually exclusive.

I continued lying on the bed, frozen with this terror, while Dawn scooted off with the determined finality of someone who'd just completed a job.

I noticed she had two or three more of those protuberances on her back.

"What are they?" I said.

"You know what they are."

"I really don't."

"Then you know what they become. Beautiful young girls. Part of me to send out into the world. My children."

Dawn left the room, leaving me with my thoughts and the final grumbling of the thunderstorm.

When I woke up the next morning, I didn't feel that great.

I went into the bathroom and vomited until there wasn't anything left, not that there was a lot in there in the first place. I couldn't remember the last time I'd eaten anything. I also couldn't remember the last time I'd had a shower and, while I felt like there were probably a million other things I should be worried about, I couldn't think of them right now. I stripped off my clothes and inspected my naked body in the full-length mirror on the back of the door.

There were more protuberances. Or, I guess, they were buds.

One was on my upper left arm and the other was under my right nipple.

I took a hot shower and tried to scrub them away.

It didn't do anything but make them hurt.

There were so many things that had been thrown my way, but this was what it was really all about. Dawn using the human race as some sort of starter culture for her monster horde. And I'd walked right into it. I really had no choice from the second I got into her car that night.

I wondered how long it would take for the buds to fully fruit and drop. I wondered what would happen to me then.

I was pretty sure I knew.

It was what was happening to everyone in Gethsemane.

You're given some material things—imprisoned by material things, nothing more than diversions—and you slowly rot away, mentally and physically, until you find yourself lying in bed and turning to rust like Mrs. Dinsmore. And then a new person moves in after you and the cycle repeats itself. This was probably how White Power Larry had managed to amass such a following. By the time people were used up, the only thing they could believe in with any certainty was the color of their skin, the shallowest form of self-identity possible.

I had never seriously questioned my sanity before but I did now.

The worst part was knowing all this and not being able to do a damn thing about it.

Being poor for most of my life had made me feel trapped, but this felt like some kind of prison. Or like being stuck in a nightmare.

The days melted away. I slept a lot. The buds grew larger. I now had five. I slept most of the days away. When I wasn't sleeping I was eating. Dawn seemed to lose all interest in me and whatever sexual attraction I'd had for her had completely disappeared. Actually, it seemed like my sexual drive had disappeared, also. The erections I ritualistically woke up with were the only ones I ever got. Many times the house was filled with the young girls, but they did nothing for me. It probably didn't help that I knew they came from people like me. They were simply there to placate people so Dawn could do her bidding. But one day they stopped showing up and I thought about Dawn saying how this was how she put herself out into the world.

I wasn't surprised to see Barcie and Sheriff Bando around the house. Of course they weren't dead. It was all just part of Dawn's script. Conveniently there to distract me when she needed them. Absent when she didn't.

And I wasn't surprised to see who Dawn had taken a shine to.

Kren.

I felt somewhat guilty for putting him in this position.

The position Travis had sold me into.

Maybe I should have been angry with Travis but I felt beyond it. Maybe he had done me a favor.

It was ultimately my fault, anyway. I was the one who slept with Stasia. That was really when it all began. I was not an attractive guy. I was not the guy who had the ability to meet strange girls in bars and sleep with them in the same night. I should have known something was up.

There was a reason I hadn't remembered sending the pictures to Travis.

Because I hadn't.

Stasia had.

She may have even taken them in the first place.

And that's what had gotten me here.

Stasia's vagina was the proverbial rabbit hole.

For all I knew, White Power Larry only existed as a threatening tool to blackmail people like me. It was entirely possible his rallies really were nothing more than redneck keggers. Stasia was the bait and Larry was the steel in Dawn's trap.

I woke up one morning toward the end of July to see Dr. Weishaupt's smiling lizard face staring down at me.

"Didn't mean to wake you there, guy," he said. "Just need to check a few things."

I tried to protest but my mouth felt dry and cottony and I was nearly certain he'd injected me with some type of sedative.

He tugged the covers down to my waist and examined my growing buds. He made sounds of satisfaction as he squeezed and prodded them.

He rolled me over to examine the three on my back.

That wasn't all.

He made grunts of satisfaction as he entered me.

I wondered who else was watching this.

It was mercifully short and, thankfully, he used lube. When finished, he felched himself from my asshole and smacked his thin lips.

The greatest mistake one can make in life is to assume he has been chosen for something. I'm not sure if this would properly be called pride or hubris or just a good old-fashioned delusion of grandeur. Yet, it completely explains why each of us stood outside Dawn's house under a late July sky full of stars for something called the End of Humanity Ball. We had all been seduced by her in one way or the other. Each of us had thought, at one point, that we were the one. Some people, the ones who were actively seeking some type of guidance, responded to her flyers for the Healing League. They were fragile people who would probably always seek some kind of healing. Others were seduced by White Power Larry's message of hate and anger. They were probably always hateful and angry people. Some people had been passively seduced. I thought about my role in this, working for Billups. The plants we'd put in people's homes. Maybe there was some brainwashing recording buried in the soil. Maybe they were coated in some sort of narcotic substance. Maybe it was something with the soil itself. Maybe it hadn't affected me too much because I wasn't around them all the time and had never put one in my home because I was too lazy to take care of things. Maybe it *had* affected me and I was too delusional to realize it. Others, like me, were actively seduced.

We were all guilty of thinking we were somehow more important than the next person.

And that's why we were all here, nude, neon green buds bulging from our skin, throbbing with the terrible energy of the evening amidst deafening electronic music and constant fireworks and a catapult periodically launching dead dogs into the lake behind Dawn's house.

Nearly everyone from my route was there. Even the Gundersons, stretched out on their mobile hospital beds like quivering puddles of vanilla pudding. White Power Larry and Stasia and their skinhead group, which now included Donnie and Kren.

All naked.

All budding.

I wondered how long this ritual had been going on.

How had I ignored it for so long?

In the end, it turns out we may have had the right to feel like we were somehow chosen.

The music cut off and the last firework exploded in the sky. The final dog made its sad splash in the lake.

And I felt it.

I think we all did.

Some type of collective anticipation.

We turned toward the house.

The outdoor lights cut off, leaving us with the glow of the half-moon and the stars.

Until an image flickered to life on the massive screen spread across the back of the house.

The image divided repeatedly until the massive screen was covered in smaller squares.

We all moved closer.

In each of the images was someone's front door, all different, but still similar.

We all knew what we were watching. Dawn's army of girls had cameras for eyes. Maybe not actual cameras. Maybe we were just somehow linked to them through biology, through Dawn, through that cosmic thing living inside her. We were seeing what they saw.

We watched as they easily opened doors and calmly strolled through houses, some large, some small, some messy, some spotless.

We watched each of them lean over a sleeping person.

Our buds twitched and stretched, all part of the same flesh, all waiting to be born, all needing what only these sleeping victims' pain could supply.

We watched the sacrifices.

Maybe if there was someone in the bed with the sacrificed, they would feel a few moments of confusion upon waking, but it wouldn't take them long to understand. It wouldn't take them long to accept their new reality.

Just like we'd all accepted our new reality.

And when the screen was nothing but a sea of red, we all made our way to the lake, filled with the pain of who knew how many dead dogs, because that's where the buds wanted us to go. That's where Dawn wanted us to go. And we lived to serve Dawn.

The buds began dropping from our flesh, plopping onto the ground and wriggling toward the lake like glowing, bloated slugs.

Eventually the lake glowed a dull neon green.

We knew it would gain in intensity each successive night and, when it no longer glowed, a new Dawn army would emerge from the pond.

And this would be the future.

The lights came back on.

The music started back up.

We felt free.

What we entered into was not a living death.

It was freedom.

Free to repeat these actions year after year.

Free to lose ourselves completely.

Free to serve Dawn and only Dawn.

Free from poverty and boredom and judgment and the struggle to make our own choices.

I felt good for the first time in years.

Other Grindhouse Press Titles

www.ingramcontent.com/pod-product-compliance
Lightning Source LLC
Chambersburg PA
CBHW051634180726
48284CB00006B/1724